NOW SHE'S GONE

Alison James

bookouture

Published by Bookouture in 2017

An imprint of StoryFire Ltd.

Carmelite House
50 Victoria Embankment
London EC4Y 0DZ

www.bookouture.com

ISBN: 978-1-78681-414-2
eBook ISBN: 978-1-78681-413-5

Dedicated to the memory of my wonderful father.

PART ONE

'A lily of a day
Is fairer far in May,
Although it fall and die that night—
It was the plant and flower of Light.
In small proportions we just beauties see;
And in short measures life may perfect be.'

from 'The Noble Nature', Ben Jonson

PROLOGUE

She took a mouthful of the sweet liquid, then another, and started to feel a pounding in her head. The bottle was slipped from her hand, and she became aware of a faint, gentle murmuring as she collapsed onto her right side. She tried to open her eyes, but couldn't. Then arms went around her waist and she was half-lifted and half-pulled until she fell over the bed and onto the carpet. The grip shifted to her thighs, pulling her flat, then to her ankles as she was dragged across the floor. The last thing she was aware of was her head hitting a step, and the low voice talking to her. Reassuring her that she would be fine.

ONE

It looked all wrong.

DI Rachel Prince fixed her gaze on the file that lay open on her tray table, staring at the photos of the perfect, broken body. She went over the accompanying statements not once but twice – then three times – re-reading the same paragraph several times in an attempt to make sense of it.

She had been trying to get up to speed on the case for the past twenty minutes, since the plane had taxied along the runway bound for Edinburgh. The prospect of a hot train in the height of the summer holidays had not appealed, so she was flying there instead. Okay, so the plane was also full, but at least the journey was only a bearable fifty-five minutes. It would be okay.

But this – the story outlined in her briefing note about a beautiful young woman randomly falling to her death – this was not okay. The component parts of the account did not add up. The case had been sold to her as something of a diplomatic mission, but this didn't look like a mere box-ticking exercise. Far from it.

Twenty-four hours earlier she had received an early morning phone call from Commander Nigel Patten, her boss at the National Crime Agency, asking her not to go into the office in South London, but instead to meet him in leafy, upmarket Kensington. This was an unusual request, to say the least, but she had driven straight to 35 Hyde Park Gate.

Leaving the force field of her car's air-conditioning, Rachel had immediately been too warm in her informal work uniform of black trousers and long-sleeved white shirt. An August heatwave was suffocating London, and although it had only been 8.30 a.m., it was already well over twenty degrees centigrade. She had rolled up her sleeves as far as they would go, wishing she'd worn sandals instead of trainers. By the afternoon it would not only be hot, but uncomfortably humid too.

The building she had been summoned to turned out to be the Embassy of the Netherlands, occupying the whole of a red-brick mansion block. A red, white and blue flag and the insignia of the European Union flew above the front entrance. This was certainly not a normal work venue, Rachel had thought, but then arriving at a job without a clue what was involved was hardly normal either.

Patten had intercepted her as soon as she came into the foyer. He had seemed jumpy, uncomfortable. He was in his late forties, losing his hair and looking a little weathered, but slim and fit for his age. He needed to be: he had recently remarried and started a new family with a much younger second wife.

'There's no time to brief you, I'm afraid, so you'll just have to listen in for now, and we can talk properly afterwards.' He had looked Rachel up and down, taking in her bare forearms. 'And you might want to roll your sleeves down.'

She had duly adjusted her shirt, and he had led her into a high-ceilinged, thickly carpeted room, where several people were seated around a large oval table. Without exception their expressions were grave, strained.

A tall, distinguished man with greying hair stood up and extended a hand.

'This is His Excellency Mr Carolus Visser, the Dutch Ambassador.' Patten had made an obsequious movement that was not quite a bow as he said it. 'Your Excellency, this is my colleague Detective Inspector Rachel Prince. She's one of our international liaison officers here in London.'

Rachel shook the man's hand and sat down next to Patten.

'Detective Prince; we've arranged this meeting on behalf of one of our nationals, Dries van Meijer.' The ambassador, whose English was fluent and barely accented, had indicated the man sitting on his left. He was younger, equally tall, with square horn-rimmed glasses and dark blonde hair slicked back in the manner favoured by City financiers. His pale-grey suit, Rachel had assessed with a practiced eye, was custom-tailored and expensive, as were the cutaway-collared shirt and the diamond-studded cufflinks. The stark black silk tie had made a discordant note in his urbane appearance.

'I'm afraid we're here under what are the most unfortunate – tragic – of circumstances. Mr van Meijer's daughter was visiting the Fringe Festival in Edinburgh last week when she sadly passed away.'

Rachel had looked again at van Meijer, and took in the pink-rimmed eyes behind the glasses, the unhealthy tinge to his tanned skin. He looked down at his hands, twisting a gold signet ring.

'The Procurator Fiscal in Edinburgh has concluded that my daughter's death was an accident,' he said. His voice was strained, tinged with anger. 'They said there was no need for a formal enquiry. The police are unwilling to take the matter further, but I – we – find this totally unacceptable.'

'Mr van Meijer asked us to approach Interpol on his behalf, and I explained that in this country, Interpol is now part of the National Crime Agency,' Visser had continued, pausing briefly to rest a hand on top of van Meijer's. 'My contacts at the Foreign Office put me in touch with Commander Patten.'

Patten had given a brief nod of acknowledgment. 'And I've offered our assistance in establishing the facts, as far as we are able.' He looked round the table. 'DI Prince is one of our most experienced investigative officers, and we would be very happy for her to go to Edinburgh on Mr van Meijer's behalf and find out as much as possible about the circumstances surrounding the death of his daughter.'

'Emily,' van Meijer had said bleakly. 'Her name is Emily.'

'It's a tricky one,' Patten had offered as they left the building together. 'Not to mention a bit of a political hot potato.'

'Yes, I can see that.' Rachel's tone had been dry. 'Otherwise why would we be acting as private investigators on behalf of a foreign national?'

They had reached Patten's car at this point: his driver waiting patiently with the engine running to keep the air-conditioning circulating. The sun was climbing behind a thin veil of heat haze, and Rachel could feel her armpits growing damp.

'Can I give you a lift?' Patten had asked,

She shook her head. 'I drove here.'

'Okay, well… it's too hot to stand around on the street and talk.' Patten said, ducking his head to climb into the back seat. 'I'll see you back at the office and we can go into it all properly then.'

Rachel had arrived at the office to find that her Detective Sergeant, Mark Brickall, had rigged up a desk fan that blew air directly into his face, and was sucking ostentatiously on a strawberry ice lolly. The NCA building in Tinworth Street was supposed to be air-cooled, but the ventilation system was outdated and only circulated stale, lukewarm air.

'Bit early for sweet treats, isn't it?' Rachel had indicated the lolly. 'Even for you. It's not eleven o'clock.'

'Temperature's going to get up to thirty-five centigrade today, loser.' Brickall had wiped his mouth with a paper towel and tossed it into his waste bin. 'I'm just making like a boy scout and being prepared.'

'In that case,' Rachel had stood up again and adjusted the fan so that it blew air over her desk too, 'how about you behave like a proper boy scout and do a good turn.'

Brickall had put out a hand to move the fan back again, but having caught sight of her expression changed his mind, taking a file from the heap on his desk and studying the contents earnestly. This was New Improved Brickall. He had recently been reinstated following a six-month suspension for professional misconduct. Since his return he had been making a show of working hard and playing strictly by the rules; with every piece of paperwork checked and double-checked to make sure it was absolutely correct. It was out of character – Old Brickall was slapdash about paperwork and had little time for protocol.

'Where have you been, anyway?' he had enquired. 'I asked Margaret but she denied all knowledge of a meeting. Not that I expected her to know.' He had made this jibe warmly: their clerical assistant Margaret was popular, if not a titan of efficiency.

'Something Patten sprung on me out of the blue,' she told Brickall. 'I need to go and have a debrief with him now, in fact.' She picked up her notebook and a pen. 'Tell you about it later. Mine's an orange Solero, by the way, on your next ice-cream run.'

'Dries van Meijer is not just any foreign national,' Patten had spoken heavily as Rachel sat down on the chair that faced his desk. 'He owns one of the world's biggest marine engineering companies, so he's hugely powerful. That's why we find ourselves in this situation.'

Rachel nodded. 'Ah. I see.'

'If van Meijer tells him to jump, the Dutch ambassador has no choice but to ask "How high?" He can't just fob him off: it's out of the question.'

'So what happened to his daughter?'

'I only have the few details I was given before you arrived this morning. The girl was on a cultural trip to the Edinburgh festival, along with a group of other teenagers, all from European countries. She seems to have gone out walking late at night after drinking and suffered some kind of fall. The Dutch ambassador promised to send over a more detailed briefing note later today, so I don't know the full story. Not yet. Anyway... the Procurator Fiscal has the option to order a Fatal Accident Inquiry in the event of an unexpected death, at his discretion. Following enquiries by Edinburgh police, he declined to do so. As you probably know, in Scotland they don't have coroners or inquests like we do south of the border. The system is quite different to ours, where an inquest would have been inevitable.'

'But if I go up there asking questions, implying the local police have fallen short... well, as you said yourself sir, it's politically extremely awkward.'

Rachel had been referring to the fact that the National Crime Agency had limited jurisdiction in Scotland. Operating there at all was conditional on authorisation from the Lord Advocate and could only be done with approval from Police Scotland.

'You're absolutely right, DI Prince.' Patten had poured himself a glass of water from the jug on his desk and taken a sip. He offered the jug to Rachel, but she shook her head. 'It is awkward. It's going to require very careful handling indeed, but I have full trust in your abilities. And in reality it boils down to a box-ticking exercise; you just need to go up there and confirm that it was indeed a tragic accident. That way we've done our bit and the Dutch will be satisfied that their concerns have been heard.'

Even then, Rachel had been doubtful that reality would align with Patten's glib summary, but had not said so. 'I take it I need to go straight away, sir?'

Patten had nodded, dabbing the sweat from his forehead with his pocket square. 'Janette will help sort arrangements. Look on the bright side: at least it will be cooler north of the border.'

As she had stood up to go, he added, 'And take DS Brickall with you. You're perfectly capable of handling this alone, but after his recent… history… I want him where you can keep an eye on him.'

TWO

By the time her flight landed at Edinburgh Airport, Rachel had read the brief file from cover to cover several times, and knew the contents off by heart. The many gaps in the information had thrown up even more questions. But that was what she was here for: to find answers.

Emily van Meijer, aged seventeen, had been attending the festival as part of a group organised by a travel company called White Crystal Tours. They brought teenagers from all over Europe on cultural trips to Edinburgh. Accommodation and half-board was provided, and they were chaperoned to appropriate cultural events. Alcohol consumption was strictly against company policy, but on the evening of Monday 7 August a half-empty bottle of Southern Comfort was found in Emily's room. The girl was missing, having apparently said earlier in the day that she wanted to climb Arthur's Seat to take photos. After several hours, when she failed to return, the tour organisers alerted the local St John mountain rescue team, who found the girl's body at the foot of a sheer rock face at Salisbury Crags. Police Scotland were called, but after examination of the scene and a routine post-mortem, decided against initiating further enquiries.

Case closed.

Except that the van Meijers were unwilling to accept this conclusion, insisting that their daughter didn't drink, wasn't particularly interested in photography and was not the sort of girl who bent the rules. In short, she wouldn't have behaved in this way. *But all parents would say that about their child's accidental death*, thought Rachel. *Wouldn't they?*

Finding accommodation in Edinburgh during the festival was notoriously tricky and expensive, not least at twenty-four hours' notice. The city centre itself lacked even a bed in a shared hostel room, but nothing was beyond Janette's organisational powers. At the NCA they joked that Janette could airdrop you into a warzone and still secure you three-star accommodation. She had managed to source an empty room in the Avalon Guest House in Coates, less than two miles to the west of the city centre, and Rachel took a cab straight there from the airport. The decor in the public areas was fussy and overly grand, and the room was tiny, but she was grateful to have somewhere central to make her base. As soon as she had unpacked, she texted Brickall, who had elected to travel on the train, claiming it would be easier than flying.

Just arrived. ETA?

He replied a few seconds later.

We're on the train. Due in to Waverley at 14.17.

Rachel drew back from her phone screen, startled.

We??

Me and the female in my life.

No idea what you're talking about, but will meet you at Waverley anyway.

*

Rachel recognised the confident, swaggering walk straight away, even though Brickall was not tall enough to stand out in the crowd of disembarking passengers. He was alone.

Or not exactly alone. There was no human female companion with him, but trotting along beside him on a red lead was a small sandy-coloured dog. She had a silky coat, soulful eyes and a melancholic expression.

'This is Dolly,' Brickall introduced her.

'You've got a bloody dog?'

'Not exactly. She belongs to a mate of mine, only he's emigrated to New Zealand. So I said I'd mind her until he could make a more permanent arrangement for her.' He reached down and fondled one of her floppy ears. 'She's a good girl, aren't you Doll? She won't be a problem.'

Rachel doubted this. 'So that's why you wanted to take the train up here?'

'Exactly, Sherlock.'

'Okay, well… I was going to suggest we visit the scene, but I suppose the dog can come with us. We'll need to drop your stuff first. Where are you staying?'

'In the arse end of beyond. It was tricky finding a place where I could bring Dolly. But we can get the tram most of the way, I think.'

They emerged up the station steps to a slow-moving swell of people. Festival madness was peaking, and the pavement was thick with dawdling tourists, buskers and jugglers. Every few steps they took, someone approached them and thrust a flyer into their hand, inviting them to attend a satirical review, stand-up comedy, a poetry reading, a conceptual art show.

Dolly quivered and tried to melt into Brickall's ankles. He handed Rachel his backpack and picked up the dog to carry her. Eventually they fought their way along Princes Street to the tram stop. As Patten had predicted, the temperature was almost fifteen degrees lower than in London, with a pale blue sky only just visible behind voluminous grey-white clouds.

They left the tram at Balgreen and walked for fifteen minutes to the outskirts of Corstorphine, with Brickall using Google Maps on his phone to navigate. His digs were in a pin-neat, one-storey villa, where the landlady, Mrs Kilpatrick ('Call me Betty') immediately gushed and fussed over Dolly as if she'd acquired a new grandchild.

'Oh, the wee dote! Look at her: she's gorgeous. What sort of dog is she?'

'An American Cocker Spaniel,' said Brickall, like a proud parent. Dolly stared at the middle distance with a worried expression as she was stroked.

'She'll be hungry perhaps?' said Betty. 'Or thirsty after the journey.' She fetched two bowls, one filled with water and one with kibble. Dolly lapped at the water noisily then ate a single biscuit, as though determined to be polite.

'The wee darling! Now, can I get you and your girlfriend some tea? And maybe some fruit cake?'

'She's not my girlfriend.'

'I'm not his girlfriend.'

They spoke in perfect unison.

Brickall reluctantly declined – or at least deferred – the tea and cake, explaining they were there to work, and planned to start immediately. He also declined Betty's offer to mind Dolly, on the grounds that she had been on a train for over four hours and needed a good walk. He and Rachel, along with the dog, set off back to the tram station, taking it to the eastern end of the line, walking another mile through the unrelenting crowds to Holyrood Park, and then hiking up the looming, volcanic Salisbury Crags. The scrubby grassland gave way abruptly to a sheer, 150-foot rocky drop.

'Amazing view,' observed Brickall, reaching down to pat Dolly, who had flopped down, exhausted, at his feet. As he spoke, the clouds thinned and parted and they were treated to a spectacular view over the city. It was even cooler than street level, and breezy.

'I think I prefer it up here,' said Rachel. 'All those people do my head in. I don't know how people who live here cope with it every summer.'

'Money,' said Brickall bluntly. 'It brings in hundreds of millions to the city every year. They kind of have to put up with it.'

He handed Dolly's lead to Rachel and walked right up to the edge of the crag.

'Careful,' Rachel said instinctively. The dog pinned back her ears and whimpered.

Brickall peered over the edge, being careful to plant his feet and keep his body weight tipped back.

'You could see how it could happen,' he said as he walked back to Rachel. 'It's dark, you lose your footing…'

'But if it was dark, why would Emily have wanted to take photos?' Rachel asked. 'It makes no sense.'

'Unless you're a pissed teenager. Then any crazy shit makes sense. I did a bit of research of my own on the way up here: people fall off here and Arthur's Seat,' he pointed to the dormant volcano looming above them, 'all the time. Multiple fatalities every year. Especially at night, when tourists come up here to admire the city lights. The local plod were spot on: it was just an all-too-predictable accident.'

'Looks that way,' Rachel agreed. 'But to complete Patten's diplomatic mission, we still need to go and speak to Police Scotland. And maybe make a few enquiries of our own into what happened that night.'

Gusts of wind swirled around them, and Dolly quivered.

'Like I said; just a kid who couldn't hold her drink and paid the price.' Brickall turned back down the path. 'Come on. Doll here has had enough, and there's a piece of fruitcake with my name on it back at Betty's.'

*

They beat a path back through the city centre, past queues of event attendees that seemed to spill out of every building, blocking the pavements.

Once they reached the western edge of the city, Rachel and Brickall parted company, and she returned to her guest house and took a long hot shower. There was no such refinement as a minibar, but a pleading phone call to the front desk resulted in a waitress bringing a vodka and tonic to her room. She sat on the edge of her bed, sipping the icy and pleasantly bitter liquid and staring at her phone.

Her ex-husband Stuart Ritchie lived in Edinburgh, and they were now on friendly terms after a long estrangement. Much as Rachel was glad that she and Stuart were speaking again, there was something faintly awkward about landing an investigation on his home turf. Especially as she had declined the invitation to his wedding earlier that year. So in case she bumped into him in what was, after all, a small city, she should really let him know she was here.

She considered phoning him, but in the end took the easy route and sent him a text saying that she was unexpectedly in Edinburgh for a few days. The reply arrived a few minutes later.

Splendid news, Rae! You must, of course, come over and have dinner with us tomorrow night. I'll email you details. S.

So, she was now committed. Rachel pulled on T-shirt and jeans in readiness to descend to the gilded, swagged dining room in search of food. Her phone rang just as she reached the door, and she picked up, expecting it to be Brickall.

'Hey, you!'

Howard Davison. Her former personal trainer and boyfriend of six months.

'Hi.'

'I thought I'd just check up on you, since you haven't been answering my texts. Is everything okay?'

Rachel flinched at the words 'check up on you' but managed to keep her tone non-combative.

'I'm fine. I'm in Edinburgh: flew up this morning.'

'Edinburgh? You never mentioned Edinburgh.'

'Last minute job. Very last minute.'

'How long for?'

'I'm not sure: probably only a few days.'

'I could go in and water the plants for you if you like?'

Howard had a spare key, which as far as Rachel was concerned was only for emergencies, like her locking herself out.

'Okay... listen Howard, I'll call you when I'm back.'

The truth was that she was glad of the chance for a break. When they first got together, Howard had recently come out of a difficult relationship and Rachel herself had not wanted anything too serious. At first this had worked well, with them spending a couple of week nights together, and most weekends.

But then she had discovered his penchant for home improvement.

Yes, in theory, it was a good thing for her functional flat conversion to be looking a bit less sterile. However, she would rather stick sharp objects in her own eyeballs than spend time trawling a DIY superstore at the weekend. Howard, on the other hand, loved it. He had continually suggested small upgrades she could make to her home and then set about installing them, extending the time they spent together to a degree that Rachel was now finding uncomfortable. The occasional weekend had morphed into every weekend. All weekend. And after the third project he had embarked on – some shelving in the entrance hall – the penny finally dropped.

He wants to move in with me.

And for Rachel, that was a step too far. For a start, she was simply not ready for that. Possibly never would be. And also, when it came to her work, Howard was not exactly on the same page. He had always worked regular hours, and when he left the gym, that was it. He was off-duty. His resentment of her late nights, irregular hours and last-minute trips was starting to corrode their relationship. For the last few weeks she had been seizing any and every opportunity to cool things off.

You bottled it, she told herself as she hung up and stepped out onto the headache-inducing swirls of the landing carpet. *This is the perfect opportunity. You should have told him. You should have broken up with him.*

But after steak and chips and a glass of red wine, she had persuaded herself that, on the contrary, it would be completely wrong to break up with Howard over the phone. Cowardly. She owed him a face-to-face. And that inevitably meant leaving the status quo as it was until she was back in London.

Her phone pinged, and this time it was Brickall, with an uncaptioned photo. It showed Dolly sitting in a plush, red dog bed, provided by the attentive Betty.

Rachel couldn't help smiling as she typed a reply.

Tell her not to get too comfortable – we're here to work! See you in Gayfield Square at 9 a.m.

She looked at the picture again. It was a fun touch, but she was all too aware that they were not in Edinburgh for the photo opportunities. Tomorrow, the difficult questions would have to be asked.

THREE

'At least you haven't brought the mutt.'

Rachel took in Brickall's smart appearance, and the absence of his canine companion.

'I'm playing by the rules now, remember?' he responded cheerfully. 'Can't afford to attract any negative attention, especially given the awkward vibe of this job. I'm just grateful that Betty offered to mind Dolly.'

'I'm sure she was delighted,' murmured Rachel as they walked into the Police Scotland building in Gayfield Square and presented themselves at the front desk with matching professional smiles, despite the surliness of the desk sergeant.

'You'll be wanting DI Sillars,' he informed them after they explained the reason for their visit. 'She handled the Dutch kid's death.'

'Could you tell me if she's available?' Rachel enquired pleasantly.

'No I couldnae,' the desk sergeant growled, 'because I've no idea if she is or if she isnae.'

He made them sit and wait in the public reception area amongst the bail reporters, document producers and people with petty complaints. After nearly an hour a diminutive figure walked into the room. A woman the size of a twelve-year-old, but with the lined face and the voice of a navvy with a sixty-a-day habit. This, it turned out, was DI Morag Sillars.

'Yous wanted to see me?' The accent was pure Glasgow.

Rachel reached out her right hand, which wasn't shaken. So instead she used it to produce her warrant card. 'Is there somewhere we can go for a quick word?'

Bristling with reluctance, Sillars led them back to her office and climbed into a chair which seemed far too tall for her. The packet of Mayfair and lighter on the desk confirmed the habit that had honed her deep, rasping Glaswegian tones. Her thin, dirty-blonde hair was scraped back into a short ponytail and she wore a skirt suit that was far too large for her, with laddered tights.

'So, what d'you want?' Professional niceties were going to be dispensed with, it seemed.

Rachel introduced Brickall and explained that they had been tasked with making enquiries about Emily van Meijer's death on behalf of the Dutch Embassy.

'Nothing to do with me anymore,' Sillars shrugged. 'The case is closed. The Fatalities Investigation Unit looked at it on behalf of the Procurator Fiscal, like they do with all sudden deaths in Scotland, and they were confident it was an accident.'

'I'm sure it was; really all we're doing is seeking some reassurance. Call it a diplomatic exercise.'

'I dinnae give a fuck about your diplomatic exercise,' Sillars rasped. 'Have you any idea what a bag of shite it is policing the fucking festival? Every year nearly three million morons pitch up in the city, getting wankered on cheap lager, pissing – and worse – in people's gardens, getting their phones mugged, cracking their heids open on the pavement, getting into fights and breaking their necks while taking arseing selfies… have you any idea how much extra work that is?'

Rachel and Brickall treated this as a rhetorical question.

'Well, go on, have you?' Sillars snarled. 'It's over a hundred extra call-outs a week. So yes, it's a shame that some rich kid fell off the Crags after a late night ramble, but trust me, it's nothing new. It certainly doesn't require any more "reassurance".'

She made sarcastic quote marks with the last word before picking up her lighter and flicking it aggressively, sending out sparks.

'DI Sillars… can I call you Morag?' Brickall was at his twinkling, charming best. Rachel noticed the tiny woman's body language soften a fraction. 'We're certainly not going to add to your workload. But if we could just review the file—'

'Look, pretty boy, even if I wanted to – which I don't – your lot have no jurisdiction on my patch. So no you can't, not without sign-off from the Lord Advocate's office.'

'Fine,' said Rachel, forcing another smile. 'Thank you for your time. We'll be back for the file once we've cleared it with the Lord Advocate.'

'Forget "Morag",' muttered Brickall as they left the building. 'More like "More-hag". Just as well I didn't bring Dolly – she'd probably have turned the poor mutt into a pair of gloves.'

They found a café a few yards away on Gayfield Place. It was far too congested with tourist trade to provide a table, but they bought two takeaway cups of coffee and a brownie for Brickall, and sat on one of the benches in the grassy centre of the square. It was a clear, sunny day, but the breeze had a distinctly chilly edge.

'So what now?' asked Brickall, spraying chocolatey crumbs over both their legs.

Rachel glared at him as she brushed them off her thighs. To bolster their credentials as envoy she had worn her best silver-grey Joseph linen suit; a rare designer splurge.

'I'll speak to Patten, and he'll have to request formal authorisation from the Lord Advocate for us to work on the case. There wasn't much in the briefing note I was given before I left London, but even with the little I've read about the case so far, there are some things that just aren't sitting right with me.' She gave Brickall a look that he knew all too well. It was a look that told him that now she had sunk her teeth into the case, she would not be letting go. 'I honestly don't see how we can go back to London without at least having a look at what's in the police file.'

'How bloody long's that going to take?'

Rachel drained her coffee cup. 'Who knows? Hopefully no more than a couple of days or so. A bit of diplomatic pressure should expedite things.'

'So we're going to stay here in the meantime?'

'We might as well. That okay with you? And Betty? I've got my room booked for another couple of nights.'

'Fine.' Brickall launched a half-court volley with his coffee cup, landing it squarely in the rubbish bin. He held up his hand for a high five, which Rachel ignored. 'At least it's not as hot and sweaty as Calcutta up here. Dolly's happy, and Betty does a cracking Scottish breakfast. You've not lived until you've tasted her tattie scones.'

'I never will figure out how you're not twice the size,' Rachel sighed. 'You eat enough for five people.'

'It's all the energy I burn… How about you?' Brickall asked, with a sideways glance. 'You okay to be here for a bit longer? Got much going on back in London?'

'Not much,' Rachel admitted. 'And, as you say, the weather's less hellish here.'

'What about the personal trainer?

Brickall still refused to call Howard by his name.

She sighed.

'Given him his marching orders?'

'Not yet. But… let's just say the writing's on the wall.' She lobbed her own coffee cup, but it landed a few inches short. Brickall gave a snort of contempt as he picked it up and kicked it cleanly into the bin.

'Time to channel some of that energy you're bragging about into being an investigating officer,' Rachel told him. 'Come on, Wayne Rooney.'

*

They arranged to meet a couple of hours later, after Rachel had changed out of her suit into jeans and T-shirt, and Brickall had fetched Dolly. She spent some of the intervening downtime on her bed with her laptop, checking out the White Crystal website. It looked outdated, with clunky links and graphics and a few amateurish photo galleries of beaming groups of teenagers in cagoules, against classic Edinburgh backdrops. They claimed to offer *'a fully integrated and supervised Festival experience, with secure and comfortable accommodation where a team leader is present at all times'*. The emphasis appeared to be on wholesome fun, and reassuring parents that their little darlings would be safe. It wasn't cheap either, costing €6,000 plus VAT for a ten-day tour. No wonder their target audience was wealthy Eurocrats.

'Where are we going this time?' Brickall asked, as they walked down Dundas Street.

'We're paying a friendly visit to White Crystal Tours,' Rachel told him. 'Only, remember, we don't have authority to operate here yet, so we've got to keep this strictly informal. That's why I asked you to bring Dolly. As a prop. She reinforces the idea that we're off-duty.'

The company's offices were on the first floor of a classic New Town terrace in Drummond Place. The interior reminded Rachel of her childhood dentist's waiting room: the smell of furniture polish and quality carpeting that had definitely seen better days. The combined reception and outer office was graced with an arrangement of silk flowers, and manned by a woman of indeterminate years with curls firmly hair-sprayed into place, a double strand of pearls and a cashmere twinset. She was transferring what appeared to be data from a set of forms into a spreadsheet, her face so tight with concentration that she failed to notice her visitors for several seconds.

'Oh dearie me,' she said, her hand flying to her throat when she spotted Dolly. 'I don't know about bringing dogs in here.'

Brickall gave her his most disarming smile. 'She doesn't bite, I promise.'

Dolly positioned herself at his feet, her tail thumping the carpet on cue.

Rachel produced her warrant card. 'Could I have a word with your chief executive… or whatever he or she styles themselves?'

'You'll want the managing director. Kenneth Candlish.' The woman directed this at Dolly, who looked back at her with sad eyes.

'Is he available?'

'I don't know about that,' the woman said sternly. 'You've not an appointment.'

'Is he free by any chance?' asked Rachel, employing more patience than she would have done when working south of the border. They couldn't afford to throw their weight about; not yet.

The woman darted out from behind her desk and tapped on one of the two doors that adjoined reception, before slipping through it. A few seconds later, she opened the door wide and ushered Rachel and Brickall in.

'You can leave the dog here; it'll be fine.'

Kenneth Candlish was a short, square man who Rachel put at about sixty, although his prematurely white hair and goatee beard made him appear at least a decade older. He wore a floral silk cravat in the open neck of his shirt, and had beautifully manicured hands. The overall effect was more suggestive of a theatrical agent than a youth-tour leader. He smiled broadly when he saw them.

'Do come in, officers.' Candlish waved to two rickety velvet-covered chairs opposite his desk. He had a genteel Edinburgh accent: precise and studied. 'I'm guessing your call is in connection with poor wee Emily van Meijer.'

Rachel confirmed this, and stressed that their call was purely informal.

'In that case, I expect you're having to cross the t's and dot the i's,' Candlish said astutely. Behind the grandiose manner, his deep-set eyes were sharp. 'But really, I'm afraid there's nothing to add. The local constabulary dealt with the matter perfectly appropriately, and the Procurator Fiscal declared it death by misadventure. I am aware though,' he steepled his fingers to add gravitas to his words, 'that the van Meijer family are still not satisfied. Perhaps not surprising, but there's really nothing more that we're able to do for them. They have all the facts.'

'Which are?' asked Brickall.

'That on the evening in question, Emily stole a bottle of liqueur from Mr and Mrs MacBain – the house parents in charge of the students' residence – drank quite a bit of it and took herself off out to Holyrood Park, where she slipped and fell from the edge of the Crags. The post-mortem confirmed this. It's all very distressing, but I must stress it was a one-off. Alcohol consumption is strictly banned in the student residence. We're highly safety conscious, and White Crystal have never had any problems of this nature before.'

'What kind of a girl was Emily?' asked Rachel. She tried to forget the images taken post-mortem and instead conjure a mental image of the other photo that had been in the briefing notes: a tall, blonde girl with model good looks; serious but with a confident air.

'I didn't get to speak with her personally, but apparently she was a pleasant young woman. Polite, not rowdy or disruptive, but certainly one of the more confident members of the group. They're only with us for a period of ten days, so we don't really get to know them well as individuals.' Candlish smiled blandly.

'And where are the kids based?' asked Brickall.

'At our residential dormitory, in Murrayfield. My assistant director, Will MacBain, lives there with his wife. Will's also in charge of organising the students' visits to the various festival events.'

Candlish spoke complacently, as though Rachel and Brickall were themselves parents of a prospective tour participant.

'May we speak to them?' Rachel asked. 'The other children in Emily van Meijer's group?'

'I'm afraid that won't be possible.' Candlish sighed regretfully and spread his hands over his waistcoated midriff, where a gold watch chain was just visible. 'The rest of the group have all returned home to their families. Their ten days were over the day after the incident. We do three tours of ten days over the festival period, with approximately twenty participants each time. The students we have currently are the second group, who obviously didn't know Emily and weren't here when… it… happened.'

Convenient, thought Rachel. But because she had no official authority, she kept this thought to herself.

'Where do most of your punters come from?' asked Brickall.

'From all over. We have some from the Netherlands, from Spain and Italy. And quite a lot from the Irish Republic, obviously.'

'Obviously?' repeated Rachel.

'They all come from Roman Catholic backgrounds: we're a Catholic organisation. We have more applications than places, so we're fortunate to be able to pick the brightest, most diligent students, all from good Catholic homes.'

He sounded so smug when he said this that Rachel grimaced involuntarily. 'If we could speak to your house parents before we wind things up here in Edinburgh, that would be very helpful.' She stood up, suddenly desperate to get out of this stuffy room.

'Of course, anything to help. Jean will give you their details on the way out.' Candlish crinkled his narrow eyes in a smile, remaining seated.

'One thing,' said Brickall, pausing as they reached the door. 'Why White Crystal?'

'Because white crystals are the emblem of unity, of purity. They symbolise innocence.'

*

'So – all fairly straightforward,' Brickall said a few seconds later as they clattered down the stairs and out onto the street, Dolly padding after them.

Rachel shot him a look. 'Funny, that. I was thinking exactly the opposite.'

FOUR

According to its website, Van Meijer Industries was the largest oil and gas industry contractor of its kind in the world. They were by far the biggest employer in the Leiden metropolitan area, but their reach was global, and the company's worth was estimated at a billion euros. Rachel sat at the table in the window of her room for a while, reading about how they provided offshore drilling platforms everywhere from north Norway to Mumbai, and had offices on every continent. For the van Meijers, the steep fee for the White Crystal trip would be a mere drop in the bucket.

She googled Dries van Meijer, and discovered a flamboyant playboy past in the years before he took over from his father as CEO of the company. There was a sequence of paparazzi shots from nightclubs in Cannes, Monaco and New York, with various actress-slash-models draping themselves over him. Eventually there were pictures of a wedding, at the Catholic Cathedral of St Catherine in Utrecht. His bride – in a Valentino gown and accompanied by ten bridesmaids – was an Austrian aristocrat called Annemarie von Burgau. Later there were charming baptism shoots captured in the European editions of *Hello* magazine, first of Willem, then Sem and finally baby Emily. There was so much pride on Dries's face as he cradled his daughter in the traditional lace christening gown: it made Rachel's heart ache.

After looking at the family photos, she regretted not talking to van Meijer properly before leaving London. One on one. To better understand just why he was so sure this was not an accident. Know your victim: that was always the starting point in any enquiry, and who better to paint the picture than Emily's own father? She found the email address for the Dutch ambassador's assistant in the briefing file and sent a brief request for a phone conversation with Dries van Meijer, before putting her laptop away and getting ready to go out.

Choosing the right outfit for meeting your ex-husband's new wife was always going to be tricky. Self-respect had to be maintained without appearing to try too hard. It didn't help that she hadn't brought many clothes in her carry-on luggage. In the end, Rachel settled on the trousers from the grey linen suit, worn with a loose, semi-sheer blouse with voluminous sleeves and a ruffled front. She put on the only pair of smart shoes she had in her case – cream kitten heels – let down her blonde ponytail and applied her make-up to look as though she wasn't wearing any, even though she was. *Was the new Mrs Ritchie right now engaged in a similar exercise*, she wondered. *Did she mind the ongoing contact with the first Mrs Ritchie?*

The answer probably depended on how Stuart had framed this evening's socialising for his new bride. He and Rachel no longer had financial ties or joint property, and he had no need to keep her on side. The only possible reason to do this, now they had all moved on, was in the spirit of remaining friends. Of demonstrating that there were no hard feelings.

Stuart and Claire Ritchie lived in a pleasant stone terrace in Inverleith, overlooking the Botanic Gardens. The pretty, tree-lined street was luminous in the setting sun; an oasis away from the frantic festival activity. Rachel paused and enjoyed a moment of peace before walking up the front path and ringing the bell.

Stuart must have seen her approaching, because the door was immediately flung open. 'Welcome, welcome!' he boomed effusively, while Claire kissed Rachel on the cheek saying, 'So nice to finally meet you.' She didn't add the cliché that she had heard a lot about her husband's first wife, but it was implied. Claire had a smooth chestnut bob and a gentle, open face that was attractive but not quite beautiful. She wore jeans and a striped Breton top and her feet were bare, making Rachel wish she had opted for a more low-key look.

Rachel deflected the awkwardness by handing over a bottle of wine, expensive enough to impress even Stuart. Claire put it in the kitchen and led Rachel into the bay-windowed sitting room while Stuart organised drinks and snacks. It had a stripped wooden floor and open fireplace and was decorated with contemporary oil paintings and discreetly expensive furniture.

'Dinner won't be very long,' Claire said, as though anxious to placate her guest. 'I hope you eat fish? Stuart says you do.'

'Fish would be great,' Rachel assured her with a smile.

Stuart came in carrying a tray of drinks and a large bowl of tortilla chips. He handed Rachel a vodka and tonic, took a large glass of white wine for himself and gave Claire what looked like fizzy water.

'I'm not drinking,' Claire explained when she saw Rachel's sideways glance. 'We're going through our second IVF cycle, and the embryos are due to be implanted tomorrow.'

'Goodness!' said Rachel, at a loss to be confronted with this personal information. What was the standard response? Congratulations? Commiserations? 'How's that going?'

'It was tough when the first cycle failed,' Claire said softly, glancing at Stuart. 'But we re-grouped and… we're hopeful things will work out this time. The doctor says my HCG levels are perfect.'

Claire beamed, and Rachel did her best to look as though she understood what this meant. 'Well, that's great. Exciting. I'll keep my fingers crossed.'

Claire sipped her water. 'Stuart feels that now he's reached the big five-oh there's no time to waste, if he's ever going to achieve his dream of being a dad.'

Was this a dig at her? Rachel glanced in Stuart's direction to gauge her ex-husband's reaction to this rather pointed remark. He, in turn, busied himself with putting a vinyl record onto a state-of-the-art turntable. Vinyl, of course: that was Stuart all over.

'Sadly, Rachel and I weren't together long enough to have a family,' Stuart said smoothly. There was the faintest hint of chill in his voice. 'It never really came up.'

Rachel nodded. Only this wasn't quite true. Stuart had been very keen to start a family from day one.

'I see,' said Claire, sensing tension and making a show of handing round the tortilla chips then fetching a dish of guacamole. 'These things have a way of working out for the best.' She smiled, and offered the guacamole to Rachel, whose hand was shaking so much she narrowly avoided spilling the green paste on her pale trousers.

'I expect it will,' said Stuart, with forced cheeriness. 'Top-up, anyone?'

They ate dinner in the handsome breakfast room that had been extended from the kitchen into the garden. The bi-fold doors were open to the outside, and a phalanx of solar garden lights gave the room a pleasant glow. Claire served roasted sea bass and fennel, a selection of pungent fresh cheeses with grapes, and a home-made white chocolate ice cream with frozen berries. It was all delicious, and Stuart didn't attempt to hide his pride in his wife's culinary accomplishments.

Keen to avoid more scrutiny of their former marriage, Rachel turned to the conversation to the reason she was in Edinburgh. She told them about her quasi-diplomatic mission, outlining the facts but not giving Emily's name.

'That young Dutch girl… I know the case all too well,' said Stuart, who was a professor of pathology. 'In fact, my department performed the PM at the Western General. It wasn't me who did the work; it was one of my junior colleagues, but I remember everyone talking about it. There was an awkward interaction with the girl's father, who was reluctant to accept the findings.'

'Dries van Meijer,' supplied Rachel.

'That's the one – big player in the oil industry. One of the reasons it's stuck in my mind was because we had a very similar case a couple of summers ago. That was during the festival too: a young French lad in town for the festival who had a skinful and fell off the docks at Leith one night.'

The back of Rachel's neck prickled. 'Can you remember his name?'

'Not off the top of my head, but I could look it up for you later; it'll be in our online case records.'

'Thank you. I'd be really grateful.'

Rachel offered to help with the clearing up once the meal was over, but was relieved when Claire refused. 'Och no, don't worry Rachel: our cleaning lady comes in the morning, so I'm going to leave it.' She had a pretty, lilting Scottish accent.

'Claire needs to be at the clinic first thing, so we'll be heading straight to bed.'

Rachel seized this as an excuse to turn down the offer of brandy or coffee and ask her hosts to order her a cab. 'Best of luck tomorrow,' she said, embracing Claire, and meaning it. Claire seemed to make Stuart happy, and the evening had been a pleasant one. Even if the only thing she could now think about was the death of a second teenager.

It must have been on Stuart's mind too, because by the time she had reached the Avalon Guest House there was already an email from him in her inbox.

The French boy's name was Bruno Martinez. Date of birth:
23 April 1999, Lyon. Let me know if I can do any more to
help. And lovely to see you tonight. S

Rachel kicked off her heels, stripped off her smart trousers and
top, and climbed onto the bed with her laptop. She had taken
to wearing just her underwear around the room in an attempt to
extend the wear of the few clothes she had brought with her. She
googled Bruno Martinez and found a Facebook tribute page. She
wasn't able to translate all of the adolescent outpourings, but she
got the gist even though they were in French. Bruno was missed
beyond measure, gone too soon, one of God's angels now.

And, of course, at the top of the page there was a photo of
Bruno. Rachel drew in her breath when she saw it. The boy was
exceptionally good-looking, just as Emily van Meijer had been
exceptionally beautiful. He had perfect bone structure, huge
brown eyes and a shock of wavy dark-gold hair.

'Shit,' Rachel exclaimed to the empty room. 'What happened
to you?'

She returned to the White Crystal website and started scrolling through their archive pages. Each student group in each year
was given a set of thumbnail pictures: carefree group shots with
exaggerated and sometimes frankly daft poses. Typical teenage
stuff. She clicked on the file for August 2015 and worked her way
through the photos. And sure enough, there he was at the centre
of one of the groups: mane of hair flying, arms spread wide as he
did jazz hands.

Bruno Martinez.

FIVE

Rachel woke to teeming summer drizzle and a headache from the wine she had drunk at dinner.

She had hoped to go for a run, but instead shuffled down to breakfast in leggings and a now slightly grimy T-shirt. She sat with the other guests, nursing a coffee and listening to them chatter about the shows they planned to see that day as they tucked in to toast and porridge.

Her phone pinged. An email from Patten.

Good news: the Lord Advocate has given his permission for you to review the file and conduct secondary enquiries into the van Meijer case. The Dutch Prime Minister personally put in a call apparently – I'm not sure it would have come together so quickly without that. I'll see you in London for a debrief in due course, but take as long as you need. Nigel.

Rachel went back up to her room and phoned Brickall.

'Are we going to go and see the students' dorm?' he asked. 'That was what we planned for this morning wasn't it?'

'It was. But we've now got access to the file, and I think we should look at it first before tackling the other members of staff. Turns out Candlish wasn't being completely straight with us when he said that nothing like Emily's death had ever happened before at White Crystal.'

She told him about Bruno Martinez.

'Christ – another one? That doesn't look good.'

'It certainly adds another layer to the puzzle. So, let's go straight to Gayfield Square to collect the paperwork, then we'll have a better idea what we're dealing with.'

'Looking forward to seeing the charming More-hag.' Brickall snorted as he rang off.

Rachel found another email when she had hung up, this time from the Dutch Embassy providing van Meijer's personal phone number. She left a message for him, saying that she would appreciate the chance to talk to him about Emily, but that she would understand if this was not something he felt he wanted to do. Then she grabbed her trench coat, which was the only waterproof clothing she had brought, and set off to meet Brickall.

This morning he was accompanied by Dolly, also dressed in a raincoat. Rachel looked askance at the dog.

He shrugged. 'No need for a charm offensive anymore, so fuck it. Dolly's now part of the team.' They trudged along Gayfield Square through horizontal rain. 'Sodding Scots weather,' Brickall observed. 'I think I'd rather have the London heatwave.'

Morag Sillars was her gruff self when she met them in reception. 'Thought I'd seen the back of yous two,' she said sourly, pulling a Mayfair from the packet despite the '*No Smoking*' notice on the wall.

'DI Sillars!' reproved the desk sergeant.

'I'm no going outside in this pishing rain,' she squawked. She thrust the file at Rachel, putting the Mayfair packet away and instead rummaging in her pocket for an electronic cigarette. 'I wish you luck with it,' Sillars said with a grim smile. 'But you'll no find anything.'

Rachel and Brickall took shelter from the rain in a café adjoining George Square, at the heart of the fringe festival hubbub. Through the window they could see a long line of tourists queuing to collect their tickets from the box office beside an upturned purple inflatable cow. They were handed yet more event flyers as they waited to be served: for a Maori *a capella* group, a female Liberace impersonator in cabaret and a *Game of Thrones* puppet show.

'Couldn't we have gone somewhere a bit quieter?' Brickall grumbled. 'Away from this arse-wit carnival.' Dolly cowered at his side, wrapping her lead around his ankles.

'I wanted us to get a feel for what the students experienced,' Rachel explained. 'It's an important part of the context of this case.'

'If they've never been to the UK before they must have come to the conclusion we're all fucking mental.' Brickall pointed out of the window at a human flame thrower with precipitation dripping off his naked, gold-painted torso, as a group of Japanese tourists in rain ponchos took photos of him.

They worked their way through the contents of the file, which were scant, taking it in turns to read through the statements. There was one from each of the house parents, Will and Hazel MacBain, one from the mountain rescue volunteer who led the search for Emily and was the first to discover her body, and one each from the first two police officers at the scene. The other students in the house at the time were all spoken to, but none of them heard or saw anything, with the exception of an Irish girl called Niamh Donovan, who said she thought she heard Emily banging around in her room in the middle of the night, and someone talking to her just before that.

Hazel MacBain said she had given Emily some paracetamol tablets earlier in the evening when she complained of feeling unwell. She smelled alcohol on her breath but didn't think to act on it. It was only when she checked Emily's room later to see if she was feeling better that she found the Southern Comfort bottle, and that she was missing. Will MacBain, only recently back in Murrayfield after taking a few of the students to a late-night concert, searched the immediate neighbourhood and alerted the mountain rescue team.

According to MacBain's statement, Emily had enjoyed a trip to Salisbury Crags earlier in the week and talked about returning there to photograph the city lights. Since this was the last night of the trip, it would have been her last opportunity to do so. The police officer's statement confirmed that a selfie stick and her phone had been found next to the body.

The pathology report, completed by a Dr Fraser Dewar, found evidence that supported these statements. The stomach contents contained both paracetamol and an amount of alcohol, and her injuries – a skull fracture, shattered spinal and cervical vertebrae, multiple contusions, broken right clavicle, humerus and femur and a ruptured spleen – were consistent with a fall from over a hundred feet onto her right side.

'And the French kid? He fell to his death too?' Brickall asked once they had both finished reading the contents of the file. The rain had stopped, and pale, milky sunshine was breaking through the cloud. Someone in a Tellytubby costume was now playing the bagpipes outside the window of the café.

Rachel shook her head. 'Drowned, apparently. I don't have any details, but it's on my to-do list to ask Stuart if he can give me a look at the PM report.'

'Ah yes,' smirked Brickall. 'Ex-husbands in high places – incredibly useful. How was dinner with your old man last night?'

'My *ex*-old man. And it was fine,' said Rachel calmly. 'In fact, it was better than fine; it was a nice evening. His new wife is lovely.'

'So all that toxic relationship history is in the past now? Buried?'

Rachel hesitated a beat. 'More or less.' She bent down to fondle Dolly's silky ears. 'Come on, this dog needs some exercise. Let's start walking, as far as a tram stop at least.'

*

The White Crystal student residence was a substantial detached sandstone house on Campbell Road, in the upmarket suburb of Murrayfield. A red family-sized estate car was parked on its drive, and the doorbell was above a brass plate that said 'Enquiries'. While they were waiting for it to be answered, Dolly squatted to pee on the front lawn and then lay down on her side, too tired to move further.

'A doggie!' squealed a delighted voice as the door was opened. A small blonde child ran out and attempted to pat Dolly. The dog rolled her eyes up into her head and played dead.

'Esme, don't touch the dog; you don't know who it belongs to! It might not be friendly.' A young woman with another child on her hip came out onto the front step.

'It's fine,' smiled Brickall. 'She won't hurt your little girl, she's far too knackered. In fact, if you could see your way to giving her a drink of water, that would be greatly appreciated.' He pulled out his warrant card as he spoke. 'I'm DS Mark Brickall, and this is DI Rachel Prince. Are you Hazel MacBain?'

She nodded, and smiled shyly. She was of medium height and build, with sandy-blonde hair, fair freckled skin and the sort of watered-down prettiness that made a face hard to recall later.

'We'd like to speak to you and your husband about Emily van Meijer, if that's convenient,' said Rachel.

Hazel nodded, clutching the toddler closer her chest. 'But Will's not here,' she said, her eyes darting from Rachel to Brickall and then over to Dolly. 'Esme, I told you, leave the doggie alone!'

Brickall walked over and separated dog and child, hauling a reluctant Dolly to her feet.

'Could we come in and have a quick word anyway?' asked Rachel. 'We can always talk to Mr MacBain another time.'

'Yes of course.' She smiled hesitantly. 'Though I'm not really sure why it's necessary.'

'If we can come in, I'll explain,' said Rachel firmly, employing her best door-stopping technique and walking past Hazel into the hall before she had a chance to refuse.

'Let's go up to the kitchen,' said Hazel, pulling her daughter back inside and steering her towards the staircase. 'Then I'll be able to get your dog a bowl of water. But I'm afraid it'll have to be quick, the baby needs a nap and I need to get the children's lunch.'

She led them up a wide staircase to the top floor. 'The student's communal areas – TV room, refectory, kitchen and a laundry are on the ground floor,' Hazel told them on the way up. 'Their bedrooms are on the first and second floors,' she pointed to a series of doors as they passed them, 'and Will, the kids and I are on the top floor.'

They had reached the attic floor. It was spacious, but sloping ceilings made it feel cramped. There was a square kitchen-dining room, a small sitting room, two double bedrooms and a third room no bigger than a box room which contained a cot. Hazel put the toddler in to it and closed the door on his fretful squeals.

'He'll settle,' she assured them, leading Esme to the kitchen table and giving her crayons and paper before filling a bowl with cold water for Dolly. 'It takes Angus a few minutes to burn himself out before he'll sleep.' She placed her hand strategically on her abdomen. 'I'm not sure how I'll cope with three when this one arrives.'

Rachel noticed the early signs of a pregnancy bump for the first time.

'Another ankle-biter, eh?' said Brickall tactlessly. 'You must be a glutton for punishment.'

Hazel responded with a beatific smile. 'Not at all; I love having wee ones around… I hope you don't mind if I get on,' she added, busying herself with peeling fruit and buttering bread.

'So where's your husband?' asked Brickall.

'He's taken the students over to Glasgow to visit the Science Centre. We try and fit in a few educational outings if we can, in addition to the festival shows.'

'When you say "taken them", what do you do for transport?'

'We've a twenty-seater minibus.'

'So that's your car parked outside?'

The skin on Hazel's neck grew slightly pink, as she concentrated on the chopping cheese into toddler-sized cubes. 'It's our family car, yes, but we only use it when Will's here. I don't drive, so everything to do with transport and activities off site are his domain. I just take care of the meals and the pastoral care, and supervise the cleaning.'

'So, the night Emily died, for example,' Rachel said. 'You said she reported feeling unwell, and you gave her some paracetamol?'

'That's right.' Hazel kept her back turned. 'She told me she had a bad headache.'

'And she'd been drinking?'

She hesitated. 'I thought she smelt of alcohol, but I wasn't certain. I rarely drink myself, you see.'

'How many pills did you give her?'

'I left the whole packet with her.'

'And that was the last time you saw her alive?' asked Brickall.

'Yes.' Hazel's voice was meek. 'It was. I went back to check on her a few hours later, before I turned in, and she wasn't in her room. That's when I found the bottle of Southern Comfort. I realised where it had come from straight away: it was ours. We don't drink spirits ourselves, but we're often given bottles as gifts by students, and we keep them in the cabinet up here in the flat, for guests.'

'How would she have got hold of it?' asked Brickall. 'If she came up here, surely you'd have seen her?'

'Will was out, and I would probably have been downstairs preparing food for the students. It's all there in my statement… After I found she was missing, it was Will who took charge and organised everyone to start looking. As I said, I don't drive, and someone had to stay here to mind the children.'

She kept her back turned as she arranged sandwiches, cheese and fruit on a plate, placing it in front of her daughter. Dolly positioned herself next to the table, and Esme dropped a cube of cheddar straight into her mouth.

'And what can you tell us about Bruno Martinez? I believe he was one of your students two summers ago.'

Once again, Hazel's translucent skin coloured. She was one of those women whose complexions were like Belisha beacons, flaring with colour when they were agitated. 'I can't…' She drew her breath in sharply. 'I don't think it's my place to comment on that, I'm sorry. You'll have to speak to Will.'

'Oh, we're going to,' said Brickall grimly. 'Don't worry about that.'

'Can we see Emily's room before we go?' Rachel asked.

'Well, it's not Emily's room anymore. There's a Spanish boy in there now. So there'll be nothing useful to see.'

'I'd still like to take a look,' Rachel persisted.

'Of course.' Hazel managed a smile. 'I can't leave the kids up here on their own, but you could take a peep on your way out. It's room nine, on the first floor. They're not locked.'

Rachel, Brickall and Dolly made their way to room nine, which was around nine feet by eight feet, just about fitting a single bed, a small wardrobe, a chest and a built-in desk along one wall. The new occupant was untidy and the carpet was strewn with dirty clothes. Dolly trundled around the room sniffing them with alacrity. There was only a partial window: the accommodation had been created by partitioning the building's original, larger bedrooms. As Hazel had predicted, there was nothing to see.

'You're right: something definitely doesn't add up,' Brickall said firmly as soon as they were out on the street again, heading back towards Ravelston Dykes with a reluctant Dolly in tow.

'Go on.'

'It must be four or five miles from here to Salisbury Crags. If you're falling down pissed, are you really going to manage to walk all the way out there in the dark? It would take over an hour. Makes no sense.'

Rachel raised an eyebrow at him. 'Great minds think alike, Detective Sergeant. That's exactly what occurred to me when I first read the briefing note. Though I suppose – being objective – she could have taken a bus or a taxi.'

Brickall sucked his teeth. 'Still doesn't sit right. If she was set on a late-night selfie shoot, she would have roped in her mates. That's how teenage girls operate. They hunt in packs. She wouldn't have gone alone.'

They headed along Ravelston Dykes towards the city, Dolly stopping to sniff every single lamp post. Rachel's phone rang.

'DI Prince, this is Dries van Meijer.'

'Hi…' Rachel looked around her and found a stone wall to sit on, motioning to Brickall to wait. 'Is this a convenient time to have a chat?'

'I thought it would be better to speak in person,' van Meijer offered.

'The thing is, I don't know when I'm going to be back in London—'

'No, I'll come to Edinburgh.'

Rachel frowned into her handset. 'Mr van Meijer, I wouldn't want to put you to any inconvenience—'

'This concerns my daughter,' he said firmly. 'Inconvenience doesn't come into it. Besides, I have my own plane.'

Ah. Of course he did.

'I'll fly up tonight, and call you when I arrive.'

Rachel hung up, already wondering how she was going to explain to van Meijer that this case was now about far more than the tragic death of his daughter.

SIX

Dries van Meijer had secured a suite in Edinburgh's most exclusive luxury hotel, despite the city's ongoing 'arse-wit carnival', as Brickall had labelled it. But then if you could fly in by private jet, mused Rachel, as she walked into the lobby, then small details such as finding a room for the night were of no consequence. She had come alone, leaving Brickall to work his way through Betty Kilpatrick's supply of baked goods.

The woman at the highly designed glass and chrome reception desk put her straight through to the suite when she asked for van Meijer.

'You may as well come up here,' he said coolly. 'We can talk more discreetly than in one of the public bars.'

When the staff realised whose guest she was, she was assigned her own bellhop to take her up to the top floor of the building. The suite had floor-to-ceiling windows on two sides, with spectacular views over Calton Hill. Leather Eames chairs sat between modern sofas covered in grey tweed and huge statement lamps, and side tables held extravagant displays of purple hydrangea, alliums and heather.

Van Meijer had abandoned the suit and black tie for a black cashmere polo shirt, well-cut black trousers and suede loafers worn in the continental style – without socks.

'Mr van Meijer,' Rachel extended a hand. 'It would be wrong to say it's a pleasure, but I am glad you were able to come.'

'Call me Dries,' he said simply. 'There is a bar here with most of the basics, or you could order a cocktail if you prefer?' He handed her an iPad with the drinks' menu, which included at least forty single malt whiskies.

'Could I have a gin and tonic?' she asked.

'Sure. Or I was going to have some of this.' He pulled a bottle of Krug from the wine fridge.

'Well in that case, since you're opening it…'

Van Meijer popped the cork with the practised ease of a jet-set veteran and filled two crystal flutes. He raised his. 'To Emily.'

'To Emily,' said Rachel quietly, taking a sip.

There was a discreet tap on the door, and a butler brought in a silver salver of open-faced smoked salmon sandwiches.

'So, how are you getting on, Detective?' asked van Meijer.

Rachel thought for a few seconds before answering. The last thing she wanted was to promise answers if there were none. 'Things are going well so far,' she said cautiously. 'We've had permission to review all the Police Scotland paperwork, and we've made a start on our own enquiries.'

'You have a theory?' he asked, his voice hopeful.

'It's a little too soon for that,' Rachel took another sip of the champagne. It was delicious, but strictly speaking she was on duty. She set the glass down and took a sandwich instead, realising that she was extremely hungry. 'There are certainly questions that need to be answered.'

He nodded, watching her face. The sadness never left his eyes, not for a second.

'Tell me about Emily,' she said. 'It's always helpful to know a bit more about a person when conducting an enquiry.' It would have been a little tactless to use the term victimology, but that was what this was. Knowing your victim. 'What kind of a girl was she? What made her tick, what inspired her?'

Van Meijer gave a shuddering sigh, one that encompassed the depths of grief. For a few seconds he dropped his head and rested his face against his fingers. When he surfaced again, he spoke levelly. 'She was a joy from day one. A lovely, easy baby, a delightful little girl. On the serious side, but loving, caring. Her two big brothers adored her.'

'This must be terribly hard for them. And for Emily's mother.'

He nodded. 'Emily had an enquiring mind, always questioning everything. The endless questions when she was four or five years old… it could drive you mad sometimes.' He smiled at the memory. 'She studied hard at school, and was an able student, if not exceptional. She was approached by a couple of top modelling agencies, but she wasn't interested in going down that route. Her dream was to go to Harvard and study Environmental Science and Public Policy.'

There was a hollow silence as they both acknowledged that this would now never happen. Van Meijer offered more champagne, but Rachel shook her head.

'The thing about Emily: she was never a silly kid. She had a privileged upbringing, sure – travelled a lot, met sophisticated people. So she was old for her years: wordly, if you like. What they said about her drinking a load of stolen whisky and going off alone to take photos in the dark; that would never have happened. That wasn't Emily, she wouldn't behave like that. I just know it.'

Van Meijer looked straight at Rachel. 'Do you have children?'

She hesitated a split second, then shook her head.

'Well when… if… you do… you will know that child just like you know yourself. You know their heart, and you know their mind. And I'm telling you: my Emily did not do this. What they say she did, this is not what happened.' He spoke with chilling certainty.

'When did you last speak to Emily, Mr— Dries.'

'The day before she died. We Facetimed, briefly. I was at La Guardia in New York, about to fly back from a meeting.'

'And how was she?'

Van Meijer paused a beat. 'I felt like something was wrong. I asked her, and she denied it, but I could tell something was unsettling her. She had something on her mind. Again, with your own child you just know, without them needing to say anything.'

'Did she make friends with any of the others in the group at White Crystal?'

'Ridiculous name,' van Meijer interjected.

Rachel smiled in agreement. 'Did she mention anyone to you?'

'There was a boy in the same group from her school in Leiden. Luuk Rynsberger. They were good friends, and travelled over from the Netherlands together.'

'Have you talked to Luuk since… he came back?'

Van Meijer shook his head. 'It was too soon after losing our daughter. We were all in such deep shock… Emily also mentioned an Irish girl she liked. She spoke about her a couple of times; said they got on well.'

Rachel took her notebook from her pocket and consulted it, remembering the girl who had given the statement in Emily's police file. 'Was it Niamh Donovan, by any chance?'

He nodded. 'Niamh, yes, that's right. She was from Dublin.'

'I'll get hold of her details, and hopefully I'll be able to speak to her.'

'If you need to go over to Dublin, I'm happy to put my plane at your disposal. If it would make it easier.'

Rachel smiled. 'That's very kind, and it would no doubt make things easier, but my boss would never agree to it. Police officers have to act impartially, and being flown around in private jets makes would make us look… well, not impartial.'

Van Meijer nodded. 'I understand.' He walked over to the window and looked out over the dark silhouette of the city against a pink and gold-streaked sky. 'It's just my impatience, you understand. My frustration.'

'I do understand. And I will go as soon as I'm able.'

'At least let me help organise it. The National Crime Agency can bill me for any costs where appropriate. You're away from your office and your everyday infrastructure here, after all.'

Rachel nodded. 'I'll certainly be in touch if I need any help, if it comes to taking our enquiries to Ireland.'

He walked over and clasped her hand in both of his. 'Please,' he said. 'Please try. I have to know what happened to my girl.'

SEVEN

'Let me get this right: you turned down a trip in a private jet?'

Brickall looked incredulously at Rachel.

'Come off it,' Rachel scoffed. 'Seriously, DS Brickall, you're not suggesting I should have accepted? I can see the headlines in the *Daily Mail* now: LONDON COP JAUNTS IN BILLIONAIRE JET.'

They were back in Gayfield Square with Dolly in tow, this time to request the file on Bruno Martinez. Rachel took Dolly's lead from Brickall.

'Why don't you go in on your own this time? DI Sillars clearly preferred you to me.'

'She had a funny way of showing it.'

'Okay, she despised you less, then. Go in there and work your magic and we'll will wait for you here. Me and Dolly.'

'It's Saturday; she might not even be rostered on.'

Brickall went into the building anyway, leaving Rachel sitting on the steps with Dolly at her feet. Ten minutes later he emerged carrying a manila folder. He handed it to Rachel. 'Bruno Martinez's file. As requested.'

'She was there?'

'Yep. I suspect she doesn't have such thing as a personal life. Anyway, I talked about football; worked like a charm. Old Morehag's a diehard Rangers fan, hardly surprising, seeing as she's a Weegie. That's her kryptonite.' He slapped the file down next to Rachel. 'Having said that, there's not a whole lot in here.'

They walked to a café on York Place to get out of the chilly wind. Brickall ordered two coffees and a fry-up for himself, and they went through the contents of the folder. The most informative piece of paperwork was the incident report by PC Kirstie Blair, who was the first officer on the scene.

I was on patrol with PC Davey Robertson at 2.45 a.m. on the morning of 12 August 2015 when I received a radio call from despatch to say a member of the public had spotted someone in the water off Lighthouse Park in Leith. On arrival at the scene, I confirmed that there was what appeared to be the body of a young man face down in the water. PC Robertson radioed despatch and asked them to contact the Dive and Marine Unit. Approximately ten minutes later DMU arrived in an inflatable launch and pulled the body of a male from the water, pronouncing him to be deceased. The witness who phoned the police, a shift worker called Derek McGraw, was taking his dog for a late-night walk when he spotted the body in the water. The park was deserted at that time, and he reported seeing no other passers-by. PC Faulds from the Dive Unit handed me the wallet from the clothing of the deceased. This confirmed that he was a French national called Bruno Martinez, and that he was a student on a cultural tour, staying at 34 Campbell Road, Murrayfield. I passed on this information to control, who despatched a mobile unit to the address.

A police appeal for information later prompted another witness, Caitlyn Anderson, to come forward. Her statement described how at around 1.30 a.m. she was returning home from a party and saw a young woman and a younger man standing near a car parked at the end of Western Harbour Drive, near the approach to Lighthouse Park. The male – answering Bruno's description – appeared drunk and the woman appeared to have stopped to help, and to be attempting to persuade him into the car. All that she saw of the car was that it was brown coloured.

Hazel MacBain had also been interviewed, but her statement was extremely brief, merely saying that she had been suffering pregnancy problems and was on bed rest. She didn't hear or see anything on the evening of the 11 August.

'Odd,' commented Rachel. 'If it was that cut and dried, why was Hazel so reluctant to speak to us about it? Why didn't she just tell us what's written here?'

'Maybe a sense of shame that two kids have met sticky ends while in her care.' Brickall squirted more brown sauce onto his plate and set to work on a slab of fried haggis. 'This is bloody delicious; you should have some.'

Rachel shook her head in disbelief. 'Haven't you already had a full Scottish at Betty's this morning?'

'So? Stick with what works.' Brickall scooped scrambled egg onto his fork, while Rachel continued to sort through the contents of the folder. Dolly's tail swept an eager arc across the café floor, and Brickall tossed her a piece of sausage.

Will MacBain's statement was a little more detailed. He described how Bruno had seemed in a low mood on 11 August, complaining of being homesick. On the evening of the eleventh Will had been accompanying a group of seven students to a concert being held at the Queen's Hall in the city, returning in the minibus at around 10.45 p.m. The first he knew of Bruno's disappearance was the arrival of the police in Campbell Road at 5 a.m. on the twelfth, but when he subsequently looked in the boy's room he found an empty bottle of port. An identical bottle was missing from the drinks cupboard in the MacBain's private quarters.

'Leith Docks is even further than Salisbury Crags,' Brickall observed. 'Again, very odd to go that far on a late night bender. Alone, just like Emily was.'

'Hmmm,' Rachel looked thoughtful. 'I'm not sure it's quite that straightforward. Maybe he had a falling out with another student. Teenage boys are a moody lot, prone to mooching off on their own. You should know: you used to be one.'

'Touché,' grinned Brickall. 'But unless we find a link to the van Meijer case, I guess we're going to have to write it off as an unfortunate coincidence. One that reflects badly on White Crystal Tours, even if the deaths weren't directly their fault. You can kind of understand why they would want to keep things quiet. For commercial reasons if nothing else.'

'There is one thing…' Rachel pulled out the post-mortem report. It stated that death was due to drowning and hypothermia. The Firth of Forth was only a few degrees above freezing at night, even in August, and the cold and the alcohol in Bruno's system would quickly have rendered him unconscious. 'Look.' She pointed to the signature of the pathologist. 'Dr Fraser Dewar. Same one that did the PM on Emily.'

Brickall shrugged, wiping the grease from his lips with a paper napkin. 'If it's a small lab, that's probably not too surprising.'

'Maybe. I'd still like to speak to him though.'

'So what's next? That, or a trip to Dublin to talk to the Irish girl?' Brickall reached down and fondled Dolly's ears.

'Dublin's definitely for tomorrow; the pathologist can wait a bit longer. But our first priority has to be talking to Will MacBain. Let's do it this evening. That way we've got a chance of catching both the MacBains in. I want to see if talking to them together throws up anything worthwhile.'

Rachel and Brickall made the return trip to Campbell Road at seven that evening.

Hazel MacBain met them at the front door wearing a frilly apron, which was stretched slightly by her pregnant abdomen.

What woman under the age of forty owns an apron? Rachel wondered. The bleep of video games and the click of billiard balls came from the other side of the hall, punctuated by bursts of adolescent laughter.

'Back so soon?' Hazel forced a little laugh. 'You can't keep away from the place… only I'm afraid this isn't the most convenient time,' she added. 'Will's putting the children to bed, and I'm getting supper ready for the students.'

'It's okay, it won't take long,' said Rachel firmly. 'We'll just pop up and have a quick word with your husband, and as soon as you get a minute, perhaps you'd come up and join us.'

Hazel peered out of the front door. 'You've not brought the dog with you? Only it's bound to get Esme all wound up, just as Will needs to settle her.'

'No dog,' confirmed Brickall, who had left Dolly watching *Ant and Dec's Saturday Night Takeaway* with Betty.

Will MacBain was sitting on the sofa in the family living room on the top floor. He was reading a pyjama-clad Esme a story, turning the pages with one hand while propping a bottle of milk in Angus's mouth. From the doorway, Brickall waved at Esme, who stuck out her tongue.

'Just give me two minutes please,' said Will. He had the sort of blandly conventional looks that would not have been out of place on the front of a knitting pattern. His mousey hair was brushed back neatly from his forehead, and he wore glasses with square steel rims. His clothes were those of a much older man: a checked Viyella shirt and sleeveless navy sweater, and punched leather brogues. He reminded Rachel of the young male teachers at her former school.

He read the last two pages of *Peppa Pig*, prised the teat from a dozing Angus's mouth and took the children to their rooms, indicating to Rachel and Brickall that they should take a seat while he completed the bedtime ritual. There were a few high-pitched protests from Esme, but as Will came back into the living room she fell silent.

'How can I help you, officers?' He had the clear and mellifluous speaking voice of someone who also sings well.

'Just a couple of things relating to your statement about the night Emily van Meijer died,' said Rachel. 'Why did you call the mountain rescue team when you realised she had gone missing? Rather than contact the police straight away.'

'Because I had a hunch she might have gone out to the Crags.' Will spoke evenly, pleasantly. 'And when it comes to finding people in the dark, they have a greater chance of getting to them fast. They're the experts in that sort of terrain, not the police. And bear in mind I had no idea what had happened to the poor girl at that time; that she was…' His voice trailed off and he adopted a look of sorrow. 'We just thought she'd got lost.'

Brickall ignored this. 'Why did Kenneth Candlish mislead us about Bruno Martinez?' he demanded.

Will looked genuinely puzzled.

'When we visited him at your company's offices, he assured us that Emily van Meijer's death was an isolated incident. And yet you had lost one of your students in very similar circumstances the year before last.'

'I really don't know,' Will said. 'I mean, he knew about Bruno. Of course he did. Maybe he just forgot.'

'Forgot?' Brickall repeated. 'He forgot a kid that died when under your care? Really?'

Will twisted his mouth in an exasperated expression. 'I don't mean forget in that sense… Kenneth is fond of a dram, and it can affect his recall. Sometimes he's not as mentally sharp as would be ideal. I expect that's what it was.'

'He seemed perfectly sharp to me,' said Rachel, recalling the beady little eyes, the incisive summary of why the two officers were in Scotland. 'Are you sure he wasn't trying to keep us from finding out about him?'

'Quite sure,' said Will calmly. 'There would be no reason to. The Procurator Fiscal was satisfied that Bruno fell into the sea and drowned, after drinking alcohol.'

'Hardly great for business though, is it?' Brickall persisted. 'Two of your clients dead in twenty-four months. Doesn't reflect well on White Crystal.'

'No. Probably not.' Will looked suitably grave.

The smell of hot food wafted up the stairs, and Hazel appeared, without her apron this time. She sat down beside her husband, pressing herself against his side. 'Kids go down all right, love?'

Will wrapped an arm round his wife and drew her in close, kissing her on the top of her head. 'All fine darling, don't worry.' He kept her in the close embrace, looking back at Rachel and Brickall defiantly.

'How long have you two been married?' Rachel asked.

'Seven years,' they answered in unison.

'Seven years and four months of bliss,' Will said, kissing his wife again. She gave a little sigh of pleasure and snuggled against him. Rachel and Brickall exchanged glances.

'So what's your secret?' Brickall asked provocatively. 'What is it that makes you act like newlyweds after all this time? Supposed to be the seven-year itch, isn't it?'

'Will is my rock,' said Hazel, glancing adoringly at her spouse. 'And we have so much in common. Our faith for a start.' She reached her hand to her neck and fingered the small gold crucifix hanging there. 'And I like to think we have a traditional marriage. We respect the traditional male and female roles.'

'That's right,' said Will smugly. 'We've not tried to reinvent the wheel. Hazel's happy to do all the cooking and supervise looking after the house.'

'Big place to keep clean,' observed Rachel.

'We do have a cleaning lady; Mrs Muir,' Hazel said. 'She's been with us for years, and she does the students' rooms and helps me up here. I do most of the childcare, apart from when I'm cooking for the students, when Will helps with bedtime. Like today. I do all the shopping, apart from cash-and-carry runs that require the car. Will supervises the students apart from – you know – female problems and medical stuff… and the building maintenance, the vehicles and the bill paying are all his domain. It works for us,' she finished simply.

'It does,' said Will, kissing his wife again.

'How do you go about deciding which festival events the students will see?' asked Rachel.

'Well, you may not have realised it, but there are thousands of things going on.' Will's smile was faintly patronising. 'We get a copy of the programme in advance, and I go through it carefully and make selections. And obviously, a lot of the more… adult themed… fare is not appropriate for fifteen to seventeen year olds. We usually go with a couple of magic shows, a couple of classical concerts, maybe one serious play, and some physical theatre or circus acts. Those are usually popular. And then on top of the festival we do a few local trips of educational value. We find that's a balance that works out well. The students always say how much they enjoy the programme, and some come back more than once.'

'So… that's August taken care of, but how about when the students aren't here?' asked Brickall. 'What do you do the rest of the year?'

Hazel glanced at her husband before answering. 'We do another residential week in January, for Hogmanay, with eighteen to twenty-one year olds. There are usually quite a few cultural events on at that time of year. Will works as a counsellor on some Catholic youth scouting and orienteering weeks, and of course he helps Kenneth with all the business administration. He's in the office a lot in off-season.'

'I'm also very involved with the chapel,' added Will, patting his wife's shoulder. 'I lead the youth choir and sing in the baroque choral group. And of course there are the wee ones; they keep us pretty busy. And our wider family.'

Hazel flushed, reaching for her crucifix again. 'But mostly we just like being together.'

'Pass me the fucking sick bucket,' said Brickall, once he and Rachel had left the house.

'I know,' she concurred, with a shudder. 'All that marital devotion. Creeped me out a bit.'

They fell silent as they walked along Corstorphine Road in the direction of the city centre, both lost in thought.

'What d'you reckon, boss?' asked Brickall after a few minutes. 'I can practically see the cogs whirring in your brain.'

'Something doesn't feel right,' said Rachel. 'But I'm struggling to put my finger on what it is.'

'Go on.'

'Emily's father was so adamant that his daughter wouldn't act in the way the official narrative portrayed her, and I trust his instinct. And then there's Bruno… although currently we don't know enough about him to work out whether that behaviour was out of character. I need to speak to someone who did know him. Find out what sort of a kid he was.'

'That guy Candlish seemed a bit slippery too. Bit too smooth. We need to look more closely at him.'

'Maybe you could do some digging while I'm away in Dublin?'

They caught a tram from Gorgie to the city centre, and when they disembarked the crowds were building again, as the late-night show schedule got underway and the locals set about their Saturday night. Everywhere there were groups of festivalgoers consuming plastic beakers of cheap lager as they queued at various show venues. 'Fancy a drink?' asked Brickall.

'Maybe,' said Rachel. 'But not here. We're going on a little side trip.'

She hailed a cab, and asked the driver to take them to Leith Shore. They found a bar in a modern hotel and sat looking over the harbour while Rachel drank a glass of red wine and Brickall consumed two pints, a packet of crisps and some pork scratchings. Then, as it was starting to go dark, they walked along the Western Harbour Breakwater and out to Lighthouse Park, following the path to the furthest reach, where the lighthouse stood. It felt surprisingly remote and wild, for a city park. There was no lighting, and they could hear rather than see the gentle slap of the water against the rocks.

'Great spot to chuck yourself into the sea with no one to see you,' Brickall said, voicing what Rachel had been thinking. 'Or to fall when you're a bit sauced.'

'Or to be pushed.'

Brickall turned to stare at Rachel's profile in the darkness.

'Is that what you think?'

She shrugged. 'I don't currently have a credible theory. We don't really know what happened. Which is why we need to keep asking questions.'

They strolled back up Leith Walk to the city centre, and as they neared the festival hub, every few yards some eager twenty-something – usually female – thrust invitations into their hands or tried to persuade them to come with them to some late night venue. There was the Hot Dub Time Machine, where they could 'literally' travel back in time ('I doubt that,' said Rachel drily), the Rhythm Furnace, where they were promised synth boogie and new wave disco, or a private party at a club called Hades, 'where absolutely anything goes'.

'The fleshpots of Scotland,' Brickall observed. 'There is definitely a whole other side to the festival than stand-up comedy and busking.'

Rachel looked down at the party invite in her hand. 'I know. And that's exactly what I'm starting to worry about.'

EIGHT

When Rachel arrived at Edinburgh Airport to check in for her flight to Dublin the following afternoon, she was intercepted by a member of the airline's VIP services team.

'Mr van Meijer wanted us to take care of you,' the woman told her, ripping up the boarding pass Rachel had printed at the Avalon Guest House and replacing it with one for First Class. 'Please feel free to use the lounge facilities. I was also asked to pass this along when you checked in.'

She handed Rachel a padded envelope. Inside was a set of keys and a typed note on Van Meijer Industries headed paper.

DI Prince,

These are the keys for our company apartment in Dublin, and I do hope you will feel able to make use of it while you are in the city. The concierge has been informed and everything will be ready for you when you arrive, including a car to meet you at the airport. If you need any further assistance while you are there, please contact my assistant Ronan O'Connell on the number above.

Sincerely, Dries van Meijer.

Rachel had merely informed Dries van Meijer of her intended trip as a courtesy, not expecting this level of hospitality. Still, since the visit was subject to a degree of time pressure, the help was not entirely unwelcome.

When the car pulled up outside, she found that the apartment was in a modern high-rise development on Charlotte Quay, overlooking the Liffey. It was a sleek, rather soulless building mostly given over to corporate rentals, and the inside of the apartment itself was styled to resemble a suite in an expensive hotel. However, there were an umbrella and wellingtons for her use, the fridge had been stocked, there were cosy cashmere throws on the sofa, and a bottle of vintage champagne stood to attention in an ice bucket. This last touch felt a little over the top given that Rachel was in town for a police enquiry rather than a honeymoon, but she did appreciate the efforts to make her feel welcome. Should she be accepting this hospitality at all? It was a thorny question, but she rationalised it as being like staying with a friend. Staying with a friend while simultaneously saving an expense on the public purse.

But it stops here though, she told herself, changing into jeans and a T-shirt and leaving the comfort of the apartment behind. No more freebies: it wasn't exactly ethical.

Instead of heading to one of the anonymous hotel bars on the quayside she set off for a longer walk. It was a balmy evening, warmer than in Edinburgh, and even though the crowds were nowhere near as oppressive as those that had been milling around the festival, there were still plenty of tourists on the street. Rachel strolled for twenty minutes in a north-westerly direction, ending up in the former working-class suburb of Stoneybatter, where she found a traditional pub with blue-painted frontage. The area was now the preserve of hipsters, and apart from a few gnarled local drinkers who looked as though they hadn't budged from their bar stool in seventy years, the pub was wall-to-wall woodcutters' beards, plaid shirts and nose piercings. Rachel ordered herself a glass of Irish whisky with a soda water chaser and took refuge at a tiny corner table away from the noise.

Brickall had sent her an email, and she read it while she sipped the whisky.

Did some chasing up on Candlish: as much as I could on a Sunday anyway. I searched available databases and made a load of phone calls. He doesn't have a record, but you could certainly say he has form. He worked as a bursar in a private boys' school in the highlands, but was let go because of 'inappropriate conduct'. The head didn't want to tell me what it was, but after reminding him that obstructing a police enquiry was an offence, he coughed.

Rachel gave a rueful smile. Will MacBain hadn't exactly been keen to give her Niamh Donovan's address, and she had had to issue him with a similar reminder.

Apparently Candlish was accused of touching up one of the pupils. He denied it, but the school decided to take the boy's word for it. Also, pre-dating computerised records and therefore wiped, he had a historic police caution on his employee record for similar behaviour. The head said Candlish disclosed it at the time he applied for the post. Presumably because he was afraid it might come to light somehow. They hired him anyway, which tells you all you need to know about public schools, IMO. The company records for White Crystal show that he set it up himself, probably because at that point nobody else would employ him to work with youngsters. So I reckon we definitely need to speak to him again.

Tomorrow morning I'm going to bat my eyelashes at More-hag and see if I can track down the witnesses in the Martinez case.

See you when you get back. Stay away from random Irish men:
they've all got the gift of the gab. As you already know ;)

Right on cue, her phone rang. Howard. Noise levels in the pub were rising, so she took the call out into the corridor.

'Hi,' he said. 'Remember me?'

Irritation rose in her like an unstoppable force. 'I do,' she said, faking cheeriness.

'Where are you – still in Scotland?'

'Dublin.'

'Dublin? You're kidding, right?'

Rachel took a deep breath and quelled her irritation.

'Nope, not kidding. I'm really in Dublin. I'm actually in a genuine Irish pub, though I've swerved the Guinness.'

'But this is… you're there for work?' Howard sounded confused.

'Work, yes. Most definitely. Same case as Scotland.'

'So when am I going to see you?'

'I really don't know. Soon.'

'So I'll carry on watering the plants then. Anything else that needs doing?'

'No, don't worry about it.' She was starting to regret letting him have his own key. 'I'll be back very soon, so there's no need. Look, Howard, I've got to go. I'll call you as soon as I'm back in London.'

'But, honey—'

She cut the call and went back to her table. A folk band was setting up in one corner, and Rachel sat there for another hour enjoying the live music and the Irish joviality. It made her think not of random Irish men, but of one Irishman in particular, a man with eyes as dark as the ocean. Giles Denton.

NINE

Niamh Donovan lived in a handsome Victorian red-brick house in Rathgar. She answered the door herself: an extremely pretty girl of fifteen, with vibrant red hair worn in long waves and Instagram-ready make-up applied with the skill of a professional.

'Are you alone?' Rachel asked, after introducing herself.

Niamh nodded. 'My parents are both at work.'

'And they'll be back... when?'

'This evening. Seven-ish?'

Rachel calculated. She didn't have enough time to return to Rathgar in the evening. An appropriate adult was required for a formal interview. So this would have to remain informal. It was better than nothing.

'All right if I come in?'

The girl hesitated a second, looking past Rachel into the street. 'I suppose so. Just for a minute.'

'What do your parents do?' Rachel looked around at the comfortable, expensively decorated interior, as Niamh led her back into the kitchen.

'Dad's a lawyer and Mum's a doctor. Coffee?'

'Yes please.'

Niamh fired up a state-of-the-art espresso machine. 'Is this about Emily?'

Rachel nodded. 'Just a quick chat. Nothing official.'

'But you're not Scottish?' She handed over a mug of coffee and a jug of milk.

Rachel shook her head. 'I'm part of an enquiry team from London. We're looking a bit more closely into the circumstances surrounding the accident. I understand you and Emily became friendly during the trip?'

Niamh ignored this. She became very still, and her artfully highlighted blue eyes were huge in her face. 'But why? Why do they need to ask more questions? It was an accident. They said it was an accident.'

Rachel motioned for the girl to take a seat, but she remained standing.

'Why don't you start by telling me what you remember about the night Emily died?'

'I just…' Niamh brushed at sudden tears with the tips of her fingers. 'I was asleep when they went out looking for her. I only knew she'd died the next morning when Mr MacBain called us all into the refectory to speak to us. Her room was underneath mine, and I do remember hearing voices from there, just quiet talking, then it sounded a bit like the furniture was being moved around. But it went quiet, and then I went to sleep. I wish now I'd gone downstairs to check on her.'

'So do you think she would have gone out into the night to take pictures?'

Niamh shook her head vigorously. 'No. No.'

'They did find her selfie stick by— with her.'

'Emily didn't have a selfie stick!' Niamh's tone was scornful. 'Are you sure?'

'One hundred per cent. She despised them; she used to laugh at the Japanese tourists who were waving them about everywhere. Em was way too cool for one of those.'

Rachel considered this for a second, taking a sip of the coffee. 'Could she have borrowed it?'

She frowned. 'I mean, I suppose so. Someone in the house might have had one. But why? Why would she? It would be so out of character.'

'That's what her family think too. Which is why we're conducting this secondary enquiry. One of the reasons.'

Niamh hesitated, her body tensing as though she was actively trying to contain herself. Eventually she pulled out the chair opposite Rachel and sat down on it. 'Is this…'

Her voice trailed off. Rachel waited.

'Is this because of the parties?'

'The parties?'

'We were…' Niamh dragged her hand over her eyes. 'This is just between you and me, right?'

Rachel nodded. 'It's purely an informal chat, yes. I won't be writing anything down, or recording it.'

'I mean, you don't have to tell my parents?'

Rachel shook her head. 'Go on Niamh,' she said gently. 'It's really important you tell me anything you think might be relevant.'

She exhaled hard. 'Okay, well you know how you get handed flyers for events that are going on at the festival?'

Rachel nodded.

'Well me and Emily and a couple of the others were out in the city one day, on our way to a concert, and we were handed these… invite things. The people who gave them to us said they were for a private party and if we wanted to go it would be loads of fun. And back at the house, one of the French girls, Marie-Laure, saw the invite and went all weird on us.'

'Weird?' Rachel repeated.

'You know how other kids are when they don't want to talk about something, but they want you to know that they know about it, to seem sophisticated or whatever.'

'Yes,' Rachel said cautiously, casting her mind back to when she'd been sixteen.

'So eventually she said she'd been to one of the same parties the summer before. 'Cause this year wasn't her first time doing White Crystal. She said it was all a bit out of control, you know – loads of booze and people copping off – and if we were planning to go we shouldn't tell the MacBains because they wouldn't allow it. So me and Emily and Luuk snuck out and walked part of the way into town, then we got a taxi to the address on the invite. It was this big, fancy house. And then…'

'Go on,' Rachel repeated gently.

'I don't know; it was all a bit strange. There were lots of people there, but older people, no one our age. Some of them were wearing masks, you know, not like Halloween masks, like ones from a masked ball. And all these guys wanted to talk to us. They gave me loads of champagne and…'

She fell silent. The cat flap clattered open and a large tabby shot in, scuttling under the table and winding itself around Niamh's chair legs before jumping up on to her lap. She rubbed its ears absently and gave a deep sigh.

'Niamh?'

'The problem is I don't really remember what happened next. I'd never drunk champagne before. My parents won't let me drink at all. I think I remember someone trying to kiss me and touch my… chest… but I can't be sure. I think I passed out, because the next thing I knew it was literally hours later – like *hours* – and I was in the back of a taxi with Emily and Luuk, heading back to the dorm again.'

'Did the three of you talk about what happened?'

She shook her head. 'We didn't really get the chance. I felt so unwell, really mortal, and the taxi had to stop for me to get out and throw up. And I got puke on my dress; it was awful. Luuk was being like a big brother, trying to look after me, but Emily just went really quiet. Afterwards it was like it had all been a really weird dream. And I had a horrible headache, the worst. But then—' She dropped her eyes. 'Look, Ms Prince—'

'Call me Rachel.'

'Rachel; I'm not sure I'm supposed to be telling you this. I mean, aren't I supposed to have an adult present or something?'

'Like I said, only in a formal interview. You've done nothing wrong. But we may have to take another statement from you at some point. I'm just trying to get a better picture of Emily's time in Edinburgh, that's all.'

'Okay.' Niamh ran her hands over the cat's haunches and he adjusted his balance on her lap. 'Well, afterwards, Emily went really quiet. She wasn't one of the loud girls on the course anyway, but she was usually pretty cheerful. But after the party she went into her shell. I asked her what was wrong and she said she didn't want to talk about it. So I asked Luuk and—' She buried her face in the cat's fur for a few seconds. 'Oh God, this is all so awful. And poor Em's dead. I still can't believe it. I just can't.'

'Whatever it is, please tell. It could be important.'

Niamh lifted her head and took a deep breath. 'The thing is, Luuk said Emily told him her drink had been spiked. And that when she woke up she was on her back on the bed, completely naked. And some guy… some man… was standing over her. With his trousers undone.'

TEN

Rachel stared at the girl across the table.

'Let me make sure I've understood you correctly, because this is very important. You're saying Emily van Meijer was sexually assaulted at this party?'

She nodded. 'That's what Luuk was told. By Emily herself.'

'Have you spoken to him about this since? To Luuk?'

Niamh shook her head; mute.

'Or to anyone else?' Rachel asked sharply, more sharply than she intended. 'It's important that I know.'

Niamh paled beneath her peach-coloured blusher. 'Jesus, no! I was mortified about the whole thing. I didn't even dare tell my parents: they'd have gone *mental*. I'm not allowed to drink, or to go out with lads. Not until I'm eighteen. It's not just my parents. I go to a convent school and it's drilled into us every flipping day that we're to behave like good Catholic young ladies.'

'So you didn't go to this other girl, Marie-Laure, and ask her if something similar happened to her?'

Niamh shook her head vigorously.

'And just so I've got this right, you never corroborated this with Emily directly.'

'Corrobor...?'

'Checked with her that Luuk's story was true. That he wasn't just making it up.'

Niamh shook her head. 'But something must have gone on, because like I said, Emily wasn't the same afterwards.'

'Did she seem upset? Distressed?'

Niamh thought about this for a while, still stroking the cat's solid body. 'No. Not upset exactly. More angry. More like she was in a really, really bad mood and couldn't wait to get home.'

Rachel thought back to Dries van Meijer's conviction that there had been something troubling his daughter.

'And when you got back after the party and sobered up – I'm sorry, but I have to ask this – was there any evidence that anyone had touched you inappropriately while you were passed out?'

'Evidence, how?'

'Were your clothes intact, not messed up in anyway? No bruises or… bleeding?'

Niamh looked horrified. 'No, no, my clothes were fine, apart from the vomit. I was fine.'

'Okay, well I think we should leave things there. For now. I'm afraid one of my colleagues may have to take a formal statement at some point, and that will involve your parents.' Rachel stood up. 'I'm very grateful, Niamh, I know this wasn't easy. Just one last thing before I go: do you still have the flyer? With the party details?'

Niamh shook her head. 'No, sorry, I didn't keep it.'

'So let's get this straight…'

Brickall and Rachel were taking Dolly for a late evening walk around the Meadows, Brickall munching on a slice of takeaway pizza. Rachel's return flight from Dublin had landed that afternoon and she had fired off a '*We need to talk*' text as soon as the plane finished taxiing.

'… we've got a guy, Candlish, heading this organisation who – if he'd done what he did post-1997 – would almost certainly be on the sex offenders register. And two teenagers in the care of said organisation attend a sex party where they're being passed round like pieces of meat. Groomed, effectively. One of whom ends up dead.' Brickall thrust the remainder of the pizza into his mouth, wiped his hands on a paper napkin and tossed it into a bin.

'Plus this other girl, Marie-Laure, was invited to an identical event the year before.'

'I'll tell you something, DI Prince, this is turning into way more than just a PR exercise to keep our Dutch friends happy.'

'Don't I know it.' Rachel reached down and fondled Dolly's ears. 'I think we've pretty much reached the point where we have to go back to London and brief Patten.'

'I've got the details for the witness in Bruno's case: Caitlyn Anderson. Maybe we should talk to her first? The other witness – the old boy walking his dog – passed away nine months ago, apparently.'

'Agreed. And I also need to find time to speak to the pathologist who did the PMs. And to Luuk Rynsberger. Oh, and we're going to need to organise someone taking a formal statement from Niamh Donovan, with an adult present.' Rachel sighed. 'Come on, there's a hot bath with my name on it back at the guest house.'

They turned and walked back up the slope towards Morningside.

'One more thing though boss; came out by chance when I was at the cop shop.'

'Go on.'

'The PC who did the Martinez incident report was there, and we got talking. She said she already knew of Hazel MacBain.'

'Really?' Rachel stopped and looked at him. 'You sure it's the same one? She doesn't strike me as the type to have a record. Far too meek and mild.'

'Definitely the same one. I looked it up to check. Her maiden name is Nevins, Hazel Nevins. She doesn't have a record, but apparently her dad was Archie Nevins, a well-known violent offender and all round bad lot. According to this PC Blair, every cop in Edinburgh knows who Archie Nevins is. He killed his wife after a drunken row. Thumped her one, and she fell and hit her head on the hearth. Died of a brain haemorrhage. Nevins was given a whole life sentence. So young Hazel spent most of her childhood in foster homes or in care.'

'Christ,' Rachel said, with feeling.

'I know. You'd never think it to look at her.'

'I suppose it explains why she treats her husband like he's a saint or an archangel or something,' Rachel said thoughtfully. 'He really is her saviour.'

It had been several years since Rachel had attended a post-mortem, but the smell of pathology labs never changed. One whiff of that strange, sickly scent of formalin, dead flesh and chlorine-based disinfectant and you knew exactly where you were.

She was met in the ante-room of the post-mortem suite by a plump, smiling young man with auburn hair and skin so freckled that the dots of pigment had merged to give the appearance of a sun tan. He was wearing a cumbersome sterile gown over scrubs and white rubber wellies, and was peeling off a double layer of gloves so that he could shake Rachel's hand.

'Dr Fraser Dewar,' he said. 'Good to meet you. How can I help?'

Rachel explained the unusual nature of her assignment in Edinburgh. 'This isn't yet a formal criminal enquiry, so I can't demand access to your files, but I just wanted to talk to you about the post-mortems on Bruno Martinez and Emily van Meijer, to see if there's anything you think you can add that might shed further light on their deaths.'

'Do you want to come through to my office?' Dewar led her through a swing door into a small hallway, with a small cubicle to one side containing a desk and computer terminal, two chairs and a filing cabinet. Through the glass panel in a second swing door Rachel glimpsed a steel autopsy table with a half-covered corpse on it, and on the floor next to it a bucket collecting bodily fluids. There were several plastic tubs for harvested organs on the steel bench, next to an electric cutting saw and an ominous collection of chisels and shears.

Dewar waved his hand around the tiny office. 'This is the level of luxury afforded to the junior staff of the University of Edinburgh Pathology Department, as you can see. Only the Prof gets a proper office.'

Rachel considered telling him she used to be married to the very same professor, but decided against it. Better to not muddy the waters.

'You'll have seen both PM reports for the two of them?' Dewar asked. 'The unfortunate overseas students? Only I'm not sure what I can add further to what was in them. Both cases were straightforward, by which I mean there was no doubt about cause of death, and no evidence at all of foul play.' He smiled at Rachel, revealing good teeth, and lighting up his rather plain face. 'Can I offer you a coffee? It's only instant, I'm afraid.'

Rachel shook her head. 'No thanks. So, please just talk me through it. The Dutch girl, Emily van Meijer…'

Dewar turned to his terminal and clicked through screens until he found the relevant file. 'She sustained injuries that were incompatible with life: that's pretty much the size of it. Head injuries, spinal injuries, damage to internal organs. She couldn't have survived the fall.'

'And she was drunk?' Rachel persisted.

'There was a blood–alcohol level of 0.08. That's enough to impair your faculties but not to be steaming drunk.'

'Not enough to render you unconscious?'

Dewar shook his head. 'Not unless you had a very unusual idiopathic intolerance, no.'

'And the French boy, Bruno Martinez?'

'Hold on…' Dewar searched through case records. 'He was about the same when it came to blood–alcohol concentration.'

'Do you know if he was alive when he fell into the water?'

'From the amount of water in his lungs, I'd say he was definitely alive when he fell in. But the disorientation from the alcohol and the shock of extremely cold water probably caused drowning to happen very quickly, especially if he wasn't a strong swimmer. You'd be amazed how frequently accidental drowning is a cause of death. It's surprisingly common.'

'And he had no injuries?'

'Nothing sustained before he fell in. There were a few abrasions on his hands and arms from him hitting the side as he went in, or possibly scrabbling to try and get out.'

Rachel shuddered. 'Okay, well, thanks anyway, Dr Dewar.' She shouldered her bag and stood up. 'I appreciate your time.'

'I'll tell you what, Detective,' he said, his face betraying an eagerness to please, possibly even a desire to see her again. 'Why don't you give me your phone number? I'll go over the lab tests and look at the histology samples again, and if I find anything remotely worthy of a second look, I'll contact you right away.'

'Thank you. Much appreciated.'

Once she was out on the street, Rachel turned and looked up at the blocky, modern building, hoping it would give up its secrets.

ELEVEN

'Do you think we should try and bring him in?'

'Bring who in, where?' Rachel was distracted by yet another text from Howard. She and Brickall were in a coffee shop near the Western General, where she was debriefing him about her trip to the pathology lab. Dolly had been left behind to help Betty Kilpatrick weed her flower beds.

'Captain Birdseye. For formal questioning.'

'Captain Birdseye?'

'You know, cos of the white beard. Cap'n Paedo. Our man Candlish.'

'Oh, right.' Rachel deleted the text without answering it. 'I don't know whether we can. For a start, we'd have to negotiate interview facilities with your friend Morag, and that would take too long, and be a world of pain. And secondly, as far as we know he's not done anything criminal. If he were on the Violent and Sex Offenders Register and decided to work with adolescents, that would be something we could get him on, but unfortunately the 1997 Act doesn't work retroactively.'

'Bugger.'

'So we're stuck with yet another informal chat, I'm afraid. I'm getting rather tired of them.'

They walked through the milling crowds to Drummond Place. 'Tell you what I'm getting tired of: this festival clusterfuck,' Brickall grumbled. 'I'll be glad to see the back of it.'

'I know what you mean,' agreed Rachel, stepping deftly through a disembarking coach party of pensioners. 'The non-stop fun and jollity starts to mess with your head after a while.'

Jean, the White Crystal receptionist, was not pleased to see them. She informed them rather sniffily that "Mr Kenneth" was at a meeting with the accountants.

'It's okay, we'll wait,' said Rachel, lowering herself onto one of the brocade chairs and picking up a copy of *Scottish Field*.

'We could diarise something for tomorrow?' suggested Jean, who clearly didn't want two police officers cluttering up her reception area. 'Or the day after?'

'No,' said Rachel firmly, abandoning the politeness of her first visit. 'We couldn't. We're here on police business, and it can't be diarised.'

Kenneth Candlish bustled in after twenty minutes, carrying several shopping bags. 'I got your teacakes, Jean. Oh.'

'Afternoon, Mr Candlish,' said Rachel, standing up. At five feet nine, and with two-inch heels, she towered over him. 'We'd like another chat, please.'

'I really think this is ill-advised, Officer.' Candlish was polite, but disapproving. 'Taking the word of a hysterical young girl about what might or might not have happened one evening during her stay in Edinburgh.'

Rachel had repeated the gist of Niamh Donovan's story about the party she had attended with the two Dutch teenagers, without going into detail.

'Are you suggesting she's made this up?' Rachel said. 'Because with more than fifteen years' experience of interviewing witnesses, I would bet my mortgage she was telling the truth.'

'All right then, suppose she is telling the truth.' Candlish's genial Scots burr grew cold, and clipped. His eyes were like hard little pebbles. 'We make it clear in our code of conduct that consuming alcohol is not allowed. Nor is leaving the residence after seven p.m. without express permission from the house parents. If the students choose to flout those rules, then White Crystal can't be held liable for what happens to them.'

'Nice,' said Brickall. 'Great attitude to customer care.'

Candlish narrowed his eyes still further, but did not rise to the bait.

'Did you know about these parties?' Rachel asked. 'Have you ever heard of such a thing happening?'

'Why would you ask that?' He broke eye contact and fidgeted with his watch chain.

'I think it's a perfectly reasonable question. You've lived here in the city for many years; you run a business related to the fringe festival.'

'There are all sorts of late night gatherings and hospitality during the Fringe.' Candlish rearranged the letter opener and pens on his desk. 'But I don't know anything about parties down in Grange, nor would I pay attention to gossip if I did. And if you're implying what I think you're implying, then you're overstepping bounds.' He opened a silver cigarette case and then closed it with a snap.

'Oh I think we're well within bounds,' said Brickall with grim satisfaction. 'May I remind you that you have a caution for what these days would be classified as sexual abuse of a minor. You lost a job because of a similar allegation. And you're running an organisation whose customers are fifteen to seventeen year olds. So if those youngsters end up being molested while they're under the care of your company, you can be sure it's a problem.'

'I thank you for your concern,' Candlish's voice wavered slightly. 'But may I point out that I do not personally have any contact at all with our students, apart from giving them a very brief welcome talk on their first day. Their welfare and entertainment are wholly in the hands of Will and Hazel MacBain, who are devout and upstanding members of the community. I merely take care of administration and finances. Now if you don't mind, officers, I have work to do. I'd be grateful if you'd leave.'

'That was interesting,' Rachel said, as they thundered down the stairs for a second time, and out into the street.

'What – you mean the lying tells? The fidgeting and looking down?'

'That too, but I was referring to what he said about the parties. He said they were held in Grange, but I never mentioned the location, not least because Niamh Donovan was new to the city, and drunk, so was unable to give me one. And yet Kenneth Candlish seems to know exactly where she was.'

Rachel's phone rang when she was back at the Avalon Guest House, changing into her running gear. She and Brickall had walked long distances in the past few days so she didn't lack exercise, but there was nothing like moving at speed to clear the mind. At the moment all the threads of the enquiry were tangled in her brain like a ball of wool after a cat had been at it.

She glanced at the screen, expecting it to be Howard.

Stuart Ritchie.

She picked up.

'Hi Rae, glad I've caught you. Are you still in town?'

'Just about, but—'

'Only Claire and I are having a barbecue for a few friends on Friday, and I wondered if you fancied popping along? You can bring your sergeant along too, if you like.'

'That's very kind of you, but I'm flying back to London tomorrow.'

'That's a shame. Will you be up here again?'

'I'm not sure, but I'd say there's a good chance I will, before long.'

'Well when you are, don't be a stranger, okay?'

'Sure,' said Rachel pleasantly, thinking that she needed Stuart's support, if only to benefit from his pathology expertise. 'Of course. Enjoy the barbecue.'

Rachel put in her headphones and headed along the Water of Leith to Roseburn Park. She pounded the paths for several kilometres until she was breathless and sweating, but still the fragments of information she had learned in the past forty-eight hours tumbled in her head, like parts of the same jigsaw that lacked the connecting pieces in between. She had no idea what the emerging picture would look like, but the untimely deaths of Emily and Bruno were beginning to feel less like a coincidence and more like… what? She still didn't know.

It seemed unlikely that Caitlyn Anderson would provide much clarification. Rachel and Brickall arranged to speak to her the following morning, before catching their flight and train respectively. Rachel had pictured her as a tall, willowy Celtic beauty, but she turned out to be a short, rotund woman with a bowl haircut and two full sleeves of tattoos, who worked as a carer in an old people's residential home. She met them in the front hall of the home during her break, and took them out into the building's large garden so that she could smoke, carrying a tray of tea in the sort of green china cups and saucers used in hospitals. Brickall let Dolly off the lead and she truffled around between tree trunks, scenting squirrels.

'The thing is,' Caitlyn poured three cups of tea and pulled a packet of Silk Cut from the pocket of her green nylon overall, 'I'd like to help yous, but I dinnae remember much. It was two years ago now. It's all a bit of a blur… what did I say to the polis back then?'

'Look, just forget the statement you made,' Rachel told her firmly. 'Just try and picture yourself back there again, and tell us what you see.'

Caitlyn took a deep drag on her cigarette and half closed her eyes. 'There was a car, big car, sort of brownish. And this lad on the pavement in some sort of trouble. Young lad, big mop of wavy hair. And this woman was... I don't know... the car door was open... No, hold on. That's it: it was the boot of the car that was open. The hatch. It was a hatchback of some kind. And this woman, she was kind of pulling the lad out of the car.'

Rachel sat forward on the bench. 'Hold on Caitlyn, your original statement said she was putting the boy into the car – are you now saying she was taking him out of it?'

Caitlyn opened her eyes and tapped the pillar of ash onto the terrace. 'I think so, aye. I'm pretty sure now I think about it that she was getting the wee lad oot the car.'

'Could you describe the woman?'

She shook her head. 'Not really. She was under a street light, but it wasn't bright enough to see her face well. I only remember that she was a bit, you know, on the heavy side. Fat.'

'And the boy was drunk?' asked Brickall.

Caitlyn thought about this for a second. 'I think I said that in my statement, but afterwards I got to thinking that wasn't quite right. I started working here since then, and the old folks... you get used to seeing them on their medication. Some of them have stuff that sedates them. It was like that with the wee French laddie. It was more like he was drugged than drunk. But that's all I can remember. That's all I saw. I'm sorry.'

'Not at all, Caitlyn.' Rachel stood up, giving Brickall his cue to go and retrieve Dolly from the rhododendron bushes. 'Thanks for talking to us: you've been really helpful.'

'What d'you think?' Brickall asked as they left the premises and walked down the street,

'I think a trip to France is in our near future,' said Rachel, reaching down to fondle Dolly's floppy ears. 'But that's for another day. First: back to London.'

TWELVE

Nigel Patten summoned Rachel and Brickall to a meeting room on the first floor only an hour after they had returned to their office in Tinworth Street.

He gestured expansively at the biscuits and coffee urn. 'I thought it would be better in here, since I've asked someone to join us.'

On cue, the door swung open and Giles Denton walked in, senior officer at the NCA's Child Exploitation and Online Protection command.

He gave Patten's hand a cursory shake, but his attention was elsewhere. 'Rachel. How the devil are you?'

And there it was, the weapons-grade charisma. The smile that made her – and probably anyone else he bestowed it on – feel like there was no one else in the room.

'From the brief summary DI Prince gave me over the phone, I thought it was appropriate that someone from Child Exploitation be here to discuss your findings,' said Patten. 'Do help yourself to coffee, everyone.'

Brickall scowled at Giles and grabbed two chocolate digestives.

'DI Prince, would you like to start?'

Rachel went to the whiteboard and pinned up pictures of Emily and Bruno at the top of it then, further down, pictures of Niamh Donovan and one she had found online of Luuk Rynsberger. He had shiny chestnut hair shaved at the sides and floppy at the top, a square jaw and an attractive smile. In between she wrote up the names of Kenneth Candlish, Will and Hazel MacBain, and with arrows shooting down from Bruno's picture, Marie-Laure Fournier and Caitlyn Anderson. She talked through the conflicting testimony of Dries van Meijer and the MacBains, Niamh's revelation about the sex party and Kenneth Candlish's reaction to it.

'Obviously we now need to dig deeper, and to try and get further corroboration from Marie-Laure and Luuk Rynsberger.'

'I also think local law enforcement should be persuaded to come on board at this point,' said Patten.

Brickall grimaced.

'DS Brickall? You have something you want to add?'

'Sorry; it's just that we weren't exactly flavour of the month with Police Scotland.' He took a third biscuit and dunked it in his milky coffee.

'That may be so, but when it comes to intelligence regarding the people behind these parties, and who's attending them, you're going to need local knowledge. Local backup. So you're going to have to try and find a way to get them onside.'

'There is something that strikes me,' said Giles, stroking his dark stubble as he stared at the photos on the board. 'Something these kids all have in common.'

'Go on,' said Rachel.

'All four of them are extremely good-looking. Five if you include… what's her name? Marie-Laure. More so than average. Which suggests to me they might have been deliberately targeted.'

Patten nodded. 'Good point, Giles.'

'Of course this may be no more than the targeting street promoters do when they select the prettiest girls to invite into a club. Or there could be more involved. I think it's certainly something we need to look into.'

'How much longer is the festival on for?' Patten asked.

'It finishes this Sunday,' Rachel confirmed. 'Only three more days.'

'In that case, DS Brickall,' Patten said, 'I'd like you to fly straight back up there and see if you can track down the people who are handing out invites to these parties. I'm assuming they're using festivalgoers as targets, and the sheer volume of people as cover. So we need to tackle this before the festival ends.'

'But sir—'

'I'll get Janette to book you a flight now, and you can brief us here on Tuesday. DI Prince, I'd like you to follow up a formal statement from the Irish girl and try and get as much information as you can from the other two teenagers – Marie-Laure and Luuk. And, of course, to continue to liaise with Chief Inspector Denton on the potential grooming issue.'

'"Liaise with Chief Inspector Denton."' Brickall put on a childish echo as they headed back up to the third floor. 'You'll love that, won't you? Fucks' sake, I don't want to go back to the arse-wit carnival! Why can't you go?'

'Because I've got things to do here. So quit bitching – that's an order.'

'Seriously boss,' Brickall flung himself into his chair so hard that it hit the edge of his desk and knocked his fan over. 'What am I going to do with Dolly? I've left her in the flat today and my neighbour's popping in to walk her at lunchtime, but I can't take her on the plane with me tomorrow.'

'Leave her with me.'

'Really?'

Rachel nodded. 'You can bring her over this evening, as long as it's before eight.'

'And when I do get up to Edinburgh, what am I supposed to do up there on my own? It's going to be impossible with no resources.'

'Just do what you can. Ask around. You're good at getting information out of people. And see if you can get your mate Morag to lend you some manpower.'

'*Yous'll no be taking my coppers off the beat!*' Brickall did a passable imitation of DI Sillars' Glaswegian croak.

Rachel laughed. 'Seriously though; if she's awkward, get Patten to phone her and pull rank.'

'Yes, boss.'

When they left work at six, Brickall headed straight to Forest Hill to fetch the dog and Rachel sought out an off-licence to buy wine. She had put off Howard the night before on the grounds that it was late by the time she arrived back from the airport, but had agreed that he could come over that evening.

When she had unlocked the front door to her flat the night before, she had known before she was over the threshold that something had changed since she left for Edinburgh. She could smell it – literally. She switched on the lights to find that Howard had painted a black chalkboard on the section of wall behind her kitchen table. He had chalked 'Welcome Home!' onto the board, adding a heart and a smiley face.

It wasn't that she didn't like what he had done. She actually liked it quite a lot – it looked great as a backdrop to the off-white table and chairs. It was that he had come here and done it behind her back, without consultation. What was it she had said to Brickall about her relationship with Howard while they were in Edinburgh… that the writing was on the wall? Well, now it really was. Or on the chalkboard.

Of course he still had no idea that he was coming over this evening to be dumped. After she'd wiped away his chalk message with a damp cloth, Rachel set out bowls of snacks and opened a bottle of the wine that Howard liked, painfully aware that this was unlikely to soften the blow.

*

Brickall arrived at quarter to eight with Dolly on her lead and a bag containing feeding bowls and biscuits. She wagged her tail enthusiastically when she recognised Rachel.

'Sorry, I couldn't carry the dog bed as well,' Brickall told her. 'You'll have to improvise.' He spotted the wine, chips and dips. 'Drinks and nibbles! Nice of you, I must say.'

'They're not for you,' Rachel said, setting out Dolly's bowls on the kitchen floor and heading into the bedroom to find a blanket for the dog to sleep on.

'Can't be a date night, surely.' Brickall took in Rachel's leggings, make-up free face and bare feet.

'Howard's coming over,' Rachel said, with a sigh. 'I'm going to attempt to end things.'

'Fucking fantastic.' Brickall settled himself on the sofa, spreading his arms along its back. 'I'm looking forward to seeing this. Nice blackboard, by the way.'

'Don't be a dickhead,' Rachel said, prodding his trainer with her bare toes. 'Now say your goodbyes and piss off. I want you well clear of the place before he gets here.'

'Okay, but video the highlights for me.' Brickall bent and kissed Dolly on top of her smooth head. 'Be a good puppy for Auntie Rachel.'

Howard arrived ten minutes later, his face hidden behind a showy bouquet of lilies. 'How's my favourite detective?' he asked, enveloping her in a bear hug and kissing her squarely on the lips. She had always enjoyed his hugs, and felt her resolve waver fractionally as she leaned into him.

'Fine,' she said. 'Good.' She inhaled hard, bracing herself, before unwrapping his arms and going to pour the wine. She had put the snacks away before he arrived, Brickall's visit having reminded her that this wasn't a date.

Howard gave her a broad smile, his pale blue eyes crinkling at the corners. Such kind eyes. They had been the first thing Rachel had noticed about him when she met him at the gym.

'What do you think to your surprise?'

'Great. Looks great. Thank you.'

'No problem... well, I must say it's really great to clap eyes on you at last. I've really missed you.'

This only served to make Rachel feel worse. When all was said and done, Howard Davison was a nice guy. He was kind, and thoughtful, and patient. But this – whatever it was – just wasn't working. The dynamic had shifted between them, putting her permanently on the defensive.

And Rachel didn't believe in trying to right a relationship, to correct its course. In her view, if it felt wrong, then it was wrong. Howard's big mistake had been failing to grasp just how much space she needed. He was always there in the background, ready to pounce on any spare time she had. Endlessly available, and expecting to come round to her flat whenever he had free time. Needing to know her schedule, tracking her movements. And now working on the place while she was away. She felt suffocated.

'Oh wow – you've got a dog!' As Howard accepted his glass of wine, he spotted Dolly sitting patiently at the side of the sofa, as if waiting for someone to make permanent claim to her.

'She's not mine, she's Mark's. Well, actually she's not even his, she's his friend's.' She shrugged. 'It's complicated.'

Howard frowned. 'Well how's that going to work? When you have to travel for the job?'

He had a point. Rachel hadn't really thought about this. She had only taken over Dolly's care to allow Brickall to take the last-minute flight to Edinburgh.

'I could walk her,' Howard went on, pouring himself a glass of the wine. 'I've got my key and I could pop by in my lunch hour.'

'No, it's okay, she'll probably only be here for a few days,' Rachel glugged her wine. Dutch courage. 'And about the key, Howard... I'd like it back.'

He patted the sofa cushion next to him, but she ignored it and remained standing. Dolly, on the other hand, responded to the cue and jumped up onto the seat, resting her head on his lap.

'Why's that?' Anxiety tightened the corners of his mouth.

'The thing is, I've been doing some thinking while I was in Scotland … and I think we should see less of each other.' The words spilled out in a rush, not sounding at all as she had rehearsed them in her head.

'How much less?'

Rachel gulped her wine again. 'A lot less.'

'Are you breaking up with me?

Just rip off the Band-Aid, Rachel told herself. 'Yes,' she conceded. 'I think we should break up.'

Howard looked stunned. 'But why, babe? I thought everything was… it's been working so well. We have such a nice time together.'

But I don't want 'nice', Rachel thought. *'Nice' doesn't do it for me.* Instead she said: 'Look, Howard, the last six months have been great. We *have* had a really nice time together…'

There it was again. The 'n' word. It was catching.

'But I'm bang in the middle of what's turning out to be quite a complex investigation. I'm going to have to do some travelling in Europe, and I'm almost certainly going to have to spend more time in Scotland. Basically I'm not going to be around, so a committed relationship just isn't going to work.'

'But babe, I don't mind that. I don't mind waiting around for you: I'm not going anywhere. If I hold onto the key, I can come over and keep an eye on the place, walk the dog, water the plants, do any little jobs that need doing…'

He still didn't get it.

'No,' Rachel said, more firmly this time, 'That isn't what I want. And I can't give you what you want either. I just can't.'

'But we're happy, aren't we?' She couldn't bear the look of confusion on his face and looked away. 'Whatever it is, we can work it out, Rachel. Let's just take some time, and—'

'No, Howard.' Rachel spoke more sharply than she had intended, making Dolly look up, her nose twitching. She softened her tone. 'I'm sorry, I really am. And I'm happy to stay friends. But the rest of it… it has to be over.'

THIRTEEN

The following evening, after returning to the flat at lunchtime to take Dolly out, Rachel loaded the dog and her belongings into her car and set off to her mother's house in Purley.

She didn't phone beforehand to say that she was coming. She knew that her older sister Lindsay would sniff at this, pronouncing it inconsiderate to turn up unannounced. But then again, Lindsay inhabited a world where even the most mundane activity was planned with regimental precision and nobody ever did anything on the spur of the moment. Besides, Rachel happened to know that her mother quite enjoyed surprises.

'Goodness me, what have we got here?' Eileen Prince exclaimed when she opened the door and saw her youngest daughter standing there with a dog's lead in one hand and a large box of Quality Street in the other. She embraced Rachel and bent down to pet Dolly.

'This is Dolly,' Rachel said. 'I'm looking after her for a while, and I thought she might enjoy a trip out of central London.'

'Are you staying the night?' Eileen asked as they went inside. As she spoke, she was heading straight to the kitchen to put on the kettle. The predictability of her mother's response was what made visits home so comforting.

'If that's all right?'

'Of course, but you should have said, love. I've already eaten my evening meal.'

'I thought you'd enjoy the surprise.'

'Well, it is a lovely surprise to see you.' Eileen put on her apron, and Rachel had a sudden flashback to Hazel MacBain playing the surrendered wife. The meek homemaker. 'And to have this little poppet for a visit.'

Eileen bent over as far as her arthritis would allow and petted Dolly. When Rachel was a child, the family owned a Jack Russell terrier called Buster, and she knew her mother missed having a canine companion.

'Horlicks?' she asked, straightening up and taking mugs from the cupboard.

'Perfect.'

'And I've got some custard creams in here somewhere… And what about you? We can't leave you out.' This last remark was addressed to Dolly, who was presented with a saucer containing scraps of leftover roast chicken.

Eileen carried the tray through to the sitting room and they sat drinking their Horlicks, dipping into the Quality Street and watching a rerun of *Gardeners' World* with Monty Don. Eileen approved of Monty Don.

'Gosh, your dad would have loved little Dolly,' she said, looking over wistfully at the framed photograph of Ray Prince. 'It's seventeen years tomorrow,' she added, her voice cracking slightly. 'Seventeen years: I can't believe it. It still feels like it happened yesterday.'

'I know Mum.' Rachel, who had forgotten the date, reached for her hand. 'That's one reason I wanted to come down tonight,' she fibbed.

'You should stay on until the afternoon. Gordon and Lindsay are coming over to collect me and we're all going to go to the cemetery to lay flowers. And the children are coming too. Then we're going back to theirs for tea afterwards.'

Rachel shuddered at the thought of spending the afternoon in mournful observance with her sister and brother-in-law. The big age gap and their dramatically different personalities had resulted in constant chafing between her and Lindsay when they were together. 'It's a nice idea Mum, but I'll have to head back in the morning. I've got some work to do.'

This was true. She still needed to try and track down Marie-Laure Fournier, and to arrange to talk to Emily van Meijer's friend Luuk.

Eileen nodded and reached for the omnipresent copy of the *Radio Times*. 'Let's see if there's anything worth watching, shall we?'

After a sound night's sleep in her childhood bed, Rachel took Dolly for her morning outing and managed to successfully reject one of her mother's fry-ups in favour of a bowl of Alpen. Then she gathered Dolly's bowls, blanket and lead, placing them next to the front door. 'Right, that's us off. We'd better get back to town,' she said, kissing her mother on the forehead.

Eileen Prince looked wistful. 'That's a shame, she's such a sweet, well-behaved little thing. It's been lovely having her here.'

Rachel hesitated for a second. 'I'll tell you what Mum, why don't you hang on to Dolly for a few days? It'll be nicer for her to be here while I'm working, and you can take her up to the park with you. She'd love that.'

She pressed the lead into her mother's hand. Eileen beamed.

'Come on, sweetheart,' she could hear her mother saying as she headed out to the car, 'You come with me. Let's see if we can find you a bit of scrambled egg.'

Rachel's phone rang that evening as she was making herself a salad and preparing to sit down with her laptop.

Lindsay.

Of course it was.

'A dog, Rachel?! You've gone and dumped a stray dog on Mum? Have you any idea how inconvenient it was when I'd already made all the arrangements for her afternoon?'

Rachel drew in her breath and counted to five. 'Okay, first off: she's not a stray. She belongs to my sergeant. Well, she doesn't exactly belong to him, she—'

'It doesn't really matter who it does or doesn't belong to, it's the thoughtlessness.'

'Lindsay, if you would just listen a minute, instead of sounding off.' Rachel exhaled loudly. 'The dog is only there temporarily. At Mum's suggestion. And you had the option to either leave her in the house while you went to the cemetery, or take her with you. It wasn't an issue. You've got a dog yourself, after all.'

Lindsay and her husband Gordon were the owners of an elderly golden Labrador.

'But you know what Mum's like: she was dithering. She didn't know what to do with the animal for the best. It got her all stressed, which was the last thing she needed on the anniversary of Dad's death.'

'All I know is she was happy to mind Dolly. She's thrilled about it.'

'And that's the other thing: given the importance of the day, shouldn't you have stayed down longer and come to the cemetery with us?'

'I had other things I needed to do.'

'I suppose I shouldn't be surprised,' hissed Lindsay. 'But you of all people might have made the effort to fit visiting your father's grave into your busy schedule.' The last three words dripped with sarcasm.

Rachel drew in her breath hard, clenching and unclenching her fists. She should hang up now and end the conversation before further damage was done, but she just couldn't help herself. 'What's that supposed to mean?'

Lindsay didn't even pause for breath. 'That if it wasn't for your selfishness, Dad would probably be alive now!'

Rachel cut the call, her heart pounding. Lindsay's claim that her younger sister's past behaviour had somehow contributed to their father's heart attack was nothing new. But it still felt like a body blow, still made her eyes sting with tears. She had adored her father, and would never willingly have done anything to hurt him.

Rachel put her salad back in the fridge, too tense to eat, and went outside to walk by the river to calm herself down. It was only eight o'clock, but starting to go dark. The heatwave had passed and there was now, at the end of August, the faintest hint of approaching autumn in the air, a scent of cooling earth and drying leaves. In a week's time, children everywhere would be returning to school to begin a new term. But not Emily van Meijer.

She texted Brickall.

How's it going up there, loser?

Brickall replied after a few minutes.

Doing my best, but it's like trying to nail jelly to the fucking wall.

When Rachel returned to the flat, she poured herself a glass of wine and found the remains of the tortilla chips from Howard's visit the night before. She emailed Dries van Meijer and asked if he could provide contact details for Luuk Rynsberger, then set about trying to trace Marie-Laure Fournier.

She found an Instagram account, featuring many sultry, pouting photos taken in an outdoor café, usually with a cigarette in hand. The locations in almost all of them were in Lyon, and the few taken at her school were tagged 'Lycée Privé, Lyon'. So she was a native of the same city as Bruno which, given the way White Crystal recruited, wasn't that surprising. It looked as though Rachel might have to fly out there, in addition to travelling to Leiden to speak to Luuk Rynsberger.

Dries van Meijer emailed back with Luuk's details, and once again offered the services of his plane. Rachel politely but firmly refused, then received the following:

Do please contact me when you are in the Netherlands. My wife would like the chance to speak to you, and of course we are ready to offer any assistance you should need. You only need to say the word.

Rachel only remembered that it was a bank holiday when she arrived at the office and saw the drastically reduced numbers. She sat down at her desk anyway and logged onto her terminal, checking through her inbox and updating files she had been working on before her unscheduled trip to Scotland. Then she phoned Brickall.

'When are you coming back?' she demanded, her frustration making her curt.

'My flight's in a couple of hours. But hold on, where's the fire? It's a sodding Bank Holiday Monday – I'm not due in the office until tomorrow.'

'Meet me for a drink when you land. At the Pin and Needle.'

'You're joking, right? Not only do I miss the league game I was going to go to in Bromley, I have to meet my boss for a drink. At our workplace local. What's so bloody urgent that it can't wait until the morning?'

'I just want to hear how you got on, that's all.'

'Okay, but you can come to me. At the Falcon.' He named his favourite watering hole on Anerley Hill.

*

When Rachel arrived there, she was fully expecting to have to endure football on a TV screen, but it turned out to be an upmarket establishment with tasteful dove-grey wood panelling and gilt-framed mirrors, serving cask ales. The daily special on the chalkboard was confit duck.

'Very nice,' Rachel commented, as she sat down. 'It's almost… girly.'

'I'm not a total philistine,' Brickall grumbled. 'And you can get the drinks in: I'm knackered.'

As she returned from the bar with a fancy ale, a glass of red wine and a bowl of chips, he commented, 'No Dolly? I thought you might bring her along.'

'Ah… about that.' Rachel told him about leaving Dolly with her mother. 'Of course you can go down there and get her back any time you like.'

Brickall shrugged. 'No, it's fine. It's probably a good idea. It worked okay when we were in Edinburgh – the first time round,' he added grimly, reminding her that he had made a repeat trip, mere hours after their first visit. 'But when I'm in the office it doesn't really work. She needs someone with her.'

'Any luck rehoming her?"

He shook his head.

'So… how did you get on over the border?'

Brickall took a mouthful of his beer. 'Well for starters, it wasn't easy. It's all very well for Patten to say "find the people distribut-ing the flyers" but the city is full of people handing out invites to events, almost all of them completely innocent. And when you're a team of one…'

'Didn't Morag and her team help?' Rachel took a chip and dipped it into a bowl of mayonnaise.

'They came good in the end, but I did have to threaten them with Patten, like you suggested. In the end, once I'd explained it properly to little More-hag, she kind of got it. After a bit of playing hard to get, you know, to save face. She accepts that they missed a trick with both kids who died having been on White Crystal Trips, and admits there could be some sort of child exploitation happening on her patch that needs looking into.'

'And did you find anyone?'

He nodded. 'I hope so. Morag lent me a couple of bobbies, including Kirstie Blair... remember her? The one who knew all about Hazel MacBain's past. Anyway, we targeted the late-night crowd on Saturday and after buttonholing a dozen or so leafleters we eventually found one who told us who we were looking for. He said he thought they were a couple of Latvians, a man and a woman. Didn't know their names or anything, but knew a bar where they hung out. So after asking a lot of questions in the bar we were directed to the digs of these guys, in some armpit of a council estate. We found their names by going through the mail in the front hall.'

'But they weren't there?'

Brickall shook his head. 'Course not. That would have been too easy. But Morag and her team organised an arrest warrant, and they've got the beat plods and the pandas out looking for them.'

'Let's hope they find them,' said Rachel grimly, downing the last of her wine. 'I'm really looking forward to hearing what they've got to say.'

She did not have to wait long.

A call came in at ten thirty the following morning, just as Rachel and Brickall were returning to their desks following a debrief with Patten. Police Scotland had picked up Maris Balodis and Iveta Kovals at Waverley Station, attempting to board a train to Glasgow. They were holding them in Gayfield Square until someone from the NCA team could get there to help interview them, as long as this complied with the twenty-four-hour custody rules.

'Shit,' said Rachel. 'I wasn't expecting it to happen so quickly. Someone needs to get up to Edinburgh right away.'

'Not me,' Brickall said hotly. 'I've only just got off the plane back from there.'

'It'll have to be me then, won't it?' Rachel left him and doubled back to Patten's office to ask Janette to book her on a lunchtime flight. Which left her just enough time to go home and pack a bag and get herself to London City airport in time for boarding.

As soon as the lift doors opened on her floor of the Bermondsey apartment block, Rachel sensed that something was different. The first thing she saw as she rounded the corner was a shadow falling on the carpet, a man's shadow, that could only be cast by someone tall standing next to the door of her flat. Her heart started beating faster when she saw a stranger leaning against the doorframe with his back to her, scrolling through his phone screen in the way people did to kill time.

'Can I help you?'

The man turned round, and Rachel could see that despite his height – he must have been six feet three – he was young; a boy rather than a man. He had thick, sandy hair brushed back from his forehead and a dusting of acne around his jawline. And green-grey eyes. Eyes just like her own.

Her mind shot back forcibly to a ceiling with bright, clinical lighting above her, the smell of iodine and surgical scrubs, the hiss of oxygen from a mask over face. A pair of gloved hands coming into view above her, holding a bright-pink creature smeared in blood and mucus, arms outstretched in a primal instinct, mouth opening in a bleating cry.

'Are you Rachel Prince?' the tall boy asked.

She nodded slowly, frozen to the spot as a strange emotion surged through her; part panic, part deep, fierce joy. Her fingers flew to her neck, her throat closing off, as though something was artificially constricting it.

He was opening his mouth to introduce himself, but she knew. She already knew.

'I'm Joe. I'm your son.'

PART TWO

'Being a mother is an attitude, not a biological relation.'
— *Have Space Suit Will Travel*, Robert A. Heinlein

PART TWO

FOURTEEN

Rachel's fingertips tingled and went numb, and the blood sang in her ears. She clutched the doorframe as her knees sagged beneath her.

'I'm sorry, give me a minute,' she mumbled. She closed her eyes and breathed deliberately for a few seconds, in and out, in and out, until the tingling subsided. Once she had collected herself, she fumbled in her bag for her key. Her voice, when she managed to force it past the constriction, emerged as a croak. 'You'd better come in.'

Struggling with disbelief and shock, there she was, back in the hospital again. *'Congratulations,'* a disembodied voice was saying to her. *'Here's your baby.'*

She made a strangled little gasp.

'Are you okay?'

'Yes. Yes, I'm fine, it's just…'

Her voice trailed off and Joe followed her inside. He looked around the flat, weighing it, scenting it like a pet being introduced to a new home. 'Have a seat,' she said. 'Can I get you a drink? Tea? Coffee?'

'Tea would be great – thanks.' As Rachel switched on the kettle and reached out for a mug and a tea bag, he went on. 'Look, sorry, to be all like… I suppose this must have been a massive shock.' He spoke with a neutral Home Counties accent, tinged with teen patois. Rachel took in the skinny jeans, logo T-shirt and backpack.

Standard teenage stuff. Only the expensive watch and trainers hinted at privilege.

'Well yes… sort of,' she answered him. 'I mean, not entirely. Obviously I knew you turned eighteen a few weeks ago…'

'The first of August,' he prompted.

'Yes, the first of August. I remember. I was there.' The attempt at humour was risky but he responded with a lopsided smile. A smile much like her own.

She didn't tell him that every first of August for the past eighteen years she had mentally measured him against a doorframe, wondering how much he had grown in the past twelve months, how tall he was. Very tall, as it turned out.

'I knew there was a chance you might come and find me. I suppose I didn't expect it to be quite so soon.' She poured boiled water into the mug, adding hastily, 'Not that I took it for granted you would. You would have been perfectly within your rights not to want to… I suppose I assumed someone from the adoption agency would be in touch with me first.'

'If you want to find your birth parent you have to have a session with an adoption counsellor,' he told her. 'Then they allow you to send for a copy of your original birth certificate. And my mate Charlie, who's like this brilliant hacker, helped me find your address online. But I planned it ages ago. For as long as I can remember, I intended to come and find you. So that's what I did.'

The measured way he spoke reminded her of his father. So much. *Biology is powerful*, she thought. That had also been her first thought when the midwife placed her son in her arms: *He looks just like his father.*

'They always do in the first weeks,' the midwife had said with a smile. 'Mother Nature's little trick. So the dad doesn't reject them.' Then she had looked embarrassed, remembering Rachel's decision to have her child adopted. 'It's not too late to change your mind,' she had urged. 'There's no stigma in being an unmarried mother these days.'

'I'm married,' Rachel had reminded her. 'But my husband and I are separated.'

'Well, in being a single mother then. It's completely acceptable.'

The staff had pressured her. Her family had pressured her. Lindsay especially, pregnant with her own first child and committed to the concept of nuclear families, had pressured her. But she had stuck to her decision, insisting that it wasn't a social issue that was inhibiting her from keeping her baby. She just wasn't in a place in her life where motherhood was an option for her. In her mind there was no going back. It was simply too late.

'Do you live here alone?'

Joe's voice jolted her back into the present.

'Yes. Yes, I do.' She suddenly remembered why she was there and, as she checked her watch, felt a surge of panic course through her, leaving her light-headed all over again. This was a disaster: she had to go and Joe was only halfway through his cup of tea.

'Has your home life been... okay? Have you been happy?'

'Yeah great. No worries there.' He gave a broad smile meant to reassure and she felt her heart expand in her chest.

'Good. That's good. I always worried that... well, there's always a fear that things might not work out in the new family.' She closed her eyes momentarily. 'A huge fear, if I'm honest.'

'I've had the classic, secure Home Counties upbringing. Lovely home, functional family.'

'More than I could have given you. That's... great.'

She glanced at her watch again, feeling stricken at having to let him go. How could this be happening? After eighteen years this great gift was being bestowed on her with the worst possible timing.

'Joe, I'm so sorry to have to do this to you. It feels so shitty when we've only just met, but... I'm only back here from the office now because I'm catching a plane. It leaves in...' she checked her watch, 'an hour and forty minutes. I need to start packing, but you're welcome to stay and talk to me while I do it. Or at least finish your tea.'

'It's okay.' Joe shrugged, but couldn't quite mask his disappointment. 'Are you going on holiday?'

'No. No, it's for work. I'm going to Edinburgh.' Rachel went to the hall cupboard and pulled out her carry-on case.

'Couldn't you, like, get a later flight?'

Oh God, thought Rachel, *this is appalling*. He's waited all his life to meet me and now I'm fobbing him off. She felt tears pricking in her eyes. 'I can't. I'm a police officer. A detective.'

'Yeah I know that.' Joe's tone was defensive. His shoulders had dropped. She felt an overpowering need to make the situation better. *Was this maternal instinct?* Rachel wondered, relishing the grim irony. She reached a hand out tentatively to comfort him, ending up landing a half-hearted pat on his forearm.

'I'm so sorry about the shit timing, I really am. But I've got to go and interview a couple of people who've just been taken into custody, and they can only be held for limited time before they have to be released.'

'Twenty-four hours,' he supplied.

'Exactly. If it were anything else, of course I would get a later flight. But listen…'She fumbled for a solution to the problem. Years of having to think quickly on her feet were paying off. 'Are you on your holidays now? I mean, not at college or anything?'

'Gap year. I finished school in July.'

'Would you be able to come up to Edinburgh in the next couple of days?'

Joe shrugged. 'Yeah, I guess so. I guess my parents would be cool with it.'

My parents. The words sounded strange on his lips. But that's what they were; the couple who had adopted him. His parents.

'I mean, I've never been to Edinburgh, so that would be kind of cool.'

'Okay, great,' Rachel rummaged in her bag and pulled out the sheaf of twenty pound notes she had grabbed from the cash machine as she left the office. 'Get yourself a train ticket, and let me know when you're coming. But make sure your parents know exactly what's going on: give them my number and send me theirs, just in case.' She took the phone from his hand, texted herself the number, then added her own number to his contacts. The touch of his skin sent an electric current through her, and she could feel the tears of shock and emotional overload welling up again. She exhaled hard, trying to centre herself.

'Okay cool, well I'd better leave you to it.' Joe shrugged awkwardly and shuffled towards the door, shouldering his backpack. 'Sorry.'

Rachel caught him by the wrist and held him still for a second. 'Joe... you will come? I really want you to. I want us to get to know each other. Properly.'

A pair of eyes identical to her own looked straight back at her. 'I will. I'll come.'

FIFTEEN

'You all right love?'

The cabby squinted at her in his rear-view mirror as his black cab rumbled over Tower Bridge.

'Fine,' said Rachel, although she was not fine. Her heart was pounding so hard that she could hear it.

'Only you look like you've seen a ghost.'

In a way, I have, she thought. The face of that tiny baby boy she had handed over eighteen years ago had haunted her ever since. She had never stopped imagining him, thinking of him growing and changing. At least he had kept his name. That was one thing that had heartened her. She had called him Joseph after her own father, Raymond Joseph Prince.

The flight attendant also shot worried looks at her as the plane took off from London City, crouching by her armrest and asking if she needed anything. Rachel requested a whisky, and sat there for the fifty-five minutes taking slow, deliberate sips at intervals until her pulse slowed and her brain cleared a little.

She caught another cab at the airport rank as soon as the flight landed, using her warrant card to move to the front of the queue, cursing herself for not asking someone at Gayfield Square to send a squad car for her. Now that the festival had finally come to a close, rooms were easier to find, and Janette had booked her into a four-star hotel in the Grassmarket. She flung her case into a corner of the room, sat down on the edge of the bed and pressed her hands over her face, once again needing to slow her breathing. *How on earth am I going to make this work?* she wondered. *Make it fit into my already crowded life.*

And then there's his father. The idea occurred to her for the first time since Joe had appeared. What the hell am I going to say to *him*?

Rachel needed to think about all of this, and yet there was no time to think about it, any of it. So she would just have to park it for now, compartmentalise. She'd managed it for eighteen years; she would just have to keep it up for a few hours longer. She wiped the smudged circles of mascara from under her eyes, pocketed her warrant card and set off to the Gayfield Square police station.

The desk sergeant eyed her scathingly. 'It's you,' he observed unhelpfully. 'I suppose you'll be wanting Morag.'

Rachel forced a smile. 'If you'd be so kind.'

Sillars arrived exhaling smoke and smelling of nicotine. She tossed a freshly extinguished butt into the bin behind the reception desk, looked up and growled. 'You'd better follow me.'

She led Rachel to an interview suite on the basement floor. 'I'll monitor from next door,' she said without preamble, 'and you can have my colleague DC Ben Tulloch in with you.' She shoved a young man in Rachel's direction. Tulloch gave Rachel a shy grin. He was long-limbed and gangly, with greased back hair and an ill-fitting shiny suit.

The first defendant they interviewed was the woman, Iveta. She was thin, with a junkie's complexion and badly died platinum hair.

'I done nothing wrong,' she whined, before Rachel had even started speaking. 'I get work handing out pieces of paper, I hand them out. That is all.'

'What we're interested in,' Rachel said clearly and slowly, 'is where the leaflets come from.'

Iveta shrugged. 'I do not know this.'

'Who gave them to you? When visitors are given a flyer about a festival event, it's usually by a member of the production team who are running the event. So who gave you these?'

She shrugged. 'Maris get them. I don't know where. I just give them.' She mimed handing out leaflets to passers-by.

'Who were you supposed to give them to?' asked DC Tulloch. 'Anyone in particular?'

She chewed her nails. 'To young people. Young people who want to party. Is all I know.'

Iveta was returned to her cell while they questioned Maris Balodis. He was a stocky man of indeterminate age with skin the colour of putty, jet-black stubble and purplish circles under his eyes. Speaking or silent, his face remained devoid of expression.

He was slightly more forthcoming about the origin of the leaflets. 'On internet,' he said. 'I look for job, see this job. Many job like this in festival.'

'Which website was it?' asked Tulloch. 'Could you give us the site address?'

Balodis shrugged. 'I don't think so.'

'Why not?' asked Rachel.

'Is dark.'

'Dark?'

'Yes, you know is dark place.'

'I think he's talking about the dark web,' Tulloch muttered to Rachel.

'So you were on the dark web… why?'

'I buy drugs.' The expression didn't change. 'I see job when I am buying drugs.'

'And how did you get onto the dark web?'

'Andrei do it.'

'Who's Andrei?'

'Man staying in flat.'

'Do you know his full name?' Rachel demanded. 'Or where he is now?'

An emotionless shrug. 'I don't know. I think he leave town after festival.'

'So where did you pick the leaflets up from? Do you remember the name of the person who gave them to you?'

'No person,' Balodis insisted. 'Pick up from Mail Boxes 4U. Someone put papers in the box, I go and I take them out. And is instructions, too.'

'Instructions?'

'They say where to stand, what time, give us photos of which kids to look out for.'

'So…' Rachel glanced at Tulloch, 'you're saying that you were told exactly who to target in respect of these parties? Where they would be, and at what time?'

Balodis nodded. 'Yes.'

Tulloch leaned forward. 'Can you at least remember the number of the mailbox?'

He shrugged again. 'I write it down. But not here. Is at my home.'

'And how were you paid?'

'I enter bank number online, then money goes in my bank.'

They sent Balodis back to his cell, and went into the observation room, where Sillars was in a chair smoking an e-cigarette and watching the monitor screen, her feet dangling several inches above the floor.

'What do you think?' Rachel asked.

'What do *ah* think?' rasped Sillars. 'I think it would be marvellous if we could charge the shites under the Prevention of Sexual Offences Act, but we havnae got a prayer. Not as things stand.'

Rachel nodded. 'I agree. Are you happy to bail them pending further investigation though? If they were recruited via the dark web, there's something not right about this.'

'Aye,' Sillars exhaled smoke through her nose like a tiny wizened dragon. 'Clearly. Go on then.' She addressed DC Tulloch. 'Stick some reporting conditions on them and maybe we've a hope of them not fecking off out of town.'

'And are you okay if I call in one of my colleagues from the NCA's Child Exploitation and Online Protection command?' Rachel asked her. 'He has a lot of expertise in these sorts of cases.'

'I'm no gonnae stop you,' Sillars growled through the vapour. 'But you'll still have a job making anything stick. It's the same every year: you get all sorts going on during the festival and then everyone pisses off when it's over. People disappear back where they came from and things get back to normal.'

'Two teenagers are dead,' Rachel reminded her sharply. 'There's nothing normal about that.'

SIXTEEN

Back in her hotel room, Rachel composed a short email to Giles Denton, asking if he would be able to travel up to Edinburgh to assist on the case, as Nigel Patten had suggested. She was watching her phone like an expectant parent – which in a way she was – picking it up every few minutes and staring at the screen. She wasn't going to contact Joe, not yet. She had decided that if he wanted to spend time with her, then the initiative had to come from him.

Eventually, after an evening run and a nondescript meal in the characterless hotel restaurant, she received a text.

> *Okay if I come tomorrow? Planning to book train that arrives at 2 p.m. Joe*

She replied that this was fine, and she would meet him at the station.

> *Is there somewhere I can crash?*

She was so unaccustomed to the role of parent that she hadn't even given it a thought. Of course, he needed somewhere for the night. Or however long he was going to stay. She would cross that bridge when she got to it. It was one of so many bridges that loomed ahead.

*

Kenneth Candlish had not been exactly helpful about the parties attended by the White Crystal students, but Rachel was still hopeful that Will MacBain might be able to shed some light. Early the following morning, she borrowed a pool car from the police station and went to Campbell Road in the hope of finding him at home.

Both the car and the minibus were parked on the driveway and the garage door was open, revealing Will in overalls, wielding an oil can. When he saw Rachel he walked slowly towards her, wiping his hands on a greasy rag.

'Detective Prince. You're back.' He was polite, but sounded far from cheered by this development.

'I am.' It was a sunny day, but there was a sharp north-easterly wind, and Rachel pushed her hands into the pockets of her trench coat and pulled it round herself tight.

'Now that your festival students have all left, I thought you might have time for a chat.'

'Give me a minute to clear up.' Will walked back into the garage, picking up tools from the floor and replacing them in a metal toolbox on a bench, returning a bottle of screen wash to a shelf on the wall. 'I'm taking advantage of the few days' peace and quiet to do some routine maintenance on the vehicles.'

'Only a few days?' Rachel asked.

'I'm leading a Christian youth group on a walking trip in the Trossachs next week.'

I'd rather stick pins in my eyeballs, thought Rachel. She smiled politely. 'Great. Sounds lovely.'

Will finished cleaning his hands with Swarfega. 'Shall we go in and get some coffee?'

He led Rachel into the students' deserted ground-floor refectory. The carpet tiles, formerly studded with crumbs and smeared with melted chocolate, were now pristine, the gleaming wooden furniture smelled of lavender polish. Gone were the heaps of discarded sweaters, the charging cables and abandoned mugs of coffee.

'Wow – you'd never know there'd been anyone living here,' commented Rachel.

'Our cleaning lady, Mrs Muir, is a miracle worker.' He looked over at the carved crucifix on the wall and acknowledged this small blasphemy with a shy smile. 'She comes in with a couple of helpers and gives the two lower floors a thorough bottoming as soon as the last group leave. Which was over the weekend. That way it's easy to keep on top of things until the next residential course.' He went into the adjoining kitchen and filled the kettle. 'Hazel's taken the children to the park, so we may as well stay down here.'

Will made a cafetière of coffee, found the remains of a milk carton in the fridge and carried them through to the refectory, where they sat at one end of the large, empty table.

'This quiet spell after the last of the festival tours has gone is always a time for reflection.' He stared into the middle distance. 'And obviously, this year, Emily van Meijer is very much on my mind. I understand her funeral took place last week.'

'DS Brickall and I went to speak to Kenneth Candlish again before we left.' Rachel had accepted the mug of coffee but declined the milk, which didn't look fresh. She took a sip, wincing slightly at the bitterness. 'We wanted to share some intelligence we'd received about both Emily and Niamh Donovan attending a party at which at least one of them was sexually assaulted. Did he speak to you about that?'

Will kept his gaze and voice level, but some of the colour left his face. 'He did phone me, yes.' He fiddled with the handle of his coffee cup. 'But like him, I know nothing about where they went, or who was behind it. How on earth could I?'

Will made this seem more than a rhetorical question. 'And if I had done, I would have informed the police, obviously.' There was just a touch of defensiveness infiltrating the warm tones of his voice. 'I'm sorry,' he said. 'But you can see why this is so difficult. If I had known what was going on, then things might have turned out very differently.'

Rachel looked at him sharply. 'What do you mean, Mr MacBain?'

'Well knowing what happened – that Emily was the victim of sexual assault – gives us a completely different explanation as to what happened on the night of the seventh of August.'

'Why does it?' asked Rachel sternly. 'I'm not sure I follow.'

Will raised his eyebrows slightly as he lifted his coffee mug to his mouth. 'Surely it changes the accident theory?'

'Go on.'

He drained his mug and set it down. 'All the students on our tours are from devout religious families. They've all had a conservative upbringing and been very sheltered, when compared with your average 2017 teenager.'

Rachel nodded, although this description didn't entirely fit with the sophisticated lifestyle Emily van Meijer had enjoyed.

'The shame and embarrassment of realising what had happened to them at a party they should not have been at in the first place, the fear of what would happen if their families found out… it could well have pushed them over the edge.'

'You mean suicide?'

Will nodded gravely. 'It makes sense now. The abnormal mood, the uncharacteristic behaviour… and young people these days are so suggestible. Not a day goes by when you don't read in the news about a teenager killing themselves because they've been bullied, or feel under pressure in some way. It's all too common.'

Rachel nodded agreement. 'Unfortunately it is.'

'Emily had had a bit to drink, and that probably clouded her judgement. She took herself off up to the Crags, but instead of losing her footing and falling, she jumped.'

'It's certainly a possibility,' Rachel conceded. 'But that wouldn't explain the selfie stick.'

Will shrugged. 'Who knows.' He rested his hands on the table in front of him. His hands were immaculately clean, and beautifully manicured, Rachel noticed.

She took her last mouthful of coffee. 'One more thing though… you talked about "them" being pushed over the edge. Are you suggesting that Bruno committed suicide too?'

'Well, I'd say it fits, wouldn't you?' The defensive tone crept in again. 'He seemed in very low spirits, and he'd also been drinking. He might well have thrown himself off the rocks, rather than tripping and falling.'

'But we have no reason to believe that Bruno Martinez attended one of these grooming parties. It was actually Marie-Laure Fournier who claimed to have been to one last summer. Bruno was dead by then. He'd been dead a year.'

Two spots of colour appeared on Will's cheeks. 'Obviously, I don't know the facts. None of us do yet. I was merely speculating. Airing a theory.'

Rachel nodded. Then, still looking at Will's face, asked, 'How much does Hazel know about the parties?'

The pink spots intensified. 'Nothing!' He sounded offended. 'Nothing at all – why would she?'

Rachel shrugged. 'She was around the students during their time here, involved in pastoral care. She must have heard them gossiping about things like that?'

Will was shaking his head firmly. 'No. Not Hazel. She's not like that.'

'Like what?'

'One for salacious gossip. She's very… innocent.'

Rachel let this sit for a few seconds. 'I understand she didn't have such a pure and innocent upbringing. She's the daughter of a convicted murderer, after all.'

Will stood up abruptly, colour blazing in his cheeks. 'That has nothing to do with any of this. Nothing whatsoever. Now, if you don't mind, I've got things I need to do.'

'Rachel!'

She was on her way through the hotel lobby, heading to Waverley Station, when someone called out her name. She turned to see Giles Denton, shouldering a smart leather holdall tooled with the initials 'GGD'.

'How are *you*?' The emphasis was firmly on the last syllable.

Rachel looked up at him. She'd always thought of his eye colour as almost black, but up close they were quite blue. They only looked black because of the thick, dark lashes that fringed them. She hadn't noticed that during their kiss under the mistletoe last Christmas, but then she had had her own eyes closed. And been somewhat tipsy.

'Hi!' she said, aware that she seemed distracted and probably a bit ditsy. 'You're staying here?'

'Patten's PA organised it, and she said you were already here. The more the merrier, eh?'

'Indeed.' She glanced at the clock above the reception desk. The last thing she could possibly do, after eighteen years of maternal absence and the disastrous timing of their first meeting, was be late for her son's train. 'Look, sorry Giles, let's catch up later.'

'Absolutely. We need to sit down and come up with a plan of action, so—'

'I'll text you later. Sorry, I've got to go; I'm meeting someone.'

He raised his eyebrows, but there was no time to explain. Not that she owed Giles Denton any explanation about her movements, but he had a singular way of disarming her. Making her feel less than professional and together. *Get a grip, woman,* she told herself. *You're acting like a schoolgirl with a crush on a sixth former.*

Standing on Platform 2 at Waverley Station, coffee in hand, Rachel had a momentary, panicky fear that she wouldn't recognise Joe among the dozens of people spilling off the London train. She needn't have worried. The second she saw his loping walk she felt a rush of connection. What would it have been like if she'd made a completely different decision eighteen years ago? But no, she told herself. No point running through a mental *Sliding Doors* scenario: that way madness lay. Just deal with the here and now.

She wasn't sure if she should kiss him – she knew her teenage niece and nephew shrank from being kissed – so she opted instead for a brief hug. 'Let's walk to the hotel, and that way you can see a bit of the city.'

They wove their way through the tourists and crossed Princes Street Gardens before tracking around the edge of the castle. Rachel pointed things out as they walked, and received the occasional grunt or 'Cool', but no more. *This is normal*, she reassured herself. *This is what eighteen-year-old boys are like.*

At the reception desk of the hotel, she told the clerk she wanted to make a booking.

'Name?' the woman asked.

'He's Joe…'

Shit, she didn't even know his surname. She hadn't thought to ask. A faint wave of panic swept up her body, leaving her forehead damp with sweat.

'Tucker,' said Joe, calmly. 'Joseph Benedict Tucker.'

The clerk scrolled through her reservation screen. 'I'm so sorry Ms Prince, I've not a room for tonight. The last one has just been filled.'

That'll be Giles bloody Denton, Rachel thought.

'I do have a nice executive double with castle view available tomorrow.'

'Okay,' Rachel sighed. 'We'll take that.'

Her room was big enough for them both, she told herself. There was a sofa, which she could take. But wouldn't it feel a bit strange?

'We could find another place for you for tonight,' she told Joe, who was sitting patiently in an armchair with his rucksack in his lap. 'There are plenty of hotels and B and B's in this area. Or you could come in with me.'

He shrugged. 'Okay, cool. Whatever.'

They dropped off his bag and went to an Indian restaurant for a late lunch, followed by a long walk through the Old Town, dodging slow-moving Americans with cameras. After they'd listened to a traditional bagpiper and stared in the windows of shops selling tartan tat, Joe started to relax and open up. He told Rachel about his school, and about his adoptive parents, Jane and Nick Tucker. Nick was a City insurance underwriter, and Jane was a stay-at-home mother. They lived in a comfortable house with a swimming pool and large garden on the edge of the Ashdown Forest. When he was three, the Tuckers had adopted a little girl called Imogen, his sister. He was going to study Politics and International Relations at Nottingham the following autumn, and was in the process of finding himself a complementary internship for his gap year.

'Do you want to be a politician?'

Joe shook his head. 'No, an activist,' he said, with delightful earnestness.

Rachel was only too happy to listen to him talk – she relished it. But inevitably it would be her turn to tell him about her own life, and there would be questions for her to answer. Difficult questions.

They came that evening, after the two of them had eaten from the room service menu and Joe was watching *Top Gear* reruns while Rachel attempted to turn the sofa into a passable bed, using the spare pillows and blankets from the wardrobe. *This is okay*, she was thinking. *It doesn't feel too weird at all.*

'Rachel…' Joe muted the sound on the TV. 'Do you know who my father is?'

SEVENTEEN

Rachel froze as she was plumping and arranging a pillow.

'Yes, yes I do. Of course I do.'

'On my birth certificate there's a blank under the father's details.'

'I know.' She exhaled heavily and sank down onto the edge of the sofa. 'I decided to leave it blank… for other reasons. Not because I didn't know who it was.'

'So who is he?' Joe straightened up on the bed and looked straight at her. 'I have a right to know.'

'Yes, you do,' Rachel said quietly. 'You have a right. It's just hard to know where to start.'

'Start at the beginning. What's his name?'

That directness, that forcefulness. It reminded her of her younger self.

'His name's Stuart Ritchie. He's a doctor. A pathologist.' The fact that they were meeting in Stuart's home town suddenly felt acutely ill-judged.

'And how did you know him?'

'I…' She hesitated. The truth. She owed her son the truth. 'I was married to him.'

He let the shock register on his face, unfiltered. 'Hold on: you were *married* to him?'

Rachel nodded.

'So why was I adopted?' His face coloured angrily.

'We weren't together at the time. We'd separated six months before you were born, before I found out I was pregnant, and I was on my own. On my own doing a job that involved working night shifts. I just wasn't in a position to look after a baby. I made the decision to give you to people who would be able to take care of you properly. In a way I couldn't.'

Joe brushed his hands across his eyes, and she realised with dismay that he was crying. Her own tears were only just being held at bay. 'Joe, my decision wasn't an easy one. I wouldn't ever want you to think I took it lightly.'

'But you didn't want me.'

'No!' She reached for him, but he turned away. 'You must never think that. It wasn't that I didn't want you… it was that I wasn't able to care for you. Not in the way that you deserved.'

He stared at her for a long beat, as she twisted the pillow helplessly in her hands. She knew exactly what was coming: the hardest question of all.

'So why couldn't my dad have looked after me? Didn't he want me either?'

'Joe…' Rachel went over to the bed and sat next to him. 'He didn't know I was pregnant. Remember, I only found out after I'd left him. We weren't in one another's lives any more. I didn't tell him that I'd had you, or that you'd been adopted.'

Joe stared at her, appalled. 'But… he knows now, right?'

Rachel shook her head.

'*What?* For eighteen years you never told him? He has no idea I even exist?'

'We lost contact. I didn't see him after we split. Until recently.'

'How recently?'

'We got in contact again last year. I saw him… quite recently. He's remarried.'

Joe bit the corner of his thumb. She knew that he was trying not to cry, and she didn't dare touch him in case he either burst into tears, or lashed out at her. 'Does he have other kids?'

Rachel shook her head. She drew in a long breath, then looked him straight in the eye. 'Look Joe, I have to tell you this because it would be unfair and dishonest not to. He's living here in Edinburgh. He has a position at the university. It's purely coincidence that I'm working here too, but it explains why I've seen him recently.'

'Friends again, are you?' Joe snarled. 'How cosy! But he still doesn't even know he had a child with you!'

'It's a mess, I know, but—'

Joe jumped off the bed. 'I can't deal with this, my brain's fucking fried… I need to go out.'

He started pulling on his socks and trainers. There was a tap at the door.

'You'd better answer it. I'm not going to.' Joe growled, stamping into the bathroom.

Rachel opened the door. Giles Denton was standing there. 'Rachel! I was going to ask if you wanted to come down to the bar for a drink, but if it's not convenient…'

'Not really.'

'It's okay – go.' Joe's voice came through the open bathroom door.

Rachel decided this might be a good moment for a bit of time out. 'Five minutes,' she told Giles. 'Meet you down there.'

Giles nodded, cast a quick glance towards the bathroom, and headed for the lifts.

'Joe – are you sure you'll be okay?'

There was no reply. 'Joe?'

'Go and have the drink, for fuck's sake.' He remained inside the bathroom, out of sight. 'I just want to be on my own.'

'So – GG Denton. What does the other G stand for?'

They were perched on high leather stools in the hotel's gaudily decorated bar. Giles ordered a whisky sour, and Rachel a vodka and tonic. She didn't think she had ever been so grateful for the relaxing effect of alcohol.

'My middle name's Garvan. Delightfully Irish, isn't it?'

'It has a mysterious Celtic ring,' agreed Rachel.

'Speaking of mysteries… how about yourself, Detective Inspector Prince? Barely in town five minutes and already you've a young man in your room.'

'Oh, no, that's not…' She thought for a second. Was she about to tell Giles Denton that she had a son? Should she? But then she supposed that if Joe was in her life to stay, then at some point she would have to start telling people. 'That's not a young man. Well, he is a young man, but he's my son.'

Giles stared at her, not even trying to hide his shock. 'Get away! You've got a grown-up son? I had no idea. You're surely not old enough.'

She smiled. 'I'm afraid I am, although I did marry very young. He's eighteen. And he doesn't live with me.'

This was all true, and she saw no reason to elaborate further on her backstory. After all, she knew next to nothing about his own.

'How about you?' she asked, keen to deflect attention from her own personal life. 'Are you married?' She took in his appearance – dark-blue shirt, well-cut jeans, brown leather jacket – trying to gauge how old he was. He was one of those men whose hair defied greying, so it was hard to tell. He was good-looking, but more than that, he exuded an effortless masculinity. A man supremely at ease in his own skin. She remembered the heat in their Christmas kiss, and a delicious shiver rippled up her spine.

Giles shook his head. 'Not anymore. I was, for about ten years.'

'Kids?'

'A daughter, Rosanna. She lives in France with her mother.'

Rachel nodded briefly, realising it would be wise to steer away from further talk of children. Her mind inevitably wandered back to Joe, who was now furious with her. Would he be okay? Would *they* be okay?

'Do you know Edinburgh well?' she asked, dragging her mind back to the present, and picking a suitably anodyne topic.

'Quite well. I've a mate who lives here, an architect, and I've visited him a couple of times. How about you?'

'Just once, on a school trip. Aeons ago…' She realised she had veered into her own backstory and changed tack again. 'Anyway, this case… can we call it a grooming case? I guess it qualifies.'

Giles took a sip of his cocktail. 'A bit too soon to say so with confidence, but very possibly.'

Rachel then outlined Will MacBain's theory that both Bruno and Emily had taken their own lives out of an excess of guilt at behaviour their families would see as depraved.

Giles held both hands palm-side up to indicate that he was open to the idea. 'It's not inconceivable. It's a sad fact that teenage suicide rates are at an all-time high, and the aftermath of sexual assault can cause extreme anxiety. And shame. Again, it needs looking at more closely.'

'And the sharing of explicit photos online can be a trigger, too? Only I'm wondering if there could be an element of that here: if Emily and Bruno feared they had been photographed? That they might be blackmailed, even?'

Giles nodded. 'That's certainly going to be in the back of our minds as we try and identify the abusers.'

Rachel took a sip of her vodka. 'Either way, we need to try and get to the bottom of who held this party, the exact location and who attended. If they're handing out flyers according to some sort of pre-selection process, then this is a highly organised operation, not an opportunistic one-off.'

'Agreed. They don't have an equivalent of CEOP up here, but I've arranged to liaise with local Public Protection Officers. They can talk me through local sex offenders who fit the bill, and any people and places on their radar. That might give us some intel to start running with.'

Rachel nodded. 'And I'm going to try and follow up what the Latvian leafleters told me. I also need to interview Emily's friend Luuk, and the other student from Lyon, Marie-Laure. Though God knows just how or when that's supposed to happen.'

'Rachel Prince, the air-miles queen.'

She grinned. 'That's what Mark Brickall always says. However I manage to pull that particular rabbit from the hat, it obviously needs to be soon.'

Denton sighed. 'That's the joy of criminal investigations for you: everything needs to be done yesterday. Can I get you another drink? Or we could maybe have a teeny tiny overpriced one from my minibar?' He gave her a smouldering look from between his outrageously thick lashes.

Rachel hesitated. She was tempted. God, she was tempted. But there was Joe to think of. She needed to check that he was alright. Welcome to parenthood.

'Sorry.' She slipped off her stool. 'I really need to go.'

When she got back to the room, Joe wasn't there. Deciding against texting to ask his whereabouts, she showered and put on pyjama shorts and a vest, then climbed into the not-very-comfortable bed she had made on the sofa, switching off the light.

He returned an hour later, heading into the bathroom to brush his teeth, then tugging off his jeans in the dark and climbing under the covers. Rachel lay listening to his breathing, overwhelmed by the memory of the only other night the two of them had spent in the same room. The intervening eighteen years which she had worked so hard at forgetting evaporated, and she was lying on her back in a hospital bed, sore from the Caesarean section, with a tiny, snuffling bundle in the perspex crib next to her. Listening to the rhythm of his breathing.

'This is well weird, isn't it?'

Joe's voice sounded strange in the dark; older.

'It is a bit.' She needed to say it, or she wouldn't be able to sleep. 'Look Joe, I'm sorry. More sorry than you can know… for not raising you. For everything.'

'Don't be,' he said, with unexpected gentleness. 'Because if you hadn't have done what you did, then I wouldn't have had Mum and Dad and Imo.'

'And they supported you in… finding me?'

'They did. They do. They're brilliant people. They've given me a great home and a great life. I'm happy. So it's okay. Please don't wish things had been different.'

'Okay,' said Rachel. 'I'll try not to. It's me that's missed out, not you.'

'Totally,' said Joe firmly, and they both laughed. 'I do want to meet my birth father though.'

Rachel stared up at the ceiling, watching the shadows made by the headlights of passing cars. 'I understand, and you've every right to. But please, Joe, let me speak to him first. This is not going to be easy for him.'

'I know his name now, and where he works, I could just show up, like I did with you.' Joe spoke defiantly.

Rachel turned on her side, so she could see his profile in the half-light. 'You could. But he and his wife, Claire…' She realised she couldn't tell Joe they were trying to have a child; that would just be salt in the wound. 'They're going through some health issues. So please, at least let me lessen the shock a bit.'

He sighed a long heavy sigh. 'Okay. I s'pose.'

She waited, but he didn't say any more, and after a while he fell asleep and she lay there once again listening to the rhythm of his breathing.

EIGHTEEN

Maris Balodis lived in a bleak pebble-dashed block of flats in West Pilton. Its grim facade was studded with satellite dishes and behind the iron-chain fence, the stringy grass was waist-high and piled with discarded furniture.

Rachel had left Joe wolfing down the contents of the breakfast buffet table, with plans to visit the Camera Obscura museum of illusions. After the high emotion of the previous evening's conversation, she was grateful that they would have a few hours apart. She assumed Joe was too, though she was finding him hard to read. He had been polite but subdued during their brief morning interactions, and she had started to wonder whether inviting him to Edinburgh had been a mistake. Too much, too soon.

She pressed the buzzer for Balodis's flat number and waited. Ten minutes later, she was still waiting. She started trying all the other buttons in turn and eventually someone buzzed the front door open, not bothering to enquire who they were letting in. It was that sort of place.

Balodis eventually opened the door of his flat, but only after she had hammered on it hard on and off for five minutes. The curtains – more draped pieces of dirty cloth, really – were all drawn, and he had clearly just woken up. His complexion was even more waxy than before, and the purple circles round his eyes almost black. He yawned, exposing gold fillings.

'Mr Balodis – DI Prince. When we spoke to you at the police station, you told me you had a note of the mail box number you used. Could you find it for me?'

He stared at her blankly, then turned and shuffled into what could have been a bedroom: it was hard to tell through the heaps of clothes, plastic carrier bags and takeaway boxes. The outline of another human body was just discernible under a grimy duvet. It stirred and the unmistakeable platinum gleam of Iveta's hair emerged onto the pillow.

After rummaging through a few of the bags, Maris pulled out a scrap of paper and handed it silently to Rachel. It was torn from a lined notebook, and on it someone had written: *Box 235, Mail Boxes 4U, 15 South Bridge.*

'Thank you,' said Rachel. 'And don't forget, we may need to contact you again, so please don't go anywhere.'

He grunted, and pointedly went to shut the front door, only just allowing her time to squeeze out of the flat before it slammed.

The manager of the South Bridge branch of Mail Boxes 4U was a cheerful and extremely overweight young woman who introduced herself as Beth. She shook her head as she checked down a handwritten ledger, then cross-checked with her online accounts.

'No, sorry, hen. There's nobody using that box right now.'

'But there was,' Rachel persisted, 'during the festival.'

'Personal mailbox records are confidential,' said Beth proudly. 'I don't have the authority to show you.'

Sighing, Rachel fished out her warrant card.

Beth's eyes widened. 'Oh, okay, sorry.'

Beth checked the record again. 'It was rented by a Mr John Smith. Paid up until Sunday 27 August.'

Rachel's heart sank. Fake name: no surprise there. 'What ID verification do you require?'

'We ask for one photo ID – it says here he used a student card…'

Figures, thought Rachel.

'… and one proof of address. He showed a store card bill. The address is in Leeds. 99 Acacia Avenue.'

It only took a brief Google search to ascertain that there was no such address. Rachel looked around the shop at ceiling level, and spotted two security cameras.

'What about CCTV footage?'

'It's backed up every week to the Mail Boxes 4U central server, then we delete it this end and start again. I've only got a memory card recorded since Monday here at the moment, and the box has been out of use on all of those days.'

Rachel pulled a business card from her pocket. 'Okay Beth, I'm going to need you to request all the relevant footage from your head office. How long do you think that will take?'

Beth bunched her plump cheeks. 'A few days, I reckon. I can ask them to rush it.'

'Please do that. And phone me as soon as you have it.'

As she was walking back towards the hotel, Brickall texted her

How's my dog?

Oh God, Dolly. She had been so bound up in Joe's appearance in her life that she had completely forgotten about leaving the dog with her mother. And it came to her in a rush that she was somehow, at some point, going to have to tell her mother and her sister about Joe. They had been there throughout her pregnancy and had fiercely resisted her giving up her baby for adoption. Especially Lindsay of course, who had recently married and was in the process of starting her own family. Her father had been understanding, a calm voice of reason in the furore, but a year later he was dead from a heart attack. Which she knew Lindsay attributed to the stress Joe's adoption had caused.

Rachel phoned her mother now. 'Just checking how you and Dolly are getting on.'

'Oh, she's such a sweetheart,' her mother sighed with love-struck pleasure. 'She's absolutely lovely, we've become firm friends.'

'That's good.'

'Are you going to pop down and see her? You can bring your friend with you if he's missing her.'

'I'm back in Scotland, but I will come down Mum, soon. There's something I need to talk to you about. Something important.'

'Oh dear,' said Eileen. 'I'm not sure I like the sound of that. Can you give me a clue?'

'No,' said Rachel firmly. 'No I can't. Give the mutt a kiss from me, and I'll see you soon.'

She texted Brickall back.

Dolly being spoilt rotten. Custody visits available on request.

She was looking down at her phone as she walked into the hotel lobby, and collided with Giles Denton.

'Whoa there Rachel, look where you're walking!'

'Sorry,' she thrust her phone into her pocket. 'Walking and texting: a terrible habit.'

'So… you on for a catch-up over dinner?' His aquamarine eyes locked on hers with shocking boldness.

'Sounds great, but I've got plans. Let's try and get together tomorrow.'

'Ah, yes. Your boy.'

'Exactly. My boy.'

*

Joe seemed more relaxed since he had been able to check into his own room at the hotel. They still needed space from one another, it seemed. He readily agreed to go out somewhere for dinner, and he and Rachel found a table in an Italian trattoria in the Old Town. Italian food, he assured her, was his absolute favourite. His family had enjoyed summer holidays in Tuscany since he was very young.

'It's okay,' he told Rachel as she hovered over his wine glass with the bottle of Barolo. 'I can have wine. I'm an adult now, remember?'

The reminder that his childhood was in the past was like a small stab in her heart, but Rachel was determined not to show it. She smiled and poured him half a glass of wine.

'Do the rest of your family know about me?'

Rachel nodded. 'It's just my mum and my sister, Lindsay. My dad died when you were a baby. And yes, yes they do know. I mean, they did know. Back when you were… they knew about the adoption.'

'Are you going to tell them I've found you?'

'I am.'

'How d'you reckon they'll take it?'

'Honestly, I've no idea.'

There was an awkward silence. What was needed was a neutral topic of conversation. 'What do you know about the dark web?' Rachel asked, as Joe went back to shovelling down his risotto bianco.

'Not a whole bunch,' Joe mumbled through his mouthful, spraying bits of rice. He caught sight of Rachel's expression and used his napkin to wipe his chin. 'But my mate Charlie's studying Computer Science at Edinburgh Uni, and he knows loads about how it works. Why?'

'The case I'm working on has led me down that particular rabbit hole.' Rachel took a forkful of her bubbling lasagne and waited for it to cool down enough for her to put it in her mouth without risk of sustaining burns. 'I'm aware that I'm pretty ignorant about it. But I expect there are experts back in the office in London who will be able to enlighten me.'

'When are you going back?' Joe tipped his head back and tossed half of the Barolo down in one go.

'I really need to leave tomorrow. So I guess you'll be heading back too?'

'But you haven't spoken to my dad yet.' Joe's face fell. 'I was hoping I might get a chance to meet up with him before I left.'

Stupidly, Rachel had been hoping that Joe had forgotten about Stuart. Obviously not. And she owed it to her son – and to her ex-husband – to make things right.

'I'll tell you what, why don't you go and find a movie on the hotel's cable channel, and I'll go over to Stuart's house now and talk to him. If he's in, of course. After that, it'll be up to him.'

Joe narrowed his eyes slightly. 'How do you think he'll react?'

'I've honestly no idea.'

Fifteen minutes later Joe was in his room watching *Batman vs Superman* and Rachel was in a cab on the way to Inverleith. She had weighed up texting Stuart first, but remembering his overwhelming need to control, decided against it. She wanted to retain the advantage of having him on the back foot.

She walked up the flower-lined path to the front door of the house and rang the bell. Stuart looked both surprised and puzzled when he opened the door. And not, she noted, especially pleased.

'Rae… sorry, I wasn't expecting you.' Stuart kept his voice low and glanced over his shoulder, in the direction of the stairs.

'Is this a bad time?'

'It's not the best… Claire's not well: she's gone up to bed early. But come in for a minute now you're here.'

Stuart led her through into the sitting room and indicated that she should sit down. There were embers glowing in the hearth and the room felt unseasonably warm. 'Claire was chilly earlier, so I lit the fire,' Stuart explained, as Rachel tugged off her denim jacket and draped it on the arm of the sofa. 'What can I do for you?'

Where to start?

Here's the thing Stuart, remember when we separated nearly nineteen years ago? Well the stress made me lose loads of weight and I assumed that was the reason my periods had stopped, but then – hey presto! – it turned out I was around five months pregnant. Far too late to have a termination, so I decided to have the baby adopted and not tell you. It was a boy, and his name is Joe. And guess what – he's back.

'The thing is, Stuart, something's come up, and it's quite important… well, extremely important… that we talk about it…'

Upstairs a door opened and a faint voice called out, 'Stu?'

'Look, I'd better go and see to Claire,' said Stuart, standing up. He lowered his voice again. 'The IVF… we got a positive pregnancy test, but this morning she started bleeding.'

Rachel stared at him, horrified. 'God… I'm so sorry.'

I can't do it now, she told herself. *I just can't. I can't announce that he's got a child with me on the day that he and his new wife lose theirs. It's just not possible. It will have to wait.*

'Look, Stuart, I can see this is not a good time. Let's catch up soon.'

Rachel stood up and followed him into the hall. 'Be there in a sec, darling!' he shouted up the stairs before turning back to Rachel. 'Can I at least order you a cab?'

She gave him the name of the hotel and ten minutes later she was on her way back there, wondering what on earth she was going to say to Joe.

As she paid the taxi driver, she received a text from him.

Crashing out now, see you at breakfast. Night.

A reprieve, if only a brief one.

*

Rachel called at reception to settle both bills on her way to breakfast, and by the time she reached the restaurant, Joe was already there with a heaped plate in front of him. His appetite was truly prodigious, and yet there wasn't an ounce of fat on him. In that respect, he reminded her of Mark Brickall.

Brickall. She was also going to have to tell him about Joe. Even though she knew him inside out, somehow she just couldn't second-guess his reaction. Not over this.

Rachel sat down at the table and poured herself orange juice and coffee. Joe had to munch his way through a mouthful of sausage and hash browns before he could speak. 'So,' he said eventually, 'how did it go?'

Rachel opened her mouth to come out with a platitude about the time not having been right when Joe's eyes flicked away from her face and over her shoulder, distracted by someone standing behind her. A slight shadow fell over her plate, making her instinctively swivel her head.

Stuart.

Rachel could feel the blood drain from her face and her mouth slipped open. What the hell was he doing here?

'Rae, you left your jacket at the house last night, so I thought I'd drop it in on my way to the General.'

Stuart held up the denim jacket she had left on the sofa.

Joe's mouth had also opened slightly, but in his case his eyes were alight not with shock, but with delight. Before Rachel had the chance to speak, he had leapt to his feet and extended a hand. 'Hi, I'm Joe.'

The blank expression on Stuart's face stopped him, instantly, in his tracks. It was only too clear that Stuart had not the faintest idea who this young man was.

Joe rounded furiously on Rachel. 'You didn't tell him, did you? When you promised me you would! Christ, what is *wrong* with you?'

Rachel realised, too late, her grave error of judgment in not speaking to her son sooner. She had done it again. She had completely messed up their fragile new relationship. 'Joe, hang on a minute, I—'

But he had grabbed his jacket and his rucksack, and as he pushed past the table, he roughly shook off Rachel's restraining hand. Joe stormed towards the door of the restaurant past staring diners, pausing at the door to shout in Stuart's direction.

'Want to know exactly who I am? I'm *her* son. And you're my father.'

NINETEEN

Rachel woke to a bright, sparkling September day. Outside the hotel window, the city of Leiden beckoned.

There was the merest hint of autumn in the air, with the promise of Indian summer warmth to follow. She slipped into jeans, a T-shirt and trainers and headed to the Botermarkt on the edge of the tree-lined canal, avoiding the cyclists bumping their way along cobbled bike paths. The city was a lot smaller and less frantic than Amsterdam, but with the same quaint, timeless feel. Rachel bought a coffee and planted herself on one of the benches that lined the edge of the canal, watching the kayakers and rowers glide past. The faint rippling of the water was soothing. There was something about the whole place that was soothing. And she badly needed that.

She had flown to Amsterdam on Monday evening, taking the short train ride to Leiden from Schipol Airport. Patten and Brickall had both tried to persuade her not to rush straight off, that it could wait another few days, that she needed a break. But for reasons she could not explain to them, she had been anxious to get away immediately. The more distance she could put between herself and the disaster of the previous Friday in Edinburgh, the better.

And it had been a disaster. A fiasco. Joe had stormed straight off to the station and caught a train home, refusing to answer his phone. Stuart, at first thinking the whole scene had been some sort of bizarre joke, had been confused. But after Rachel had sat him down and managed to persuade him that it was true – that she had been pregnant when she left him and had given up their son for adoption – his shock and rage had been spectacular.

'It all makes horrible sense now!' Stuart had spat at her. 'You doing a vanishing act and refusing to have contact with me. You had a bloody great big secret to hide, didn't you?'

Apologising wasn't going to cut it, but Rachel had at least made an attempt to explain. Stuart had stopped her in her tracks by holding up a hand. 'You had no right!' He didn't raise his voice, but spoke with a savage disdain, which was worse. 'That was *my* child too. I had a right to be consulted about his future! I could have taken him, raised him myself if you weren't prepared to. But I wasn't even offered the chance.'

'Our marriage was over. I didn't think it was right for us to be tied together forever. I thought the best option all round was for him to have a normal life in a stable home.'

'And did your family know about this?' Stuart had snarled. 'They clearly didn't think I deserved to know, but did they at least try and make you see you were wrong?'

Rachel had hung her head, twisting her napkin between her fingers. 'They knew. And they didn't agree with me. Lindsay in particular… she wanted to tell you about Joe.'

And it's caused tension and ill feeling between us ever since. Because my family had an image of how my life should be: marriage, children. Exactly like their own. And I shattered all that. Trashed it. Trampled over their values, made them feel slighted, because I didn't conform.

'Well at least someone had some decency…' Stuart had ranted on, stared at by the waitresses and hotel guests, until Rachel had had enough. She'd stood up abruptly, knocking over the orange juice.

'It's no use, Stuart; clearly nothing I can say now is going to make things right. I can't go back and change my decision, and I can't undo the fact that Joe is here, and he wants to get to know us. The way I see it, we owe it to him to get our shit together and do our best for him now.' She softened her aggressive tone slightly. 'I'm sorry Stuart, I've got to go, I've got a plane to catch.'

'Rachel, don't you dare!' Stuart had grabbed her wrist, but she'd pulled herself free.

'We'll talk about this properly when you've had time to think, and to calm down.'

Rachel had returned to her room to fetch her suitcase, phoning Giles to apologise for being unable to meet him.

'Something unexpected has come up,' she told him. Well, that much was certainly true.

Giles wasn't the type to pry, or act affronted. 'Not a problem,' he had said in his lilting Dublin accent. 'I've been given some good leads about where these parties might be happening and who might be behind them. One of my colleagues, Sarah Pattison, is coming up here for a couple of days to give me a hand, and you and I can touch base as and when you get back.'

'Thanks Giles.' She wondered if he could hear the wobble in her voice.

'Anything for you, sweetheart.'

The 'sweetheart' was a touch overfamiliar, but at that particular moment she had been grateful for his easy warmth. On the way to the airport, that evening, and the whole of the weekend she had tried phoning Joe, but her calls only ever went to voicemail, just as Stuart's frequent calls to her went unanswered.

When Dries van Meijer heard that Rachel was in his home town, he once again leapt into billionaire super-host mode and tried to offer her the use of either the presidential suite in the Huys van Leden, an upmarket boutique hotel near the canal, or a luxury apartment that he used for corporate hospitality. She had turned him down, insisting that for such a short trip she was quite happy with her budget lodgings near the railway station.

'You must at least come to my office for some lunch,' he had told her. 'I'd like you meet my wife.'

The Van Meijer headquarters was a huge plate glass and steel monolith on the north side of the canal. It was easily the biggest building for miles, which was entirely fitting for the city's biggest employer. Rachel was escorted to a top floor office suite, where Dries van Meijer – still in a black tie – greeted her with a continental double kiss.

'We'll have some lunch in the director's dining room,' he told her, leading her through to an opulent carpeted room with vast windows where a linen-covered table had been set with crystal and silver and arranged with an array of salads and exquisite open-faced sandwiches. Rachel stared at the indulgent spread with a sinking feeling. She would much have preferred somewhere more low-key to hold the difficult conversation she now needed to have.

Standing next to the table was a tall woman in her mid-forties with long creamy-blonde hair and beautiful regular features, familiar from the pages of *Hello*. She was dressed in a pale blue Chanel dress and discreet, expensive jewellery. She smiled warmly, but like her husband, her eyes were dulled with grief.

'DI Prince, this is Annemarie.'

She took Rachel's hands in hers and squeezed them. 'I have been so wanting to meet you.'

It was a strange to receive such a greeting from the mother of a victim, and to be waited on and offered champagne by a white-gloved butler. But as they talked, there was no mistaking the van Meijers' gratitude that someone was putting considerable effort into finding out what had happened to their beloved daughter. They could not get her back, but they might at least get some answers. That was the least awful of the bleak options that stretched before them as a family.

Rachel refused the champagne in favour of sparkling mineral water, trying to find the best way to start their discussion. The facts, her police instinct told her. Facts first; speculation later. So, rather haltingly, she told Dries and Annemarie that Emily had attended a party in Edinburgh where she was probably drugged and sexually assaulted.

Annemarie's hand flew to her throat, and her face crumpled.

'I'm sorry, I know this is very difficult,' Rachel reached her own hand across the table and briefly touched Annemarie's wrist. 'But you have a right to know exactly where the investigation is taking us.'

Dries gave a brief nod. 'Are you saying he was she raped?' he asked baldly.

'I honestly don't know. I have no firm evidence that's what happened, but we don't have all the facts yet. We're still working to get the full picture. Luuk Rynsberger attended the party too, so I'm hoping he may be able to tell me more.'

'And how is this linked to her death?' Dries demanded, taking his wife's hand and tucking it into his. 'The hardest thing to take is that we insisted Emily join an organised trip to the festival, rather than just go off under her own steam, because we thought it would be much safer for her.'

'Again, we don't know yet,' said Rachel gently. 'But there has been some suggestion that the incident might have led her to take her own life.'

Dries van Meijer shook his head vigorously from side to side. 'No. Absolutely not. Emily would never do that. A boy at her school killed himself a few years ago, and we talked about it together. She was absolutely adamant that suicide was wrong. That whatever happened to you, nothing was so bad that you had to do that. Why would she?' He indicated the room, his wife, the city outside the huge window. 'She had absolutely everything to live for.'

'You're Roman Catholics?' Rachel asked, even though she already knew that this was true. 'Couldn't the faith-based guilt have been too much for her?'

This time it was Annemarie who shook her head. 'No. Not possible. Yes, we're Catholic, but in this country that's no big deal. There are actually more Catholics than Protestants in the Netherlands, but only a small percentage actively follow the teachings of Rome. So yes, Emily was nominally Roman Catholic and baptised as one, but I don't even know whether privately she believed Jesus was the son of God.' Her voice trembled and grew strained. 'I'm not sure she even believed in heaven.'

Rachel reached across the table and touched Annemarie's hand again. Her own plate of food had only been picked at. Tucking into smoked salmon and quail's eggs seemed wrong, given the subject matter of their conversation. 'Look, I know this is very hard, but as I said to Dries when we met in Scotland, any information could potentially help us find out why Emily died.'

She turned to Dries. 'Do you know what happened to the selfie stick?'

Both the van Meijers looked blank.

'There was one found… with her.'

Annemarie shrugged. 'I don't know about that… there was a parcel of her stuff that the police sent back to us, but I didn't look in it. I couldn't.'

'Would it be all right for me to take a look?'

'Of course,' said Dries. 'I will give you our home address and you can come over whenever it's convenient.'

The Rynsberger residence was a handsome red-brick house with an ornate mansard roof and wrought iron balconies, overlooking the botanic gardens from the south side of Leiden's canal. An attractive woman, who introduced herself as Mieke Rynsberger, ushered her into an airy, high-ceilinged room and brought in a tray of coffee and cinnamon biscuits.

'Luuk will be here in a second,' she said in her faultless English. It was easier to understand the Dutch than it was Glaswegians, Rachel reflected. 'This has been a very hard time for him; he and Emily were good friends.'

The door opened and her son entered, politely shaking Rachel's hand. He was tall, but not as tall as Joe. Rachel's mind instantly formed the comparison, in an unfamiliar parental autopilot.

'I will leave you two,' said Mieke, discreetly pulling the door shut.

Luuk squirmed on the edge of the linen-covered sofa, clearly uneasy. 'I have to talk about Emily?' His English was a little accented, but still clear.

Rachel nodded. 'I know it's hard for you, but it's very important that we understand what happened just before she died.'

Luuk stared down silently at his fingernails.

'Niamh told me that the three of you went to a party one night when you were in Edinburgh?'

Luuk nodded.

'Could you talk me through what happened?'

'I don't know a lot… I had a lot of alcohol and I don't remember much.'

'Well, just tell me everything you *can* remember. Anything and everything, even if it seems really small or unimportant.' Rachel took out her notebook and pen.

'We went in a taxi. It was about ten minutes from the residence – you know, the MacBains' house. It was a large house, about the same size as where we were staying, but you know, more…' He ran his fingers through his chestnut hair, struggling for the word. Rachel resisted the temptation to prompt. 'More expensive, more smart. There was a big stone wall at the front, next to the road.

And the door was painted kind of purple. Like an aubergine. This I remember, because it was unusual. And the windows had black…' He pointed to the windows of the sitting room.

'Blinds?'

'Yes, blinds. So no one could see inside. There was music, loud music, lots of chat, lots of people, a lot wearing masks over their eyes. Like birds, animals and stuff. Dark, except for hundreds of candles.'

'What kind of people?'

'There were a few people around our age, but mostly they were older.'

'How old? Like your parents?'

'Some, yes, and some even older than that. Maybe fifty, sixty.'

Rachel nodded encouragement. 'Go on. This is all helpful.'

'There were younger people dressed like waiters handing round the drinks. They were all wearing masks, and some of the guests, too. People standing in groups, talking, some sitting. Sometimes people went up the stairs in twos or threes.'

'And what did you do, Luuk?'

'We stood around, feeling a little strange, you know, a little uncomfortable. We weren't really sure why we would be invited there, to a party like that. It was weird. People kept giving us more and more drinks. Someone led Niamh away to talk and then someone else led Emily away… I was feeling drunk, I had to sit down, so I found a big sofa and sat on it and a man – an older man, quite bald – sat down and asked if I was okay, and he had his hand on my leg, stroking me here.'

Luuk indicated the stretch of flesh between his quad and his groin. 'The next thing I remember is Emily coming downstairs, looking upset, asking where Niamh was. We couldn't find her, and then she came downstairs too and I remember her hair and make-up were messed up and she seemed out of it. Emily grabbed hold of her and dragged her outside. We ran down the street and managed to flag a taxi.'

Rachel took a sip of the excellent coffee, then picked up her notebook again. 'And later you and Emily talked about what had happened?'

Luuk nodded. 'The next day, when we had slept off all of the alcohol. Emily said her drink must have been spiked. She doesn't really like to drink…' He sighed heavily before correcting himself. 'Didn't like to drink… and she only had one, but it made her pass out completely. Like, out cold. But then when she woke up, this guy was… I don't know.' He looked down at the floor. 'I guess you would say assaulting her.'

'I think you would,' said Rachel drily.

'Her shirt had been opened and also her jeans were off, and the guy had, you know… been touching her private parts, and also was touching himself.'

Luuk dropped his head and pressed his hands to his forehead.

'But she didn't contact the police?'

Luuk shook his head, then looked up. 'Not that night; she was too out of it. I guess we should have done…We should have gone to the police straight away.' He lowered his gaze again.

'You're doing really well, Luuk.' Rachel rested her own hand lightly on his shoulder. 'Did Emily remember anything at all about the man?'

He shook his head. 'Not much. She just said it was an older guy… *voornam*… professional, like a businessman type.'

Rachel put her pen down for a minute. 'Do you think Emily was sufficiently disturbed to take her own life?'

Luuk shook his head vigorously. 'No. Never. She wasn't upset, she was angry.'

Rachel thought back to Niamh saying more or less the same thing about Emily. Niamh herself had been frightened, ashamed, after the party. But Emily had been angry; she had been clear about that. 'So do you know if Emily spoke to anyone else about what happened to him? Anyone other than you?'

Luuk picked up one of the biscuits and broke it into several pieces, sending crumbs all over the pale rug. 'I don't think so, but for sure she was going to. After she had sobered up and had the chance to think about it, she made her decision.'

'Which was?'

'Emily wasn't the kind to be a victim. She was strong, you know, focussed? She was going to tell the MacBains, and she was going to make *them* tell the police.'

TWENTY

Lying on her bed in her modest chain hotel, a diet Coke on the bedside cabinet, Rachel glared at a notification lighting up her phone display.

Missed Call: Stuart Ritchie

She found herself thinking back with nostalgia to the sunlit uplands of her adolescence, when there no mobile phones and after school you chatted and giggled with friends who were focused on your face and your voice and not a five-inch pixelated screen. A time when – conversely – if you wanted to avoid someone, you could do exactly that.

But this issue could not be avoided forever, so she picked up the phone and composed a text to Stuart with one hand, holding the Coke can in the other.

> *Am abroad on a job. Will probably be in Edinburgh again soon, so let's try and make time to sit down and talk calmly and rationally about how we are all going to move forward. Meanwhile, please know that I am truly sorry for the shock and the hurt this has caused you. R.*

Once she was satisfied with the wording she pressed 'Send', took a large mouthful of the Coke and set about writing a message to Joe. This one was much harder to get right. Impossible, really. In the end she settled on:

Joe, I'm so very sorry about how things worked out in Edinburgh. I had delayed telling Stuart about you because his wife had just miscarried, but of course I had no idea he would just turn up like that. This isn't how our reunion should have gone. I realise that making the joint trip to Edinburgh so soon was a mistake. MY mistake. We needed more time to get to know one another and for things to fall slowly into place, not for everything to just collide like that. I understand if you don't want further contact with me, but I am here if you ever do. Repeating how sorry I am achieves nothing, but know that I really wanted things to work out differently. Rachel. xx

When she had sent it, she tipped her head back and stared up at the ceiling, tears stinging her eyes. She was emotionally drained. Howard came into her mind, and for a few seconds she longed for his reassuring, uncomplicated company. She could always phone him…

But no. That was a dead-end street. Instead, she pulled on a pair of leggings and her running shoes and pounded the twilit banks of the canals with The Amazons in her headphones. Joe had said how much he loved them.

'Would you like to see her room?'

After breakfast the next day, Rachel had travelled to the van Meijer residence, a huge cream villa in the fashionable suburb of Tuinstadwijk. It was set back from the road behind iron gates, and on the other side of the house the beautifully tended gardens sloped down to canal frontage and a wooden dock. The front door was opened by a uniformed maid, but Annemarie quickly intercepted her, appearing from a doorway in jeans and a linen shirt, her feet bare and her hair scooped on top of her head in a messy bun.

She led Rachel up the magnificent curving staircase and onto the landing, which had a huge arched window overlooking the garden. Rachel paused to take in the view. Extravagant displays of hydrangea in sugar pink and sky blue lined formal gravelled paths. She glimpsed ducks waddling along them, past a flagpole flying the Netherlands flag. It would have been the most idyllic sight were it not for the immense sadness that hung over the place.

There were several doors off the wide, carpeted landing. Annemarie stopped at the middle one. 'I left the parcel from the police in here,' she said, opening the door with a marked intake of breath. 'We told them we'd like them to return all her things, but I haven't opened it… didn't want to. But I do come in here. I actually like to come in here, if that doesn't sound too strange.'

'No, it doesn't sound strange at all,' Rachel said quietly.

The room was spacious and bright, with a window on the garden side and a huge pinboard on the wall above the bed. Emily had stuck up photos, posters from live shows and sporting events she had attended, rosettes and prize certificates. There were pictures of her as a little girl, blonde and cherubic, and candid snaps of her older brothers laughing at the camera. Emily and Dries trying their hand at paddleboarding in some exotic location, both tall, both tanned chestnut-brown.

Annemarie indicated the standard-issue sealed brown paper parcel that a deceased's belongings were bagged up in.

'There. Maybe it will help me if you open it.' She picked up her daughter's pillow and buried her face in it, her tears falling freely now, coursing down the sides of her nose and wetting the pillow-case. Rachel stood in silence until, eventually, she gathered herself.

'I still have my sons, and I'm grateful for that. They're both wonderful. But she was my little girl, my *schatje*…' She was taken over once more by desperate sobs. 'I'm so sorry.'

'Don't be,' Rachel reached in her pocket and found a tissue, offering it to Annemarie. 'It's okay to cry. You *should* cry.'

She looked at the pinboard, the happy summary of Emily's life and achievements, and with a rush the eighteen lost years of Joe's life crowded in on her, and she felt the searing pain of her own loss. She attempted to blink away her tears – she usually managed to maintain a cool, professional facade when dealing with bereaved relatives – but Annemarie noticed.

'Do you have children?' she asked, her voice still thick with anguish.

Rachel nodded. 'A son.'

Annemarie dabbed at her face and straightened up. 'Look at me, such a poor hostess. I haven't even offered you coffee.'

'It's fine, there's no need.'

'I need… I think it would be better if I'm not here when you open the…' Annemarie indicated the parcel.

'Sure,' said Rachel. 'I'll go through it, and I'm afraid I'm going to have to take away the contents as evidence. But you will get them back eventually. Before very long, I hope.'

Annemarie gave a brief nod to show that she understood, then left the bedroom with a last, lingering look. Rachel pulled forensic gloves and evidence envelopes from her bag. With her gloved fingers, she carefully ripped the parcel open and removed the contents. There were Armani jeans and a Chanel T-shirt – both muddied and bloodstained – a pair of scuffed and muddy trainers, a suede bomber jacket – Gucci, Rachel noted – with a rip over the shoulder and back and Calvin Klein underwear. Rachel folded them carefully and reached for the items that had fallen to the bottom recesses of the bag. A smartphone with a cracked screen, a Cartier tank watch and a White Crystal photo ID card which had the company's contact number and conferred discounts at various venues and shops. And the selfie stick, which had snapped into two pieces.

The cheap plastic accessory seemed incongruous. It was the sort of thing that street corner touts offered to tourists all over the world for a few pounds. In London you saw them at Marble Arch and Parliament Square, and there had been several sellers in Princes Street during the festival. Rachel felt sure that Niamh was right: this had not belonged to Emily van Meijer. She might have borrowed it from someone else, but from what Rachel now knew about the girl, even this seemed unlikely. So why had it been with her at the moment of his death?

Rachel dropped the plastic pieces into an evidence bag and checked through the pockets of the jeans. They were empty. If she had taken a taxi to Holyrood Park, you would have expected there to be some cash, and possibly the keys to her room. She checked the pockets of the jacket. There was no cash there either. No wallet and no keys. She could conceivably have taken an Uber: as a sophisticated young European she probably had the app on her smartphone, which Rachel sealed into a second bag.

As she folded the jacket again, she felt something crackle under her fingers. There was a zipped breast pocket on the inside. She opened it and pulled out a much thumbed and folded piece of glossy, aubergine-coloured paper. It was printed with gold lettering.

YOU ARE CORDIALLY INVITED TO LOSE YOUR
INHIBITIONS AT A SPECIAL PRIVATE EVENT!

MASKS, MAYHEM AND MISCHIEF

SATURDAY 5TH AUGUST, 22.00 TO 01.00

21 GRANGE LOAN TERRACE

… DO YOU DARE TO BE THERE?

TWENTY-ONE

'Did you bring back any weed from Holland?'

'No, I didn't,' Rachel told Brickall firmly. 'Anyway, chance to go and buy some would have been a fine thing.'

'Shame. Patten's had me working on a really dull counterfeit currency case while you've been away. Really fucking soul-sapping.' He grinned at Rachel. 'So in the absence of mind-altering drugs, if you could wangle getting me back on the Edinburgh jolly, that would be fantastic.'

The two of them were walking to the Pin and Needle for a much-needed post-work drink. Earlier, Rachel had written up her notes from Leiden and sent them to Giles Denton, and he had just phoned her to tell her that he and his colleague were launching an immediate investigation into the address where the party had taken place. A forensic courier service van was driving the items belonging to Emily van Meijer to Edinburgh, where the blood on her clothes would be analysed and the data on her phone retrieved. And Rachel herself would be heading north of the border again.

'How d'you fancy going to Lyon to question Marie-Laure Fournier?'

Brickall pulled a face. 'Teenage girls aren't really my forte. You know you'd do a much better job of it.'

They'd reached the pub and Brickall went to the bar to fetch his usual order of a pint of lager and a plate of chips, together with a glass of Zinfandel for Rachel.

'They've started doing cheesy chips!' he said, placing the gooey yellow mountain on the table and rubbing his hands vigorously. 'Game changer!'

Rachel couldn't help but smile. She had missed Brickall's infuriating mood swings: his alternating high spirits and sulking. For a few wonderfully escapist seconds, she sat watching her sergeant extracting chips from their blanket of cheese like a messy game of Jenga.

'You could try Skyping the French chick,' he suggested.

'Don't call her a chick. Seriously: this is 2017.' Rachel thought for a second. 'But that is quite a good idea, as an interim measure; I'll still have to talk to her properly at some point.' She took a mouthful of the familiar house red, pulled out her phone and scrolled through Marie-Laure's Instagram. 'Ooh… hang on, we could be looking at two birds with one stone here!'

A selfie of Marie-Laure and another girl making corny peace signs in front of Big Ben had been posted earlier that day. The caption read: *A Londres pour trainer avec ma cousine #cool #mortelle #amour*

'What we have here is something that's as rare as hen's teeth – a piece of luck in a criminal investigation. She's currently in London visiting her cousin. I'll pop back to the office in a bit and dig out her phone number.'

Brickall gave her a thumbs up. 'Nice one,' he said, before diving back into the cheesy chips. 'Sure you don't want one? You always nick at least one of my chips.'

She shook her head.

'What's going on with you? You've been quiet ever since you got back from Holland.'

Rachel drew in a deep sigh, so deep that it made her light-headed. She was going to have to confide in Brickall. Not just because he was a daily part of her life and it would be awkward not to, but because she had found the last few days isolating, and she desperately wanted his support. He had his faults, but when their backs were against the wall, he was always on her side.

'There's something I need to tell you.'

Brickall grinned. 'Let me guess: you're pregnant.'

'Not exactly.'

Brickall's mouth fell open and he stared pointedly at her abdomen. 'Bloody hell, Prince, I was joking.'

Rachel managed a small smile. 'I'm not pregnant, but… I have a son.'

'No you don't. Come off it.'

'I do. He's eighteen and he's called Joe. Joe Tucker.'

'Christ, you're not even kidding!' Brickall's eyes widened in shock. He saw the expression on Rachel's face and his tone softened. 'Well go on then, you'd better tell me about him.'

So Rachel did. All of it, from discovering she was pregnant with her estranged husband's child too late for a termination, through to the horror of Stuart finding out about his son's existence over a hotel breakfast buffet.

'I've got to hand it to you,' Brickall said with grudging respect. 'When you make a mess you *really* make a fucking mess.' He went back to his bowl of chips. 'Problem single mother – I suppose it gives you some PC cred.'

His eyes met hers over the rim of her wine glass and they both laughed. It was something she hadn't done at all in the past few days, and it felt good.

'Seriously though, what are you going to do?'

Rachel shrugged. 'At this point I have no idea. I haven't heard from Joe since he was in Edinburgh. As you say, it's a mess, and right now both of them – Joe and Stuart – probably hate me. I've got so many bridges to build, my life's a bloody construction zone.'

'Well, you've got me,' Brickall said simply, going in for another chip.

Rachel shot him a grateful look.

'I need to tell my family about Joe. I was going to do it this weekend and I wondered if you'd come with me for moral support. And it would give you a chance to visit Dolly.'

'Be glad to,' Brickall said. 'Nothing like a run out to the 'burbs. And I've missed spending time with my best girl.' Brickall caught the expression on Rachel's face. 'I mean the dog.'

After a quick morale-boosting run first thing on Saturday morning, Rachel changed into the least confrontational outfit she could find and drove to Brickall's flat, stopping for coffee and car-friendly snacks en route.

They looked at each other as he eased into the passenger seat and burst out laughing. They had both opted for dark jeans, a chambray shirt and brown leather boots.

'We look like Topsy and fucking Tim!'

'It's obviously the officially sanctioned parent-visiting uniform,' Rachel replied. 'You could go back in and change your shirt, or…'

'Or we could totally mess with their minds.'

They high-fived each other, then set off round the South Circular to Purley. *I need this*, Rachel reflected. After the overwhelming emotional stress and confusion of her foray into parenthood, the long shadow now cast by her past decisions, she needed the silliness and banter that she and Brickall had always enjoyed.

'Did you manage to make contact with the French girl?' he asked, taking a swig of his coffee and opening a bag of Maltesers.

'Eventually. After I'd left her several messages, she finally took the hint and called me back. She's leaving London on Monday, but I'm aiming to try and grab her before she gets on the Eurostar.'

'Good work.'

'Then you and I are heading straight up to Edinburgh. I cleared it with Patten on Friday night.'

'Sweet,' said Brickall with satisfaction.

They were greeted on the driveway by Eileen Prince and a delighted Dolly, who trotted up to Brickall and placed her paws on his kneecaps. He fondled her head, then reached out a hand to Eileen.

'Nice to meet you, Mrs Prince. I'm Mark Brickall. Dolly's foster dad.'

'I've heard a lot about you from Rachel.' Eileen took in their matching outfits. 'And look at you both – you two look like twins. There isn't something you need to tell me, is there?'

'No!' They answered in unison.

'Coffee?'

'No thanks,' Rachel held up her empty takeaway cup. 'Actually, Mark was hoping to take Dolly out for a walk. If that's okay?'

'Of course it is. Come inside and I'll get you her lead.'

As they trooped into the hall there was the sound of a car pulling up outside.

'That'll be Lindsay,' said Rachel.

Her mother did a double take.

'I asked her to come over. You remember I had something to say to you? Well, I need to say it to her too.'

'But you're not getting engaged?'

'No Mum, I'm not getting engaged.' Rachel sighed. 'Not to Mark and not to anyone else.' She took Dolly's lead and handed it to Brickall.

'My cue to leave,' he smiled. 'Back in a bit.'

Lindsay bustled into the hall, staring at Brickall's retreating back. 'What on earth is going on?'

'Hi Lindsay.' Rachel reached in and kissed her sister on the cheek. Lindsay recoiled slightly, caught off guard by this rare show of affection.

'I wanted to talk to you and Mum together,' Rachel told her with more calm than she was feeling inside.

'Well it's not exactly convenient. Tom has jujitsu on a Saturday morning.'

Tom was seventeen but, Rachel reflected, nothing like his cousin. He had none of Joe's charisma.

She ignored her sister's comment and indicated that the three of them should go into the sitting room. Then, without fuss or preamble, she told them that Joe had come looking for her.

Eileen's hand went to her throat, her eyes widening. Lindsay blinked and sniffed. 'He's just turned eighteen, hasn't he, so I suppose it's no great shock. Is there going to be regular contact?'

Her sister made it sound like a form of prison-visiting.

'I don't know... there's been a bit of a problem.' By which she meant that her son was not currently speaking to her.

'What sort of problem?' Lindsay demanded. 'How can there *already* be a problem?'

Rachel shifted on the edge of the sofa. 'He found out that Stuart didn't know about him, and...' she looked down at the toes of her boots, 'let's just say he wasn't exactly happy.'

'That's hardly a surprise!' Lindsay snorted. 'I told you at the time, didn't I?' Her cheeks were flushed now, and she positively bristled with self-righteous indignation. 'I wanted to tell Stuart about the baby, but oh no, you wouldn't have it. You knew better. And now look! We've once again lost a nephew and a grandson. A cousin for my two. We're back to where we were eighteen years ago.'

That's right Lindsay, make it all about you. Rachel didn't respond to her sister's catastrophising, knowing that if she did she would snap. Her fingers were clenched so hard against her palms that her nails were cutting into them.

'Give it time,' said Eileen firmly. 'It's all brand new and strange. For both of you. There are bound to be some teething problems.'

Rachel went over to her mother and kissed her. 'Thanks, Mum.'

Lindsay softened slightly, giving her shoulders a tiny shrug. 'Well... I suppose Mum's probably right. It's bound to have been a huge shock for both Joe and Stuart. There's still a chance you can patch things up when things have calmed down a bit.'

'Thank you,' said Rachel, with a smile that was not entirely forced. 'I promise I will let you both know if Joe gets in touch, and I hope eventually you'll get a chance to meet him.'

Lindsay shot a sceptical look at her mother. 'I'll put the kettle on,' Eileen said quickly, reverting to the comfort of her usual routine. 'And there's a lemon drizzle in the tin that I baked yesterday. That handsome sergeant of yours looks like he needs feeding up.'

TWENTY-TWO

Marie-Laure had asked Rachel if they could meet somewhere near St Pancras station, so that there was no possibility of her missing her Paris train. Rachel suggested a coffee shop in Granary Square, just behind King's Cross.

'I know this place,' Marie-Laure said. 'My cousin Lucienne – it is her I am visiting with – she is at Central St Martin.' She made the last word singular and pronounced it in the French way, which made the renowned art college sound exotic.

'It's a good place to meet,' Rachel smiled. She glanced at her watch, conscious there was little time for small talk. 'I think you know why I want to speak with you today.'

'About Bruno.' Marie-Laure said simply.

Rachel did a slight double take. 'Actually, I was hoping to speak to you about Emily van Meijer… Did you know Bruno from home? I know you were both from Lyon.'

Marie-Laure shook her head, a pretty gesture that involved a lot of flipping of her long, dark mane. They were seated at a table on the paved square, and she took a cigarette and lighter from her pocket and lit it with one smooth, practised movement.

'I didn't know him at Lyon,' she said, tipping back her head and blowing smoke towards the cloudy white sky. 'I know him in Edinburgh, at White Crystal.'

She pronounced it '*cristalle*'.

Rachel blinked. 'But… Bruno Martinez died two years ago, in August 2015.'

'I know, I was there. I went to White Crystal Tours three years.' She held up her fingers. '2015, when I am fifteen-year-old, 2016 when I am sixteen and this year when I am seventeen. I *adore* Edinburgh very much.' She made an expansive gesture, swinging the smouldering tip of her cigarette dangerously close to Rachel's face.

Rachel was taken aback. 'Let me get this straight – you've done three consecutive years at the festival, and you were there when both Bruno *and* Emily were there.'

'Yes. Is correct.' Marie-Laure flicked the tube of ash at her feet and returned Rachel's scrutiny, unabashed.

Rachel performed a rapid calculation. This meant that Marie-Laure was probably the only non-family member in the MacBain's house when both Bruno and Emily died. This could be significant. 'Okay, so we have quite a lot to talk about. The police haven't talked to you before now?'

Marie-Laure shook her head. 'This year I was out at a concert when Emily is missing. They only talked with people at the house.'

Rachel glanced at her watch again, pulling out her notebook, and caught Marie-Laure's look of irritation. 'Don't worry, I won't make you miss the Eurostar. So, let's start with Emily. You were with her this year… did you get to know her well?'

Marie-Laure shrugged and ground out her cigarette butt under her foot, turning her attention to the coffee, which had just arrived. 'Not really. She was a nice girl – *sympa* – but most of the time she was with her friend Luuk.'

'Luuk, and also a girl called Niamh… you know her too?'

Marie-Laure nodded. 'Yes. I know Niamh,' she said simply.

'They were all handed invitations to a late-night party when they were out at the festival and they went, on Saturday 5 August. Just to be clear: you didn't go with them?'

Marie-Laure shook her head. 'No. But I see the invitation they are given. And I know exactly what this is because I am invited last year, in 2016. Same thing.'

'In the same place?'

'I don't know if it is in the same house, but the invitation – it looks the same.'

'But this year you were not invited and you didn't attend?'

Marie-Laure nodded again, taking a drag from the cigarette. 'And in 2015?'

'I was invited, and Bruno also; we were together in the city when they give us the papers about the party. But only he went. I was…' She clutched the front of her abdomen, miming acute stomach ache. 'I was not good that day.'

'Okay,' Rachel paused, trying to tease out the strands of the metaphorical ball of wool and work out where on earth Marie-Laure might fit in. 'So last year – the year you went – did you go alone?'

Marie-Laure placed her coffee cup carefully in its saucer. 'I went with a boy. An Italian boy called Massimo. Max, he call himself.'

'Can you tell me about what happened that night.'

'I don't remember everything, because there is so much of alcohols there, and very quickly I am…' She mimed drunkenness by making herself go cross-eyed. 'I go outside and a man comes and tries to kiss with me.'

'Can you remember what he looked like?'

Marie-Laure shrugged. 'Old, grey hair. He has a strange… I don't know the word in English… in French we say *tache de vin*… is a purple mark. It was here.' She indicated the right side of her neck.

Rachel nodded. 'Ah, we say port wine stain or birth mark.'

'I tell this man no, I don't want, then Max comes in the garden and I say I want to go. So this year… when the guys are invited again, it brings back a memory.'

Rachel nodded, remembering Niamh's description of Marie-Laure acting strangely when she saw the invitation flyer. 'And going back to 2015 – to two years ago – did Bruno talk to you about the party afterwards?'

'Yes.' She checked the time on her phone. 'The train. I must go.'

'Please just tell me what you can. This was a few days before Bruno died, so it could be very important.'

'Really,' Marie-Laure gathered up her bag. 'I need to go.'

Rachel checked her own watch. 'You have two minutes. Please.'

Marie-Laure sighed and reached for her cigarette lighter, flicking the wheel on it repeatedly. 'He is very upset. He say he is going upstairs in the party house to lie down because he was feeling… *pris de vertige.*' She made an exaggerated head reeling movement to show dizziness. 'He wake on a bed and a man was with him, and he was… his boxer shorts were off… he is worried the man has had sex with him. He say he run outside and get a taxi, back to the residence.'

'Did he talk to anyone about it? Apart from you?'

Marie-Laure shrugged. 'He want to tell Hazel, but he is worried because going out at night is forbidden. So I tell him that he might be mistaken – if you are drinking too much the memory goes bad sometimes. You imagine things happen. But he say to me that what happened to him was wrong. He will tell Hazel at the end of our trip, so it doesn't matter that he has break the rules, and he will tell his parents when he gets home. But then, before this can happen…'

She dropped the lighter on the table, stopping her narrative dead.

Rachel completed the sentence. '… he fell into the sea and drowned.'

TWENTY-THREE

'So lover boy is still up here?'

'I'm not sure who you mean,' said Rachel coolly.

She and Brickall were wheeling their cases from the tram stop to their hotel. Not the one that Rachel had stayed in the previous week – she couldn't face it after the mortifying showdown during breakfast – but a similar establishment nearby. It was mid-September, but autumn had already arrived in Edinburgh, with a gusty wind blowing the leaves off the trees and intermittent horizontal drizzle.

'I mean your pet Pierce Brosnan lookalike. Denton.'

'He's not my pet anything,' Rachel corrected him. 'But yes he is. Working with the local child protection team. I'm going to meet up with him for a briefing in a bit and find out where he's got to. Feel free not to attend if you have better things to do.'

'I might as well: it's not like I've got Dolly to walk this time. Not that she would enjoy this,' Brickall indicated the weather. 'Shame she's not here, though I miss her.'

'She's fine with my mum,' Rachel smiled at Brickall. 'But I do miss the mutt too. A little bit.'

They dropped their luggage and took a cab to the Public Protection Unit's office in Dalkeith, a town six miles south-east of the city centre. Giles Denton met them in the reception area of the huge modern brutalist building and showed them to where he and his colleague had been given temporary office space. He introduced Sarah Pattinson, who turned out to be young and pretty, with a halo of thick natural blonde curls.

Giles, as ever, twinkled at Rachel and more or less ignored Brickall. 'We've managed to find out a bit about 21 Grange Loan Terrace: the location of the party attended by Emily van Meijer. It's registered as belonging to an offshore trust in Cayman. Currently rented out, but not to an individual, to a holding company in Malta. Smoke and mirrors stuff. We've also identified the firm of solicitors who arranged the lease, so I thought one of us could pay them a visit.' He handed out a set of printed sheets. 'I've also been given this list – names of some people on the local sex offenders' register who might fit the bill for this sort of high-end grooming. We could try bringing them in for questioning, though at this stage I suspect it would just be a matter of straight denials all round.'

Rachel was shaking her head slowly. 'I think we need to cover more ground before we go down that route. What kind of IT expertise can we access here? I'm thinking back to the Latvian leaflet distributors, who were recruited via the dark web… can we see if there's someone here who specialises in it, who could help us open that rather nasty can of worms?'

'I can look into that,' said Sarah quickly. She glanced over in Giles' direction, as though eager to please him. 'I'll speak to Intelligence.'

'How about setting up surveillance on the party house?' Brickall asked.

'It's currently unoccupied,' Denton told him, 'so there seems little point. If it looks like it's being used again, then yes – I'd say that would be an obvious line to pursue. We'll need to keep it under informal surveillance in the meantime.'

'He's definitely banging her,' Brickall said as they waited in reception for their taxi to arrive.

'Who is?' Rachel feigned ignorance, although she knew exactly what he was referring to.

'Old Westlife there. Bet he's putting the moves on Blondie. And I can't say I blame him; she was cute.'

'Don't be fucking ridiculous,' Rachel said, with more vehemence than she intended.

'Jealous, are you? Don't worry, he was still giving you the glad eye. He's a player, our Irish pal.'

Once they were in the cab, Brickall gave the driver the name of their hotel, but Rachel leaned forward into the front seat and asked him to do a detour.

'Where to, dear?'

'21 Grange Loan Terrace.' She sat back in her seat. 'I thought we could do a little recce of our own.'

It was dusk by the time the driver pulled up outside the large sandstone villa.

'You want me to wait here and then take you on to the hotel?' the cab driver enquired as Rachel and Brickall climbed out onto the pavement.

'Actually, no; change of plan. You can leave us here.' Rachel said, reaching into her wallet and handing him a ten-pound note.

The facade of the house was hidden behind a tall privet hedge. While the windows of the neighbouring houses glowed invitingly, those at number 21 were blank and unlit. The aubergine door that Luuk had described looked almost black in the fading gloom.

Brickall and Rachel instinctively cupped their hands against the glass of the front windows to get a look inside, but heavy wooden shutters had been bolted across them, masking the interior.

'Shall we try the back?' asked Brickall.

He vaulted over the side gate and unbolted it to let Rachel through. At the rear of the house there was a terrace arranged with expensive garden furniture and lighting, and beyond that a sloping lawn. Rachel pictured Marie-Laure sitting out there a year ago;

confused, drunk and possibly even drugged. Wanting to go home. She looked up at the imposing upstairs windows, also shuttered, and pictured what had taken place up there. She shuddered.

'You okay?'

'This place gives me the creeps.'

Brickall tried the back door, shaking the handle and then squatting down to inspect the lock. 'You up for a bit of breaking and entering?'

'Detective Sergeant, you do know it's illegal. Even for serving police officers.'

'Yes, but what if we thought we heard a member of the public inside, in a state of distress.' Brickall winked. 'We would be within our rights to forcibly enter to investigate… you got your knife?'

Rachel pulled out the Swiss Army knife she always carried and handed it to him. He inserted the reamer tool at the bottom of the lock and held out his hand to Rachel. 'Got a pin of some sort? A hair grip?'

Rachel searched her pockets and pulled out a paperclip. 'Will this do?'

Keeping tension in the reamer with one hand, Brickall unbent the clip with his teeth, bent a right angle at one end and inserted it, jiggling it rhythmically until the lock tumblers slid back. With a final twist of the reamer, the lock gave way and the door opened.

'I won't tell you where I learned to do that,' he said with a grin.

'Most of the force have been taught how to pick a lock,' Rachel observed. 'I know I have.'

Inside, the house was dark and silent. Rachel pulled on a pair of latex gloves and switched on the light in the front hall. There was a heap of mail on the front mat. Hidden amongst the pizza delivery menus were a couple of letters – probably utility bills – addressed to Sabre Holdings.

The front reception room had a huge chandelier and squashy expensive sofas arranged around a large, square coffee table. At its centre was a cluster of candleholders with half-burned candles. In fact, there were candles everywhere, flanking the edges of the staircase and full running the length of the passage that led out to the terrace. Luuk had recalled there being no light apart from 'hundreds of candles'. It must have made for a very distinctive atmosphere.

The kitchen was fitted with expensive charcoal-coloured units and state-of-the-art appliances, including an American-style fridge. Brickall opened it. There was no food inside, just neatly arranged bottles of mineral water and, in the built-in wine rack – several bottles of Krug.

'Nothing but the best for our perverts,' Brickall observed.

The kitchen was tidy and very clean, and there was no sign of anyone ever using it to prepare meals. Pinned to the side of the fridge was a typed notice with phone numbers for 'Electrician', 'Plumber' and 'Cleaner (Valerie)'.

Rachel pulled out her phone and took a photo of the notice, then turned to Brickall. 'Shall we go upstairs?'

'Thought you'd never ask.'

On the first flour there were four large bedrooms and three bathrooms, two of them *en suite*. All were well-appointed in a characterless way, decorated with shades of beige and grey as though they were hotel rooms. Candles were dotted around all the rooms and there were large, sumptuous beds with bedspreads in shiny colours and heaps of velvet cushions. Rachel opened a bedside drawer and she and Brickall peered inside. A box of tissues, condoms, a bottle of personal lubricant.

'Nice,' observed Brickall drily. 'Thoughtful'. He examined the expensive light fitting. 'I'm just trying to figure out the economics. You know the rule: follow the money. Someone's renting this place for what must be several grand a month, then leaving it empty apart from the occasional party night – how does that work financially? It doesn't feel like it's just some rich guy's hobby.'

Rachel shook her head, turning to walk up the plush carpeted stairs to the top floor, Brickall at her heels. 'I agree. Emily and Marie-Laure both described something highly organised. I'm guessing the people who attend the parties have to pay a hefty fee. Or maybe pay a subscription, like a private members' club.'

The top floor had two smaller rooms and a shared bathroom, decorated in a similar fashion, with the same 'kit' in the drawers.

'Can we go now?' asked Brickall. 'I think we've got the picture.'

Rachel nodded, pulling off her gloves. 'We certainly have.'

They returned to the ground floor and left through the back door, slamming the deadlock behind them. As they walked up the driveway, Rachel's phone buzzed with two texts. The first was from Giles Denton.

Fancy dinner tonight? G x

The other was from Joe.

TWENTY-FOUR

Rachel sat on the edge of her hotel bed and stared at the text.

I'm sorry I left when I did. I was angry, but I've thought about things, and I get that it was a situation you had no control over. Right now I'm just trying to get my head around everything. Would like to stay in touch. J

She needed to acknowledge her son's gesture somehow, without coming on too strong or crowding him. And then there was the Stuart problem. That was one colossal bridge that needed rebuilding. He had stopped the endless phone calls, but now that she was back in Edinburgh, she really ought to reach out to him, to attempt to heal that gaping wound.

But one thing at a time. Stuart could wait a little longer. She would deal with Joe first. She wrote back.

Me too, but please know there's absolutely no pressure. When you're ready. x

Having dealt with the situation to the best of her ability, she turned her focus back to preparing for her date with Giles Denton. Or was it a date? She wasn't entirely sure. Given the pitfalls of becoming personally involved with colleagues, it was probably best to treat it as an informal chat about the case. Nevertheless, she took down her hair from its ponytail and changed from a plain white work shirt to a floaty chiffon top. She hesitated for a few seconds over whether to vamp up her lipstick from her usual neutral shade to a seductive dark red. *Why worry*, she decided, as she applied the red colour. *He's a man. He won't even notice.*

'Well get you, with your Hollywood siren lips!'

It was the first thing Giles said to her, though his lilting Irish accent made it sound genial rather than sleazy. In fact, it sounded great. Rachel smiled at him, and batted her freshly mascaraed lashes. *You're flirting with him like a brainless bimbo*, she reprimanded herself. *Get a bloody grip.*

They were in a small, dimly lit brasserie in Stockbridge; a venue that Giles had chosen. They ordered drinks while they looked at the menu, a vodka and tonic for her and an Irish whisky for him ('I'm a cliché and proud of it'). It was only when she looked at the descriptions of the food that Rachel realised she hadn't eaten for nearly twelve hours.

'The food's fantastic here,' Giles said, with his usual uncanny ability to see into her mind. 'Marvellous – all of it.'

'Good, because I'm starving.'

A basket of bread arrived and she dived into it, describing her tour of 21 Grange Loan Terrace in between mouthfuls.

'I made sure I wore gloves,' she assured him when he pulled a mock-shocked face. 'But I think we should apply for a warrant and get a forensics team in there.'

'I agree. Absolutely,' he said. 'And are you up for talking to the lawyer who represents Sabre Holdings, a Mr…' he checked the note on his phone, 'Douglas Coulter? I could come with you, if you like?'

Rachel thought about this for a moment. She liked the idea of tackling a tricky interview with Giles at her side. But then she and Brickall had their two-hander routine down pat after years of working together and bounced off each other in a completely intuitive way. Partnering with Giles might introduce an unwelcome and unhelpful dynamic of sexual tension. Besides, if Brickall found out she had been 'unfaithful' to him and been out on a job with Giles, she would never hear the end of it. The sulking and sarcasm would be unbearable.

'No, it's fine, I'll cover it. But I'd be grateful if your team could drill down on the dark web angle; my instinct is that there's something there.'

'Your Spidey senses tingling?' suggested Giles.

'Exactly.'

Two heaped bowls of *moules marinières* arrived, giving off fragrant steam. Rachel picked up a shell and sucked out the meat, aware that Giles was watching her, watching her scarlet-painted mouth. She met the gaze of those intense eyes and looked quickly down at her bowl, feeling somehow vulnerable; naked.

'Tell me about Rosanna,' she said, keen to deflect attention from herself.

Giles shrugged, swirling his wine round his glass in a distracted motion, as though the topic was not a comfortable one. 'There's not a whole lot to tell. She's a great wee kid, but I only see her a few times a year, during her school holidays. We both enjoy the time together, no doubt about that, but it's hard to maintain a close relationship when you see so little of one another.'

Rachel's mind went straight to Joe and the huge gap she now had to span. If that was even possible. Perhaps it was best to switch from parenthood to a safer subject. Careers.

'And how did an Irishman like you end up at the NCA?'

'I started out in the Garda.' He took a mouthful of the wine, leaning back in the chair in his easy manner. 'Transferred to the National Bureau of Criminal Investigation, which is the Republic's equivalent of the NCA. Then my ex and I split, and I was struggling to finance two households.' He smiled ruefully. 'With the financial crash and all. It hit Ireland hard… but by then there was freedom of movement for EU nationals, so I took advantage of it and applied for a job at the NCA. And here I am.' He made a flourish with his hands.

She smiled. 'Here you are, large as life… so why Child Exploitation? Any particular reason?'

Giles turned his attention back to fiddling with his wine glass. 'No reason other than that it was something that interested me.'

Rachel's phone started ringing. She ignored it, tweezing a second mollusc with the empty shell of the first, but it rang again, straight away. It was a number she didn't recognise.

'Sorry, I'd better get this.' She wiped the garlicky broth off her mouth with her napkin, taking a smear of crimson lipstick with it.

'Never off-duty,' said Giles ruefully.

She picked up the call, twisting in her chair and leaning towards the quieter end of the restaurant.

'DI Prince.'

'Hi, this is Beth.'

'Er, hi.' Rachel's mind was a blank.

'Beth McAllister. At Mail Boxes 4U in South Bridge.'

'Yes, sorry. Of course. Hi.'

'Only you said to ring you when I had some news on the CCTV. I'm sorry to ring so late, only the IT department said they would send something over today, and I waited, but nothing happened. So I had to phone them, and they told me to phone someone in Italy, and anyways, eventually they said they'd have to resend and it's only just got here. I've been sitting here after the shop closed, waiting.'

Rachel tried to digest this slightly muddled narrative. 'So, what is it you have?'

'I've got images of John Smith. The one who opened that mail box you were interested in. Only… well, to be honest it's a bit weird. But I definitely think you'll want to see it.'

'Can you wait ten minutes, Beth? I'm coming straight over now.'

Rachel hung up, looking apologetically at Giles and sorrowfully at the bowl of cooling mussels. 'I'm really sorry to do this to you, but I'm going to have to leave.'

'That's him, there.'

Beth McAllister, dressed in a tight Adidas tracksuit top and denim skirt, bent over the computer monitor and pointed to a pin-sharp image of a man approaching the row of numbered mail boxes.

'Bloody hell,' said Rachel. 'I see what you mean.'

The figure – young from his physique and gait – was wearing a tartan Tam O' Shanter hat attached to a scruffy ginger wig.

'We call those "See You Jimmy" hats,' Beth told her. 'You can buy them in fancy dress shops, and they sell them to tourists at the stalls on Rose Street.'

The man walked over to the mail box, opened it and slid in a slim stack of leaflets and placed a dark object on top of them.

'I reckon that's a mobile phone,' Beth said in a stage whisper.

'I reckon you're right.'

The man walked out again, keeping his head down. The shaggy wig and the brim of the hat made it impossible to view his face properly. The time stamp said 5 August, 15.44.

'When I told them it was for a police investigation, they had the pictures specially enhanced,' Beth said proudly.

The images were indeed very good quality, making it all the more frustrating that the man's face couldn't be identified. The clothes definitely struck a jarring note – a smart, well-cut jacket and trousers, proper shoes rather than trainers.

'Could I take a copy of the footage?' Rachel asked.

'Sure – do yous know who it is?'

She shook her head. 'No idea. Not without the use of facial recognition software.'

Beth inhaled sharply with a little shiver of excitement. 'Oh my God, this is so exciting. Just like *CSI*.'

Back in her hotel room, Rachel slipped into sweatpants and a T-shirt, and was just picking up the room service menu when there was a loud, impatient hammering at her door. She swung it open, to find Brickall standing there.

'Fancy a pizza?'

Rachel laughed. 'Right now, I could eat three.'

'There's a place near here that does delivery, and I've already checked they do extra hot sauce, so…' He handed her his phone, which was displaying an online menu. 'Decide what you fancy and I'll order.'

Rachel was hesitating over anchovies versus olives when there was another knock at her door, more discreet this time. Giles stood in the corridor, holding two brown paper carrier bags and a bottle of wine. 'The restaurant took pity on us and packed up our dinner into doggie bags… Oh.' He caught sight of Brickall. 'Sorry, I didn't know you were—'

'That's okay,' said Brickall, his expression souring as he snatched his phone from Rachel's hand and put it back into his jeans pocket. 'We were about to order a pizza, but it seems you've beaten me to it.' He raised his eyebrows in Rachel's direction. 'With your "special" delivery service.'

'Was I interrupting something?' Giles asked when Brickall had left the room.

'No, no… it's fine. We really were just ordering a pizza; that's not a euphemism.' Rachel grinned at him, pulling foil cartons out of the bags and reaching to the bottom for the knives and forks, thoughtfully wrapped in paper napkins.

'You and Mark are very close though,' Giles observed pointedly. 'I don't like to think I'm stepping on toes.'

'Oh no, don't worry – we're not close like *that*,' Rachel said quickly and instantly regretted it. It now sounded as though she intended Giles and herself to become close 'like that'. 'We've worked together a long time and we're good friends.'

'So you *are* close.' Giles poured the wine into two glasses and handed one to her, standing only inches away.

'Yes, I suppose we are. As colleagues.'

'And what would I have to do to become… close… to you?'

He was standing dangerously near to her now, his thighs just touching hers. Rachel's heart sped up, and she could feel a delicious warmth suffusing her body. Giles set down his glass and placed his hands behind her neck, winding his fingers through her hair and kissing her with the same spine-tingling thoroughness as their Christmas kiss. Only this time it was more intense because instead of being in a crowded pub they were alone. Four feet from a bed.

Rachel felt herself melt into him, pressing her body against his, her left hand straying to his back and down to the waistband of his jeans. He took the wine glass from her right hand, putting it next to his own, and leaned forward, using his superior height and weight to shift her equilibrium and topple her back onto the bed. He was still kissing her hungrily, pulling at her T-shirt, and she tugged his shirt open. His chest was muscular, and lightly covered with black hair.

Rachel's physical instincts were taking over, but through the swirling treacle in her brain, sense somehow kicked in. This case was not only about the death of innocent teenagers, but also exposed the NCA's ability to respond to extremely sensitive material. Sleeping with a key co-worker would compromise her own efficiency, and – if it came to light – the entire investigation. Once she would have been unable to think this way, but now she was putting herself in the place of Emily and Bruno's parents. Would I want the officer in charge of finding out who killed my child behaving like this? Shagging the good-looking child protection specialist? The answer was an emphatic no.

'No!' she whispered. Her voice was so thick with desire that it emerged as a groan. With a huge effort she threw the seduction gear into reverse, scooting out from under Giles's body and pulling down her T-shirt.

'Giles, we can't. You know it's not a good idea. Not now.'

He stayed where he was for a few delicious seconds, as if unable to move out of a powerful force field. Then, with a sigh, he stood up, re-buttoned his shirt, and reached for his wine glass. He drank deeply, as though attempting to sedate himself.

'You're probably right. Can I still interest you in a spot of chicken chasseur?'

She shook her head slowly, unwilling to admit she was still hungry. A meal with wine would set the scene for the whole bed scenario to happen again. 'No thanks, I'm fine. Probably best you take it with you.'

'You said "not now"… does that mean you and I are a possibility, after…?'

Rachel gave him a half-smile. 'Never say never.'

TWENTY-FIVE

The offices of Reekie & Co were in an imposing sandstone terrace in the West End. Rachel and Brickall were led up a broad, carpeted staircase to an ante-room and asked to wait until Mr Coulter had finished with the client who was consulting him.

Brickall helped himself to coffee from a sleek machine in the corner and some individually wrapped packets of shortbread. 'So, you and Ireland's answer to George Clooney…' He sprayed crumbs on the jade green carpet as he opened the packet of biscuits. 'Hot and heavy night, was it?'

'Actually, he left about ten minutes after you did.' This was the truth, if not the whole truth.

Brickall's eyebrows shot up. 'A quickie, then.'

'Don't be a pain, Sergeant. Nothing happened.' Again, this was a slight distortion of the truth, but Rachel had no desire to discuss Giles Denton with Brickall.

After ten minutes, a female assistant called them through into Douglas Coulter's office. He was behind a huge antique desk, and remained seated, gazing out of the tall sash window to his right. Passive aggression on point, thought Rachel.

'Mr Coulter,' she extended a hand. He did not take it, but turned slightly in his chair so that he was looking more or less in their direction. 'I'm DI Prince, and this is DS Brickall.'

'You're here from London,' he said brusquely. 'Why?' He was a man in the later part of middle-age, waistline bulging slightly in his handmade suit, no doubt as a result of too many business lunches and too little exercise. His thinning grey hair was rearranged to disguise some of his bald pate.

'We're looking into a client of yours. Sabre Holdings.'

Coulter could not have looked less interested. 'May I ask why?'

'We have reason to believe that a property leased by the company has been used in the commission of sexual offences against minors,' Rachel tried to keep her impatience under check. 'If we could have sight of their file…'

Coulter gave her a thin, reptilian smile. 'You know, officer, that the solicitors code of conduct governing client confidentiality puts that out of the question. Not unless you have a Data Protection waiver from the court.'

'That's easily enough arranged,' said Brickall. His tone was bullish.

'Not necessarily,' Coulter said smoothly. He barely moved in his chair, merely sliding his fingers to and fro along a wooden pen holder on his desk. 'Under the Police and Criminal Evidence Act, you will have to issue me with a subpoena, whereupon I will request the court to decide client privilege.'

'Can you tell me anything at all about why Sabre Holdings are renting 21 Grange Loan Terrace?' Rachel persisted. 'What is the purpose of the tenancy? Who approached you about it? Do you have a name, at least?'

Coulter did not even bother looking in their direction, turning again to look out of the window. 'Again – I would like to remind you of client privilege.'

Brickall approached the filing cabinet to Coulter's left. 'Keep the records in here, do you?' he asked, reaching for the top drawer.

'Don't touch that!' Coulter's head whipped round, animated at last. 'Not without a court order.'

As he glared at Brickall, his face in profile, Rachel caught sight of something just visible above his shirt collar, on the side of his neck that had been nearest to the window. A port wine stain.

*

'Christ on a bike!' Brickall said. 'So you reckon that dusty old stick was at one of the parties himself?' He and Rachel were holed up in a café on Lothian Road where, despite the shortbread, Brickall had just ordered a full Scottish breakfast.

'Let's see now…' Rachel mimed stroking her chin. 'Marie-Laure describes a port wine mark on the right side of the man's neck. An older man with grey hair. And Coulter is the one who helps lease the house where the parties took place.'

'That's no fucking coincidence.'

'Exactly. So you know who we have to talk to next,' Rachel told him, helping herself to a triangle of toast. 'Whether we like it or not.'

'Our mate Morag Sillars.'

Rachel nodded. 'And unfortunately Police Scotland don't seem to have made the link between Bruno Martinez and Emily van Meijer both dying while in the care of White Crystal Tours, so we're now being forced to play catch up.'

Brickall gave a small shrug. 'Given the two-year time lag between the two deaths, I think that's just an unfortunate oversight.'

'Maybe. But we still need their help. We've got enough circumstantial now to start putting a formal investigation together, but we need resources. Normal, everyday stuff. Like desks.'

'And constables,' agreed Brickall, munching on a piece of bacon.

'So, hurry up and finish stuffing your face.' Rachel drained her cup of coffee. 'All roads lead to Gayfield Square.'

One of the things that Rachel's police career had taught her was that despite its endless vagaries, human nature could still surprise you.

On this occasion, the surprise was that DI Sillars was not only helpful, but almost apologetic that the potential links had been missed. She listened – e-cigarette in hand – while Rachel relayed the substance of her meetings with Niamh, Luuk and Marie-Laure, and the mysterious set-up behind the house where Emily and Bruno had been assaulted.

'I agree it's well dodgy,' she rasped. 'Dodgy as fuck. Definitely worth taking a closer look at this Coulter character too. How about some covert obs on his home address?'

'If you could spare the manpower, that would be great,' Rachel shot a grin at Brickall, who discreetly raised his eyebrows in a silent 'who knew?' gesture. 'And we need to get one of your intel boys – or girls – looking at Emily van Meijer's mobile.'

'Aye, I will.' Sillars breathed vapour like a small, belligerent dragon. 'And we'll check the selfie stick for latent prints. Anything else?'

'We need to apply for a warrant to do a full forensic search on 21 Grange Loan Terrace.'

'I'll get DC Tulloch onto it. And I suppose yous'll be wanting desk space while we're sorting all this lot?' She directed this at Brickall, with what Rachel thought was almost a hopeful look.

'That would be great, Morag.' Brickall gave the diminutive woman his most disarming smile. 'At the moment we're wandering the streets, like—'

'Like the useless soft southerners you are.' Morag completed his sentence with the ghost of a grin. 'Let me speak to Sergeant Finlayson and see what I can do.'

Forty minutes later, they were given the key to a room in the basement. It was small and badly lit, but there were three basic desks — two with phone lines, one with a computer terminal — a whiteboard and a cupboard with some basic stationery supplies. Even better, DC Tulloch was allocated to help them, when his other duties allowed.

'Good old More-hag,' Brickall said, swinging his legs up onto the desk as he tried one of the chairs for size. 'She really has come through.' She had even applied to the approved police list for a formal name for the investigation. They were now Operation Honeycomb.

'That's because she's an old-fashioned copper at heart,' Rachel told him, rummaging through the cupboard for some coloured pens to use on the whiteboard. 'And her instincts are telling her that something that smells this fishy, probably *is* this fishy.' Rachel pointed to the computer terminal. 'How about you try and find out a bit more about our pal Douglas Coulter? And work through that list of local sex offenders that Giles gave us.'

'Aye aye, boss.' Brickall did a mock-salute.

Rachel pulled out her phone and scrolled to the screen shot she had taken in 21 Grange Loan Terrace.

Cleaner (Valerie).

Rachel tried phoning the mobile number. It rang out, so she left a message.

There was a repeat offer of a pizza blow-out from Brickall once they had returned to the hotel, but Rachel declined. There was something that needed to be done that she couldn't put off any longer.

Stuart was grim-faced when he opened the door to her. He led her wordlessly into the sitting room. This time the lamps on the side tables were off, and there was no welcoming warmth from the fire.

'Claire's not here,' Stuart explained. 'She's gone to visit her mother in Dumfries for a bit. I'm hoping to join her, once you and I have sorted a few things.'

'Does she know… about Joe?'

Stuart shook his head. 'I will tell her, of course. I'll have to. But right now she's understandably devastated about losing the pregnancy. I just can't do it.'

Rachel nodded. There had been no invitation to sit, but she lowered herself onto the edge of one of the squashy sofas. Stuart remained standing.

'Have you heard from… our son.' The words sounded unnatural coming from his mouth, and he showed he was aware of this, grimacing slightly.

'Yes. He has been in touch, which is good. And I hope to see him again at some point. So when I do…' She attempted a smile, but it met with a stony stare. 'I imagine he'll still want to meet you.'

'We've already met, remember?' Stuart spat. 'In a hotel dining room.'

Rachel looked at his face, and for the first time she looked for Joe's features there. The hairline and the jaw were the same. She let out a long sigh.

'Stuart, there's no point me apologising to you. It doesn't change anything. I know you're completely blindsided by this, but I can't go back and do things differently. It's not possible to rewind the past eighteen years. As I said in my text, at this point we owe it to Joe to think about how we move forward.'

'I know there's no merit in re-hashing the past,' Stuart's tone was a little gentler, and he sank down into an armchair, his shoulders curved forwards. 'But Rae, I just need to understand how we got to this point at all. How you could discover you were pregnant and not tell me?'

'The fact is, if I'd discovered I was pregnant sooner, I would undoubtedly have had a termination and we wouldn't be having this conversation. My body, my choice.' Rachel spoke firmly. 'You and I were over, Stuart. For me anyway. I'd already come to the conclusion that marriage wasn't for me. In my head, there was no going back. I couldn't come running home with a baby in my arms.'

'Why the hell not?' Stuart raised his voice again. 'I would have looked after him. I would have looked after both of you.'

'But that's the point: I didn't want looking after. And I didn't want to raise a child in a relationship that was already broken.'

'But… this is what I can't get my head around,' Stuart put his hands to the back of his neck. 'You could have raised Joe alone. Thousands of mothers do.'

Rachel shook her head. 'I would never have been there. You know the hours I have to work, the unpredictability.'

'You could have switched to desk-based work, with regular hours.'

'I didn't want to.' Stuart opened his mouth but Rachel cut across him. 'And yes, I *know* how selfish that is, but it's the truth. It was better for him to be in a stable home, with two parents who could give him the time I couldn't.'

'So you chose your career over your own baby?'

Rachel closed her eyes. She was back in that hospital with the hours-old Joe in his clear plastic bassinet, trying not look at him, because if she looked at him she might love him. And she had been so afraid of loving him.

'It wasn't that simple. I think you know that.' Rachel looked straight into Stuart's face. 'Handing him over was excruciating. It was the hardest thing I've ever had to do. You have no idea of the agony I felt. The guilt.' Her voice broke and tears started running down her cheeks to her lips.

Stuart handed her a tissue. They were both silent, apart from Rachel's gulping breath. Eventually, he reached over and squeezed her hand. 'Okay… that's got everything out. Which is a good thing. Now let's think about what we do now.'

'When I hear from Joe, I'll ask him how he feels about seeing you. But before that can happen, obviously Claire has to be involved.'

Stuart looked stricken. 'Do you know what the worst of this has been? Feeling guilty that Claire's still childless, and I'm not. Most of my life I've wanted to be a father, and now – miraculously – I have a son. You and I have a son.'

'We do,' said Rachel gently. 'And he's wonderful.'

TWENTY-SIX

Rachel and Brickall were in the Operation Honeycomb office the next morning when Sillars marched in, not bothering to knock. She must have been fresh from an outdoor cigarette break, because instead of clutching a vape she wafted the aroma of nicotine, which lingered in the windowless room.

'Morag!' Brickall addressed the tiny woman with a flirtatious tone. 'How lovely to see you.'

'Ah've set up that surveillance for yous,' Morag said brusquely, in her grating voice. 'There'll be an unmarked car outside of Coulter's house in Comely Bank for the next forty-eight hours. But if that disnae give us anything, we'll have to review.' She made an attempt at a smile, then marched out again.

'That voice! Like sandpaper to the ears,' observed Brickall. 'Listen, I think I might have something here. Coulter's a member of the Edinburgh St Andrew Masonic lodge, and so were a couple of the men on the list, before they were presumably drummed out of the freemasons.'

'Or were they?' Rachel mused out loud. 'That's the problem with secret societies, you just can't be sure.'

'Anyway, these two nonces—'

'Sex offenders, Sergeant.'

'These two – Dr Neville Robbins and Eric Gourlay – presumably they would know Coulter. And it looks like they share a hobby.'

'Get their details, and maybe we'll pay them a visit,' Rachel told him.

Brickall went back to sorting through the papers on his desk. 'How did last night go? The big "Oh-whoops-I've-had-your-baby" convo?'

Rachel was spared answering this question by her phone ringing in her hand.

'Is this Detective Inspector Prince?' The voice was older, slightly querulous. 'You rang me. My name's Valerie.'

The house was one of an unassuming row of pebble-dashed bungalows in Corstorphine, this morning looking drab and grey behind a curtain of relentless drizzle. The woman who answered the front door was also unassuming. She had a dated perm, and a generally careworn look. Rachel judged her to be in her late sixties.

'Valerie? I'm DI Prince.'

'Come in out of the rain dear, come in,' she said, taking Rachel's trench coat and hanging it on an old-fashioned hall stand. Brickall had stayed behind doing research into Edinburgh's roster of sexual predators, disgruntled because Rachel had lent her own desk space in the Operation Honeycomb office to Giles Denton while she was out.

Valerie led the way through a passageway laid with a swirly burnt-orange carpet that made Rachel think of marmalade. Her own grandmother had had a similar carpet. They ended up in a tidy little sitting room filled with reproduction antiques and china ornaments. A wire-haired dachshund sat on a blanket on the sofa.

'Can I get you some tea or coffee, dear?'

'No, don't worry,' Rachel said, with a polite smile. 'This will only take a minute.'

'I must say I'm very puzzled as to why a detective from London would need to talk to me.' Valerie sat down carefully next to the dog, her body language betraying that she was on edge.

'I found your phone number in a house in Grange Loan Terrace. You were listed as the cleaner. Is that right? Have you cleaned that property?'

Valerie's hand went to her necklace, and she twisted her fingers through the beads. 'I have done, yes, a few times. But not as a regular job, no.'

Rachel was watching her carefully, but keeping her expression neutral. 'Do you know how many times you've worked there?'

'It would be three, or possibly four. I'm not sure exactly.' She reached across out of Rachel's eyeline and started rearranging a set of porcelain figurines.

'And how did you come by the work? Who told you about it?'

Valerie kept her focus intently on the porcelain birds. 'I really don't remember. I work for several people, and they recommend me to other people, and so on. Word of mouth sort of thing.' Spots of colour appeared in the centre of her cheeks.

'So, who paid you?' Rachel persisted.

'No one, not in person as such. There was just an envelope of cash in the kitchen, and a key left under the mat, which I was to put back through the letterbox when I was done.'

'And there was no one there when you were working there?'

'No dear, the place was always empty.'

'You're quite sure? There was nobody in the house at any time?'

Valerie shook her head firmly.

Rachel patted the dog to try and dispel her rising frustration. 'Surely an exceptional property like that… you would remember who suggested you for the work?'

Valerie gave a little laugh and patted her perm. 'I'm not as young as I was, dear… I have what you might call "senior moments". Especially when it comes to remembering names and the like.'

Valerie was lying, Rachel knew that. She decided to change tack. 'And when you were working there… what was your impression of the purpose the house was being used for? It's not a family home, is it?'

Valerie fidgeted with the china ornaments on a side table, clearly embarrassed. 'Well, there'd obviously been parties when I went in there… there were empty drink bottles and… such like. You know.' She cast her gaze down.

'"Such like" being?'

She lowered her voice almost to a whisper. 'Used contraceptives.'

'Anything else?'

'Once there were some… ladies underthings. Left on the floor near one of the beds.'

'And you didn't think that was odd?'

Valerie pressed her hands into her lap, her fingers still folded round a porcelain robin. 'I suppose so, but it's a well-to-do area. People with a lot of money live there. I put it down to some sort of… professional entertaining. That's really all I can tell you. I was just there to clean.'

Rachel sighed, and stood up. 'Well, thank you, you've been very helpful.'

Valerie led her back into the hall a little too quickly, as though eager to get rid of her guest. 'I'm sorry I couldn't remember more, dear.'

'No problem,' said Rachel, still convinced that there was nothing wrong with Valerie's memory. 'I'll just grab my coat.'

She fetched it from where it hung on the hall stand, next to a brass plate with a pile of unopened post on it. Seeing the letter reminded Rachel of something. *Basic error*, she told herself sternly. *You'd call out Brickall for that.* She whipped out her notebook.

'If I could just have your full name before I go, Mrs…?'

'Muir. Valerie Muir.'

Mrs Muir. Rachel's memory stirred, then she felt the jolt of adrenaline in her chest as she realised where she had heard the name. The MacBain's cleaning lady. Their 'miracle worker'.

*

When she returned to Gayfield Square, PC Kirstie Blair, Giles and Brickall were all huddled round the computer screen.

'We've got back the analytics on Emily van Meijer's phone,' Kirstie told her, looking up at Rachel.

'Anything interesting?'

Giles made a so-so gesture with his hand. 'Most of it's pretty standard teen chat.'

'I think this one could be significant though.' Brickall pointed at the screen. 'It's a text to Luuk, and the time stamp is only a couple of hours before she went missing. Only problem is, it's in Dutch. Except for the word "dude" which I guess is international teen-speak.'

Rachel leaned forward and pulled up a page for Google Translate, cutting and pasting the message into the text entry box. 'And as if by magic…'

> *Dude, you know what we were talking about before? Well can you get the number for Markus Baas from your mum? I think I need to speak to him, but I don't want to freak out my parents by asking.*

'Do you have any idea who Markus Baas is?' Giles asked, turning round to glance at Rachel. Their eyes met, and he held her gaze a fraction too long, throwing off her equilibrium. The room suddenly felt too warm.

'I don't, but I can certainly find out. Give me a second.'

Rachel headed out of the basement and out to the front porch of the building where she not only had better signal on her mobile, but was also away from the laser beam of Giles Denton's eyes.

She phoned Dries van Meijer. He had given her his personal number, and although an assistant answered his phone, when she heard who was calling she put Rachel straight through.

'How's the investigation going?' was the first thing he said.

'I can't give you details at this stage, I'm afraid, but I can tell you I'm in Edinburgh again with a team of five and back-up from Police Scotland, and we're actively pursuing several lines of enquiry. I'll update you as soon as we have anything concrete.'

'Good.' Van Meijer sounded relieved. 'How can I help you?'

'Do you know of someone called Markus Baas?'

There was a loaded pause. 'I do, yes. Can I ask how he's relevant?'

'We've found evidence that Emily meant to talk to someone of that name, but of course we have no idea—'

'He's my lawyer,' Dries interjected. 'His practice has taken care of my family for decades. But why would Emily need to talk to Markus?'

'That's what we need to find out.'

'Can you hold the line just a second? I'll speak to Baas myself.' There was a pause of around a minute while van Meijer went to another line and left Rachel on hold. Then he cut back in. 'Hi… I just got through to Markus Baas and he said he definitely didn't hear from Emily in the week before her death. Or at any other time.'

Rachel returned to the basement and relayed the substance of this conversation to the others.

'So she wanted to talk to a lawyer… to make a complaint of sexual assault?' asked Brickall.

Rachel shrugged. 'Since she didn't get as far as speaking to him, we don't know. We can check back with Luuk to see if he at least had a chance to pass on Baas's number… But I'll tell you what else came up this morning.' She went over to the whiteboard and selected a red pen, writing 'VALERIE MUIR' in large letters. 'The mysterious "Valerie" who cleans at 21 Grange Loan Terrace is none other than the cleaning lady for the MacBains. The hosts of White Crystal Tours.'

TWENTY-SEVEN

Come to my room, lardass.

Rachel stared at the text for a second, then headed down the corridor to Brickall's room. He opened the door to her with an open pizza box in the other hand; half of it eaten. He shoved it towards her.

'No thanks,' Rachel wrinkled her nose. 'Not if it's drenched in hot sauce. I was about to order something from room service.'

'Hold off on that for a second... you know how we love a stakeout?'

Rachel sighed. 'You mean *you* love stakeouts. Because you're a weirdo that way.'

'Whatever... the plod who was designated to watching Coulter's house this evening has had to pull out – his missus has gone into labour – and I said I'd do it. Want to come along?'

Rachel didn't want to, not really. On the other hand, Giles Denton was off the menu and an evening alone in her hotel room with a limp club sandwich did not appeal.

'Oh go on then.' She helped herself with some reluctance to a slice of Brickall's pizza.

'Car's outside.'

'Give me two minutes to fetch my coat and bag.'

*

They stopped for Brickall to bin the pizza box and buy 'siege snacks' – fizzy drinks, crisps, sweets and chocolate – then he drove the unmarked car to a pretty Georgian stone terrace in Comely Bank, parking it a discreet distance from Coulter's smart black door. It was just starting to go dark, and office workers were returning to their homes, some on foot, a few on bikes. The next morning was clearly recycling collection day, because blue plastic boxes punctuated the pavement.

Twenty minutes later, by which time Brickall had consumed a packet of crisps and two chocolate bars, a sleek dark-blue Jaguar pulled up and Coulter climbed out of the driver's door. He was carrying a briefcase and a newspaper and he let himself into the house, leaving the front door ajar. A few minutes later a middle-aged woman, with blonde hair in a straggly bun, emerged carrying a blue recycling box piled high with wine bottles.

'That must be the wife… looks like she's fond of a tipple.' Brickall observed. 'Or someone in that house is, at least.'

'If I were married to that snake, I reckon I'd be hitting the bottle too.'

The stream of workers returning home petered out, lights went on behind curtains and shutters, and the street became still. It came back to Rachel with clarity that the golden ratio in police operations was ninety-five per cent boredom, five per cent action. She was already getting uncomfortable, squirming in her seat to try and make room for her legs.

'So… what's the story with you and Denton then?' Brickall asked, keeping his eyes straight ahead as he munched on a fun-sized scotch egg.

'There is no story,' Rachel sighed.

'But you guys like each other. Even a fucking blind man would know that.'

'Yes, we like each other.' Rachel's tone was belligerent. She grabbed a packet of wine gums and shoved one in her mouth. 'But

I'm not about to start sleeping with him when we're working on a high-stakes case together.'

'Oh come on… people do it all the time when they're working together. And you at least admit that you fancy Denton?'

'I do. But that's hardly news. Now can we please change the subject?'

'How's your lad?'

Rachel shrugged. 'I wish I knew. I'm waiting for him to get in touch with me… I reckon it needs to be that way round.'

After three hours, just as Brickall was making plans to go and empty his bladder, a man walked down the street towards them. It was still raining, and his face was partly obscured by his umbrella. He ran up the steps to Coulter's front door and rang the bell. The door opened and he slipped inside.

'Was that…?' breathed Brickall.

'I don't know, it could be.' Rachel leaned forward to check that the camera on the dashboard was switched on and recording.

Forty minutes later the teeming drizzle had stopped, so when the front door opened the man emerged with his umbrella down. He wore an old-fashioned Gannex raincoat over a tweed suit and a moleskin waistcoat. The groomed white hair and goatee beard were unmistakeable.

It was Kenneth Candlish.

It was with a sense of grim satisfaction that Rachel and Brickall returned to the offices of White Crystal in Drummond Place. There were to be no polite exchanges in Candlish's cosy, over-furnished office. This time he was coming with them to Gayfield Square, for a formal interview.

Jean, his faithful secretary, clutched at her pearls in dismay as Candlish was ushered out. He didn't resist, or protest: he was far too wily for that. Having been in trouble with the law before, he probably knew to stay silent. Only when he was installed in the interview room with tea in a plastic cup did he speak, to ask for his solicitor to be present.

'And who should we contact?' Rachel asked, pulling out her notebook. 'It will save time if you can give me their number.'

'Heather Kinnaird, at Reekie.'

She froze, pen poised over her notebook. 'You mean Reekie & Co? In Atholl Crescent?'

'Yes, that's right.' Candlish stroked his goatee and smiled insincerely. He'd decided on a charm offensive. It wasn't working.

'I'm afraid that won't be possible,' said Rachel coldly. 'One of their partners is a person of interest in this investigation. There'd be a clear professional conflict.'

'You're referring to Douglas Coulter?'

'Let's wait until you have a lawyer before we get into this. DS Brickall – would you go out to the front desk and contact the duty solicitor, please.'

A solicitor arrived fifteen minutes later, looking fresh out of law school, and Rachel started the recording equipment, doing the formal introductions.

'May I ask what my client is charged with?'

'He's not charged with anything yet. At the moment, Mr Candlish is merely assisting with our enquiries. He doesn't need legal representation; that was his choice.'

The baby-faced lawyer took off his coat and sat back in his chair, looking relieved.

'So, Kenneth… you've already admitted to knowing Douglas Coulter, senior partner at Reekie & Co. In fact, you just mentioned him yourself as a possible person of interest.'

'I did not say that.' The flinty little eyes gave nothing away. 'I just named him as partner at the legal firm I use. Douglas is a well-respected member of Edinburgh society. We go way back. Old family friend.'

'And what was the purpose of your visit to him last night?' Brickall spoke this time, pushing a still from the dash cam footage across the desk towards the solicitor. It showed Candlish walking down the steps of the Coulters' house.

'As I said, we're friends. It was a social visit.'

'Bit late for that, wasn't it?' Brickall asked. 'By the time you arrived, most people would be turning in for the night. Or was that the point? You needed to wait until Coulter's wife had gone to bed.'

Candlish's small eyes flicked from side to side, but he held onto his composure. 'Like I said. A social visit, to a friend.'

'What did the two of you talk about?' Rachel asked.

'This and that. Golf. Holidays. Mutual friends.'

Brickall put his elbows on the table and leaned forward so that he was only a couple of feet from Candlish. 'Mutual friends who have an interest in underage sex?'

The solicitor raised his biro feebly. 'I have to object to that line of questioning. Mr Candlish is not charged with anything of that nature, nor can he be expected to testify about his friends' sex lives.'

Brickall snorted. 'If he's prosecuted for arranging or facilitating sexual services by a child, then trust me, he'll have to.'

Candlish paled slightly.

'Okay, so here's our problem, Kenneth,' Rachel said, leaning back in her chair, adopting contrasting body language to Brickall's. 'When we asked you about certain parties featuring teenagers on White Crystal's own tours, you denied all knowledge of them. And yet you knew one of the parties took place in Grange. And – guess what – the person who drew up the lease on the Grange property where these parties took place is none other than your pal Douglas Coulter. Who in turn matches the description of someone seen attending one of these parties and molesting a young girl. A girl who was a student on one of your company's courses. A rather troubling series of coincidences, isn't it? So what are we to think when we find you calling on Coulter late at night?'

'As I said, he's a friend. That's all.' A sweaty sheen broke out on Candlish's face, and he reached down and fidgeted with his watch chain.

'We're obviously wondering why the conversation between the two of you couldn't be held over the internet or a mobile phone, which would make it potentially traceable.'

'That's speculation,' Candlish said, his voice thin and strained. 'You've no evidence either way about what we talked about. The subject matter of our wee talk was entirely innocent.' He looked desperately in the direction of the boy solicitor.

'Unless you're going to charge my client, I think this interview should end here.' There was a scraping of chairs as Candlish and the lawyer stood up.

Rachel switched off the recording. 'I'd be grateful if you would inform us if you're leaving Edinburgh for any reason. We'll need to speak to you again.'

As she watched DC Tulloch escorting Candlish to the front lobby, her phone bleeped. It was a message from Joe.

Where are you?

TWENTY-EIGHT

It took Rachel a while to decide what to do. Her parenting instincts were lagging eighteen years behind, and she was not sure how to interpret this communication from her son, arriving – as it had – without preamble. Was it a cry for help?

She went to a higher floor in the building to find a signal sweet spot. Whatever instinct she did possess told her to call rather than text.

'Hullo.' The tone was nonchalant.

'Joe. Are you okay?'

'Yeah, fine.'

'Only I wasn't sure what you meant in your text.'

'Oh right… yeah… I just meant are you in London or Scotland.'

'I'm in Edinburgh at the moment.'

'How long for?'

'Several more days at least… why?'

'I'm visiting a mate in Newcastle and I thought I could maybe, like, come up for a bit.'

Rachel's mind raced. She wouldn't have time to chaperone a teenager. And then there was Stuart. He would have to be told Joe was coming this time. That was unavoidable.

'It would be great to see you,' she said, meaning it. 'I'm really busy with the case, but—'

'I could help you with that if you want.'

Rachel's heart gave a little surge. 'That's very sweet of you, but unfortunately police investigations don't quite work like that. We can certainly talk about it. Some of it. I'm usually around in the evening.'

And there's your father, she thought.

'Cool, but don't worry about a hotel or anything, yeah? I've got another mate who's about to start his second year at Edinburgh Uni, and I'd be crashing with him.'

'Great,' said Rachel. 'It would be really lovely to have you up here. Let me know when your train gets in.'

When she returned to the basement, DI Sillars was there.

'Just briefing your sergeant here,' Morag croaked, giving Brickall a sidelong glance that was almost flirtatious. She pulled out her pack of Mayfair and lighter. 'He can fill you in: I'm off out for a fag.'

'Morag's got us a warrant for a forensic search on 21 Grange Loan Terrace,' Brickall said, once she had gone. 'And she's going to apply for one for the White Crystal offices, so we can look at Candlish's computer.'

'We'll need his home address too,' Rachel pointed out. 'Anything dodgy is more likely to be on his personal electronic devices.'

DC Tulloch looked up from the computer terminal. 'Ma'am, I've tracked down the municipal street camera footage for Grange Loan Terrace. It gets deleted every four weeks, so we don't have the night of the party, but here's something from three weeks ago you might want to see.'

The others huddled round the screen to watch grainy black-and-white images from in front of number 21. At 23.11, the front door opened and two people emerged. One was a tall, slim man with a sleeve tattoo whose face was obscured by a baseball cap. The other had luminous hair that looked bright white under the street lamps.

'That's Iveta Kovals!' breathed Rachel. 'Looks like she was doing more than handing out leaflets.'

The two figures were having a discussion that became heated, with a lot of arm waving. The man loomed over Iveta's slight frame in what was an unmistakeable gesture of threat, seizing her wrist. Iveta pulled away from him and hurried away up the path.

'Is that the other one you interviewed?' asked Brickall.

Tulloch shook his head. 'Balodis? No, wrong body shape. Too slim. Might be the mysterious Andrei though? The one who pointed them to the job advert.'

Rachel walked over to the whiteboard and started adding names, linked with arrows and questions marks, starting with Maris Balodis and Iveta Kovals. Her metaphorical ball of wool now resembled a large, complex spider's web.

'We need to make re-interviewing our Latvian friends a priority,' she told the others. 'And Giles,' she turned round and addressed Denton, 'how did Sarah get on with her dark web research?'

'She spoke to a contact in Police Scotland's Intelligence Support Division.' He looked through a notepad on his desk. 'Tom Wallace. But here's the thing –' he pronounced it 'ting', Irish fashion – 'Wallace walked Sarah through how the networks operate, and there's no doubt a big percentage of their traffic is child pornography and marketing of illegal services. Trouble is, the officers who can penetrate the dark net and track what's going on there need special training, and they're all in the joint NCA and GCHQ cybercrime cell.'

'In other words: back in London.'

'Exactly.'

Rachel palmed her forehead in frustration.

'But here's the other thing – I've got to go back to London for a top-level Command meeting, so I could have a go at digging out one of these experts for you and see if I can persuade them to make the trip up here.'

'That would be great. And make sure they know it's top priority. Please.'

'Of course.' Giles attempted to subject her to more smouldering eye contact, but Brickall had been scrutinising their interaction, so she ignored it. 'Come on,' she said briskly to her detective sergeant, pulling on her coat. 'You and I need another little chat with Hazel MacBain.'

'No doggie?' Esme MacBain did not hide her disappointment when she saw Rachel and Brickall on the doorstep of the Campbell Road house.

'No doggie,' confirmed Brickall.

Dog or no dog, Hazel MacBain greeted them amicably. Her blandly pretty face had grown rounder since their last visit, and she wore a denim maternity smock over her pregnant belly.

'My husband's not here, I'm afraid. He's on his outward bound course.'

'It's not Will we want to talk to,' said Rachel with a perfunctory smile. 'Can we come in?'

They went up to the top floor sitting room, where Angus had been left in a playpen, munching solemnly on a crayon.

'This won't take too long will it?' Hazel said nervously, lifting Angus from the pen and sitting down with him on her lap, like a human shield. 'Only, I've got more on than usual, with Will being away. When you rang I was about to get Angus into the buggy and walk up to the shops for some groceries.'

'Go shops!' Esme beamed, handing Brickall a book about a baby dragon.

'She views it as a treat,' explained Hazel. 'Normally Will does a run to the cash and carry, or drives me up to the supermarket and amuses the kids while I do a whip round with the trolley.'

'You should have a fair idea by now why we're here,' said Brickall, mollifying Esme by turning the pages of her book and pointing silently at the dragons.

'Well no, not really,' said Hazel. A faint blush of pink was visible just above her collarbone. The gold crucifix flashed as she turned it round between her fingers. 'I mean, the enquiry into Emily's death must surely be done with now.'

'I'm afraid not,' said Rachel. She kept her tone pleasant, her expression neutral. 'The enquiry is very much open. For example, last week I spoke to Marie-Laure Fournier. About Bruno Martinez.'

The flush on Hazel's neck crept a little higher. She bent her head and rested her lips briefly on the crown of her son's head.

'She confirmed that Bruno attended a party in Grange during his stay. And that he was very distressed about what happened to him there.'

'Which is why he ended up taking his life. You went over this with Will the other day: he told me. We discuss everything.'

'No,' said Rachel. 'What Marie-Laure said was that Bruno had no intention of bottling things up. Quite the opposite: he wanted to talk about what had happened. With you.'

The crimson stain spread up to Hazel's cheeks. She shook her head vigorously. 'He never spoke to me. I only ever heard about the parties after you discussed them with my husband last month.'

'And Emily van Meijer,' said Brickall, taking the next book Esme shoved at him. 'Did she ever speak to you about sharing what had happened to her with his family's lawyer?'

'No, no she did not. She never mentioned a lawyer. Or the party.'

'Might she have spoken to Will about it?'

'No, I'm sure she didn't. Will would have told me. He tells me everything.' Her tone was oddly insistent. She let go of her son and gripped the crucifix again.

Rachel changed tack. 'One other thing… your cleaning lady is Valerie Muir?'

'Mrs Muir, yes.'

'Were you aware that she has been employed to clean the house where these sex parties took place?'

Again, the colour blazed on Hazel's face. 'No. No I'm not. Why would I be?'

'You said she'd worked for you for years.'

'Well, yes, but…' Hazel busied herself with finding Angus a truck to play with. 'She's not full-time with me. She has other work.'

'So you didn't put her forward for the job?'

'No!' Hazel pressed her palms to the warm patches on her cheeks, as if trying to make them fade. 'That's nonsense. Now, if you don't mind, I need to get the shopping done before Angus is ready for his nap.'

Rachel stood up. 'Of course. We'll leave you in peace. If you wouldn't mind just giving us the details of the trip Will's gone on.'

'It's the Hibernian Catholic Boy's Club… he's given me the name of the place they're staying, and the landline, in case he lost service on his mobile. One second…'

Hazel put Angus down and reached for her handbag, pulling out a large leather purse. She unzipped it and thumbed through the section where cards were stored. She pulled out a business card and handed it to Rachel, who used her phone to take a photo.

Angus, who was starting to fret, pawed at Hazel's purse, attracted by the shiny gold zip.

'Me! Me have!' he whined, as Hazel tried to keep it from his grasp.

'Here, let me put this back for you…' Rachel took the contested purse and slid the card back into place. But not before taking a look at the contents, as she had been trained to do. She zipped it up and put it back into Hazel's bag, out of the reach of the clamouring toddler.

'Thanks,' Hazel managed a wan smile. 'Like I said, I need to get him out for a walk.'

'I'm sorry we've held you up: we'll leave you to it.

'What was that about?' Brickall asked as they walked out of the front door and into Campbell Road. 'Suddenly coming over all softly-softly?'

'Because I want to get a warrant and search that bloody place from top to bottom,' said Rachel grimly. 'But if we spook Hazel and she realises what's coming, I have a feeling potential evidence might end up being disposed of.'

'You think she's hiding something?'

Rachel thought back to the skin-flush of deception that Hazel hadn't been able to control, and to what she had just spotted in her purse. 'Oh, I'm quite sure of it.'

There was no reply at the West Pilton flat formerly occupied by Maris Balodis. Rachel left Brickall putting in a call to Gayfield Square to check the relevant PNC file, while she knocked on the doors of some of their neighbours. This was a transient community, the run-down flats rented by people on the margins of society, and there was either no reply, or the residents spoke no English. Eventually one of the doors was opened by an elderly woman who had the dubious fortune of being a long-term resident of the block. She nodded when Rachel asked her if she knew anything about the Latvians in Flat 5.

'Gone, hen,' the woman said. She was tiny and wizened, but her clothes were clean and her hair had recently been taken out of curlers. 'There was a polis car here one night and the man was arrested and then the young girl with the silver hair, she took off somewhere. The place is empty now. Though no doubt they'll put more foreigners in there before long.' She set her lips firmly in disapproval. 'They always do.'

The results of Brickall's phone call backed up her story. Maris Balodis had been charged with actual bodily harm after a fight in a pub and was currently on remand in HMP Dumfries.

'And Iveta's done a bunk,' sighed Rachel.

'A criminal evading law enforcement agencies: who'd have thought it,' Brickall jibed. 'So what now?'

Rachel checked her phone. There was a message from Joe.

Getting in to Waverley at 15.56

'First: an arrest warrant for Iveta Kovals. Second: go back and chase up the forensics on 21 Grange Loan Terrace. And third: get your girlfriend DI Sillars to apply for a warrant to search Campbell Road. Discreetly: we don't want them getting word of it.'

'A dawn raid job?'

'Possibly.'

'How about you? You coming back with me'

Rachel looked up from the taxi app on her phone. She shook her head. 'Not this time. I'm on mummy duty.'

An hour later, standing under the departure boards at Waverley, Rachel spotted a familiar figure.

Giles Denton.

He was waiting for the King's Cross service to announce boarding, about to catch the train that Joe would be disembarking. She was on the point of walking up behind him and sneaking her arms round his waist when she saw another familiar outline: a tall, loping figure hefting a large rucksack. Joe.

Forgetting about Giles immediately, she stood on tiptoes and waved like an excited child. He was wearing a short-sleeved grey T-shirt over a long sleeved white one, and there were newly acquired knotted bracelets on both wrists. As Rachel stepped forward to hug him, she took in the heady and now familiar boy smell. And she time-travelled back with a jolt to the maternity hospital once more, lying in bed next to the baby she was trying so hard not to love. A new midwife on shift, unaware of her adoption plans, had taken in her air of detachment and said reassuringly, 'Don't worry, being a mum doesn't all fall in to place immediately. It takes a while for the love to come in.'

And now at last, the love had come in. This was the strange expanding sensation in her chest as she reached up to place her hands on his broad, T-shirted back. He was her child, and she loved him.

TWENTY-NINE

'I'm not going to call you Mum or anything.'

Rachel and Joe were walking to Dundas Street in the New Town, where his friend rented a flat.

'That's absolutely fine,' Rachel replied. In truth, she hadn't earned the title. A mum was someone who packed lunchboxes and waited at the school gate. 'Nick and Jane are your Mum and Dad.'

'And Stuart will never be Dad either, even if I do get to meet him properly.'

'That's also fine,' Rachel reassured him. 'I'm going to give you his number and leave it to you to make an arrangement with him if you want. Best I stay out of it, I reckon.'

Joe dropped his rucksack at his feet and turned to look at her. 'It is good to see you though.'

Rachel patted his arm. Keep it light, the voice in her head told her. 'You too.'

Joe pointed at the front door of a solid Georgian house, now converted to flats. 'This is where Charlie lives, so…'

'He's the one who knows all about the dark web, right?'

Joe grinned. 'Well remembered. But I guess it's your job to remember details and stuff.'

'Maybe we could grab something to eat later?' she added hastily. 'But if you have plans with your friends, that's fine.'

Her phone rang, an Edinburgh number that she didn't recognise. 'I'd better get this…'

Joe gave her an awkward squeeze and a salute, then turned and pressed one of the doorbells.

'DI Prince, this is Fraser. Fraser Dewar.'

Rachel's brain performed a quick search. 'Oh yes, at the pathology lab.'

'That's right… only I thought I'd better ring you. I went back to the lab results on the two deaths we discussed, and there's something… unusual.'

All of Rachel's senses tingled. 'I'm on my way over to you now.'

She found Fraser Dewar in his tiny office in the post-mortem suite. This time he was in cords and a checked shirt rather than scrubs and rubber apron. His plump face broke into a broad smile.

'Lovely to see you again!' he said, sounding as though he meant it. 'Can I get you a drink?'

Rachel requested tea, and Fraser disappeared back into the lab, re-emerging with a grimy mug in his hand. She sipped it tentatively, hoping that given its provenance, it hadn't been in contact with bodily fluids.

Fraser clasped his hands over his knees with the gleam in his eyes that Rachel had often seen on the faces of people breaking important news.

'So… I went back to the blood and urine samples from van Meijer and Martinez and re-tested them. I did some gas chromatography on the blood samples… and in both of them, I found calcium oxalate crystals in the urine, and abnormal acidosis in the blood.'

'What does that mean?' asked Rachel, though she had a strong suspicion after attending many post-mortems and inquests during her career.

'Ethylene glycol poisoning.'

'As in… anti-freeze?'

He nodded. 'Exactly. That's where it's most commonly found anyway. It has a sweet taste, but it's colourless and odourless, so makes a very effective poison. As a safety measure, most modern anti-freeze is made with propylene glycol, which has an unpleasant taste, but the other kind is still available. Mix that with alcohol – sweet-tasting alcohol particularly – and you won't know it's there.'

'Like Southern Comfort.'

'Like Southern Comfort. Exactly. You remember we talked about how neither of the deceased had drunk very much… not enough to cause them to pass out or completely lose their coordination?'

'Yes – you said a blood–alcohol level of less than 0.1.'

Dewar's smile was admiring. 'Well remembered.'

Rachel gave a small nod of acknowledgement, using it to mask her reaching her right arm back to the desk and ditching the acrid mug of tea among the pile of papers. 'It's my job.'

'The thing is, in the early stages of ethylene glycol poisoning, the symptoms are the same as extreme drunkenness. Dizziness, nausea, headache, lack of coordination.'

'And these tests – they're not done routinely? Only I'm wondering why this wasn't spotted before.'

Dewar shook his head. 'It's not something we'd normally look for unless there was active suspicion of foul play. And both these deaths were presented to us as death by misadventure. There was no Fatal Accident Inquiry ongoing, otherwise we would undoubtedly have run more blood analysis.'

Rachel thought back to Caitlyn Anderson's allegation that on the night she died, Bruno seemed more drugged than drunk

'So is that what killed them? The ethylene glycol?'

Dewar shook his head. 'It will eventually be fatal, even after ingesting quite a small amount, but it takes at least twenty-four hours to reach that point. So Emily died from her fall, and Bruno drowned. That hasn't changed.'

'But...' Rachel was trying to process this new information. 'Help me out here – are you saying they both took the ethylene glycol as part of a suicide attempt?'

Dewar shook his head vigorously. 'No, that's exactly the point. Of course people do kill themselves by drinking ethylene glycol; hundreds a year. But there'd be no point in mixing it with alcohol, given it has no taste – you'd drink it down straight and wait until you lost consciousness. In both these cases, the victims have had just enough of the stuff to make them appear drunk, and it's been hidden in the alcohol. Not a great deal of alcohol, as we've already established.'

Rachel was staring at him. 'So someone else gave it to them?'

'They had to have done. Because the effects kick in within thirty minutes, and there would be no way that the victims would then have set off to Salisbury Crags or Leith Docks alone. They wouldn't have been able to get themselves that far. There had to be someone with them.'

'So this someone else didn't give them the anti-freeze to kill them?'

Dewar shook his head. 'That's why this was so clever. A straightforward overdose of anti-freeze would have been picked up in a hospital, and by our initial post-mortem tests. It could still be a possible suicide, sure, but questions would have been asked about where it came from. So put yourself in the shoes of the perpetrator...'

Rachel smiled. 'Hold on; isn't this bit *my* job?'

'Go on then.' Dewar held out a hand to indicate that she had the floor.

'You need these teenagers to be incapacitated so that you can get them to these locations.' Rachel spoke slowly. 'So you want them to look and act as though they're drunk, but they're in an environment where they're not *allowed* to drink... and in Emily van Meijer's case, she didn't much like alcohol. So you give them a modest amount of Southern Comfort – port for Bruno – with a slug of ethylene glycol in it. And that way they act like they've drunk a whole bottle. They're pretty much out of it.'

'And presumably could easily be persuaded or pushed into a car.' Dewar suggested.

'Oh God…' Rachel tipped her head back and covered her face with her hands. 'It all makes sense. But the idea of it is…' She shuddered. 'It's too awful to contemplate.'

Dewar nodded. 'It is. And it looks like you've got a double murder on your hands.'

PART THREE

'Do you believe that evil and tragedy are always planned?
You don't think Fortune has anything to do with it?'

The Ferryman, Amy Neftzger

THIRTY

On Saturday morning, Rachel allowed herself the luxury of a lie-in.

She did this with absolute certainty that it would be interrupted. Sure enough, as she climbed back into bed with a cup of tea made using the in-room kettle, her phone rang.

'Prince?'

The word came out as a breathy croak, with exhaled smoke round the edges. Morag Sillars.

'DI Sillars,' said Rachel with a smoothness that belied the fact that she was reclining naked on four plump hotel pillows. 'What can I do for you?'

'That wee Latvian tart,' Sillars rasped. 'Picked up tricking in Coburg Street last night. She's in one of our cells, if you want to take another crack at her.'

'Great, thank you.'

'Or maybe you can give yourself a day off, and send your DS,' she said craftily.

You'd like that, thought Rachel. *Having Mark Brickall all to yourself.*

'No it's fine, I want to be there,' Rachel had already set down her tea and was struggling into a bathrobe. 'And I need to talk to you about results of the repeat pathology tests on the two teenagers… But I'll probably bring DS Brickall too.'

'Aye, well, good.' Sillars grunted, before cutting the call.

*

After Rachel had briefed Sillars about Fraser Dewar's suspicions, and been promised more manpower, she went upstairs to join Brickall in the interview room.

'It's all kicking off now,' she murmured to him as she slipped into her seat. 'Operation Honeycomb is now suspected murder. I'll fill you in later.'

'Category A,' said Brickall, rubbing his hands briskly. 'Now you're talking.'

Iveta Kovals was huddled motionless in the corner of the room, a police-cell blanket round her shoulders, covering a skimpy top and mini-skirt that revealed too much blue-white flesh. Once the services of a solicitor had been refused and the interview had been formally started, Brickall wasted no time in playing Kovals the CCTV footage of her outside 21 Grange Loan Terrace with the unidentified man.

'This is you, isn't it?' he asserted.

'No comment.'

'And this man you're talking to… what's his name?'

'No comment.'

'Look, Iveta… the more you help us, the quicker this will be over. You clearly know the guy, so who is he?'

'No comment.'

Rachel had sat through countless 'no comment' interviews in her time, but this was different. Usually the suspect was parroting the phrase on legal advice, or was too bored to engage, or was playing the system in the hope a future jury would not have the confidence to convict. But this was different. Iveta's eyes flicked constantly around the room, and her body was taut with fear.

After the interview was ended and police bail had been arranged, Rachel left Brickall to help Sillars organise an upgraded incident room for Operation Honeycomb and followed the Latvian girl out of the building.

'Iveta – wait, please!'

Iveta stopped in her tracks, arms folded across her chest, shivering in the chilly breeze.

'Look, I know you're scared to talk. I get it. But we can't help you – we can't protect you – if won't tell us who's behind these parties. Because you know, don't you? Some of it, at least.'

Iveta dropped her chin and stood there, mute.

'Just a name. That's all we need. Is it Maris's contact Andrei?'

Iveta shook her head vigorously, then turned and started walking away.

Rachel followed her. 'Here –' she fished in her pocket for one of her cards – 'if you change your mind, call my mobile number and we can talk, okay.'

Iveta still did not speak, but she took the card and thrust it into the back pocket of her tiny denim skirt.

'We thought we'd get Chinese,' Joe said. 'That okay with you?'

Rachel was at Charlie's flat in the New Town, and feeling very honoured to be included in the boys' Saturday evening plans. The place was a typically chaotic student share, with drying laundry and discarded dishes everywhere, but the flat itself was spacious and airy, with tall sash windows.

'Fine,' she agreed, pulling out two twenty-pound notes from her purse. 'As long as you let me pay.'

Charlie phoned in an order and they sat drinking bottles of beer while they waited for the food to arrive. The boys were eager to learn more about the case ('Upgraded to a double homicide? Sick!') and Rachel told them as much as she was allowed. Which was not much.

'Charlie's studying Informatics,' Joe said proudly. 'That's how he knows all about the dark web.'

'Can you actually get onto it yourself?' Rachel asked him.

'Sure,' said Charlie. He was as short and square as Joe was rangy, with black hair worn in an undercut and the beginnings of a hipster beard. 'We learned all about it on my course. I've got a Tor browser installed on my computer.'

'A Tor browser?'

'It has a search function that allows me to browse the dark web completely anonymously.'

Rachel raised her eyebrows. 'And that's legal?'

'It's perfectly legal to look, as long as you don't do anything illegal when you're on there. Like buying class A drugs or looking at child porn. I mean, you come across dodgy sites all the time, but I never click on the images. As long as you don't open them, you're okay.'

Their food arrived, and they feasted on crispy Peking duck and chilli prawns, sitting around the coffee table with food on their laps. The boys chatted and joked as if Rachel wasn't there, which she interpreted as a good thing. Then when the detritus had been bagged up and the dishes slung into the kitchen sink, Charlie sat on the sofa with his laptop with Rachel and Joe on either side of him.

'So is there a lot of child porn on the dark web?'

Charlie looked sideways at her, as though she'd just asked if water was wet. 'There are something like one hundred million sexually explicit images of children,' he told her sternly, 'and about forty thousand chat rooms dedicated to exchanging child porn.'

Rachel raised her eyebrows and sat back. 'Wow. I had no idea.'

'A lot of it is webcam stuff, from countries like the Philippines. And the most extreme content is… well, it's really sick.'

'And he doesn't mean in the millennial sense of sick, as in "cool",' Joe interjected, fetching himself another beer. 'He means fucked-up.'

'Yes, I got that,' said Rachel.

'There are sites offering kids as young as one or two.' Charlie went on. 'Sites specialising in torturing children, or deflowering little girls. You imagine the most perverted thing ever, and it's out there.'

Charlie pulled up the browser and there it was, with a search box function, just like any other.

'It looks kind of innocuous,' Rachel observed.

Charlie nodded. 'It works in exactly the same way as a normal browser, but once it's accepted the connection it then bounces the signal around the world through a chain of encrypted connections, so no one can tell who the original user is, or where they're located.'

'And how do people pay for the child porn? Do they use credit cards?'

'Sometimes,' Charlie said. 'What's happening more and more is that it's becoming a barter system – paedophiles have to trade content of their own to access other people's content. That cuts out any potential entrapment, because if an undercover cop offered content for barter, he would be committing a crime himself.'

Rachel though about this for a moment. 'So if you had a video of a girl being raped but your interest was little boys, you could use the video to access stuff you were interested in. Without money changing hands.'

'Exactly.' Charlie grinned at Joe. 'She's clever, your mum.'

Rachel felt herself turn pink with pleasure, not at the compliment but at the acknowledgement of her status as 'Joe's mum'. 'Can we take a look?' she asked hurriedly.

'What do you want me to search for?'

Rachel considered this. 'Try combining "Edinburgh festival" and "party".'

Charlie typed the words into the search box and started scrolling through pages of content, most of it in baffling beta format.

'Here's something… on this forum called "Edinburgh Extra"… *"Ed Festival: staff wanted to help recruit and entertain YFs at exclusive gatherings catering to Minor-Attracted Adults. Fresh fruit included."'*

'YFs?' Joe asked.

'Young Friends. It's code for abuse victims.'

'And "Minor-Attracted"…'

'Code for paedophile.'

'And why the hell is fresh fruit included?'

Charlie grimaced. 'That means some of them are guaranteed virgins.'

Rachel winced, re-reading the ad. 'Hold on, this could be…'

'What?'

'Nothing.' She was wondering if this was the ad that Maris and Iveta had seen when they were hired to distribute the flyers. 'Is there any way you can tell who posted this?'

He shook his head. 'Only if you have a very sophisticated forensic set-up, like the FBI or something.'

'Okay, well… this was very interesting. Thanks Charlie.'

'If you like I can bookmark this site and check back on it for you. See if there's any more activity.'

'Only if you have time: your studies need to be your priority.'

'Spoken like a parent. Classic.'

Joe's words were uttered instinctively, without guile, and for the second time that evening Rachel felt the warm glow of acceptance.

Once the laptop had been put away, the boys played Rachel some of their favourite tracks. The music was so loud that it was only when she had wished them good night and stepped out into the silent street that she noticed a missed call and a voicemail from an unrecognised number.

She played the voicemail. The recording was poor quality, due to lack of signal or background noise, or both.

'Miss Prince… is Iveta… I think I need talk to you… these are very bad men involved… Scaring me very much… is called –' she then said a name that sounded like 'Georgie' – *'make threats to me. Can you meet me?'*

The message ended abruptly. Rachel tried calling back the number, but it rang out.

She tried again several times once she had returned to her hotel, leaving her mobile under her pillow before finally switching off her light at midnight. Just after she had descended into a deep sleep, it rang. At precisely the same moment, there was a brisk knock on her door.

'Hello?' she answered the phone and the door simultaneously, admitting Brickall, dressed in a sweatshirt and joggers.

'Prince,' Sillars barked down the phone line. 'We've a body, found on the West Approach Road. I think it's one of your pet Latvians. I'm sending a panda for you and Mark.'

'Oh it's Mark now, is it?' Rachel addressed Brickall as she hung up. 'And I presume the only reason you're in my room in the middle of the night is because Morag's already told you. Before she told me. Which figures.'

'Well come on then, put some fucking clothes on, you spanner!'

Rachel was suddenly aware that she was wearing nothing more than a T-shirt and knickers. She pulled on black jeans and a grey sweatshirt, dragged a brush through her hair and followed Brickall down to the waiting car. She was tired and disorientated but he, by contrast, was bristling with energy.

'We've gone from a double to a triple body count in a matter of hours,' he observed as a uniformed officer drove them west out of the city, past the noisy Saturday-night partygoers.

'It's hardly cause for celebration,' Rachel snapped. All she could see in her mind's eye was Iveta's cowering figure.

He looked askance at her. 'Who rattled your cage, Prince?'

'Iveta tried to phone me, this evening. If I'd picked up, maybe this wouldn't have happened.'

Brickall turned and gave her a long look. His eyes glittered in the passing lights of oncoming traffic. 'Rachel…' Brickall never called her Rachel. It was 'dickhead' or 'loser', or occasionally 'Boss'. 'Fuck's sake, you don't know that!' He grabbed her by the shoulders and twisted her round so that she was looking at him. 'You don't even know if it's her. But if it is, you don't want to fall into the trap of thinking that if you didn't prevent a crime then that crime was your fault.'

She felt tears prick at the edges of her eyes. What was wrong with her, for God's sake? Since Joe had come back into her life she was an emotional jelly.

Reading her mind as ever, Brickall went on: 'Now get a fucking grip, Prince. Morag already thinks we're a pair of soft jessies; don't give her any more ammunition.'

The car came to a halt on the edge of a brownfield site, its hoardings announcing the imminent construction of executive apartments. A white tent had been erected, and several other squad cars were parked with their blue light bars still flashing. The site was essentially little more than a huge hole in the ground and Rachel and Brickall had to pick their way across the muddy, uneven ground in a torch beam directed by one of the uniformed police officers.

Morag Sillars emerged through the white tarpaulin tent flaps with paper overshoes over her tiny feet. She immediately lit a cigarette, dragging on it deeply. 'Yous two'll want to see,' she growled, exhaling smoke at them.

Inside the tent, the body lay partially covered by a piece of blue plastic sheeting. A kneeling SOCO in a hooded Tyvek suit stood up and backed away to give them room.

'Oh Jesus… fucking hell!' Brickall, never one to be squeamish, flinched. The throat had been slit so wide and so deep that the head was hanging by mere tendons, amid glistening viscous burgundy clots. The pungent, ferrous smell of blood was overwhelming. The SOCO adjusted his lighting unit so that it picked out the platinum white fronds of hair. Now that her death had smoothed the pinched tension of her face, it was clear how young the girl was. Probably no more than twenty.

'I'm sorry,' Rachel addressed Iveta Kovals. 'I'm so sorry.'

THIRTY-ONE

The new-look Operation Honeycomb incident room at Gayfield Square had windows. It also had half a dozen desks, multiple phone lines and several computer terminals. A couple of uniformed officers had been allocated to help with administrative jobs.

Rachel called a briefing there first thing on Monday morning, outlining the mechanics of the ethylene glycol poisoning of Bruno Martinez and Emily van Meijer. Both of whom had threatened to blow the whistle after being sexually assaulted at a party for anonymous but apparently well-connected patrons.

'… A party at this address.'

Rachel pinned up a picture of 21 Grange Loan Terrace on the new, improved whiteboard.

'And then in the early hours of yesterday morning, a young Latvian woman recently seen at the property,' she added a mugshot of Iveta Kovals, 'was found with her throat cut. We've not found the knife, but there seems to have been a struggle before it was used, so forensics are hoping the recover some DNA from under the victim's fingernails. DC Tulloch – can you chase that? She worked for the organisers of the same parties, and was about to name the person – or people – behind them. The link between Iveta and the teens appears to relate in some way to White Crystal Tours.'

One cue, Brickall pinned up photos of Kenneth Candlish, and Will and Hazel MacBain. 'This couple hosted the dead teenagers and their director, Kenneth Candlish, was actively associating with at least one suspected party guest, a top lawyer called Douglas Coulter.'

Rachel added his photo.

'His firm arranged the lease on this house.' She tapped the photo of Grange Loan Terrace. 'The problem we have at the moment is that these links are very tenuous. Too tenuous. We need to dig up more substantial evidence to make a conspiracy stand up. That's going to be our starting point.'

DC Tulloch raised an arm. 'Boss?' Sillars glowered at her own DC addressing Rachel in this manner. 'We've got back the results of the forensic search on Grange Loan Terrace.'

Rachel motioned for him to stand up and come to the front and address the room.

'Okay…' Tulloch took a deep breath. 'The place had been very thoroughly cleaned. Professionally cleaned. So basically evidence was on the thin side… we did find a few sets of prints that the cleaner had missed, but as yet no matches on IDENT1. However, we also found hidden cameras in the bedrooms. The sort that record onto a remote device, so there were no actual recordings we could look at.'

'So the pervs were filming what they got up to,' rasped Sillars.

Rachel's mind flashed back to her informal tutorial from Charlie. 'It's likely that footage was then sold on the dark web,' she said. 'But we need input from our cybercrime unit to move that line of enquiry forward. My priority now is to get in and search the property where the teenagers were staying in Campbell Road.'

'A Spanish special?' Brickall used the slang for an unexpected raid. 'Pre-dawn?' he added hopefully.

'Not sure about pre-dawn, given they have small children who would be fast asleep and potentially distressed… but early, yes. When we can be sure the whole family's there, and unprepared.'

*

Soon after six the following morning, just as the first gold and grey streaks of sunrise were appearing on the horizon, Rachel, Brickall and DC Tulloch hammered on the door of 34 Campbell Road. There were officers in tactical gear with manual battering rams standing by, but Rachel felt strongly that a more low-key approach was called for. Not only were there children present, but neither Will or Hazel MacBain were being arrested.

A shocked Will answered the door in pyjama bottoms and a towelling dressing gown. His normally tidy hair was ruffled, and his face puffy with sleep.

'What's going on?'

The three detectives, already gloved, pushed past him and ran up the stairs, followed by PC Blair and a male constable in combat boots and stab vest.

'You can't do this!' He followed Rachel, trying to make eye contact. 'Please – DI Prince – stop! We haven't done anything!'

There was the sound of a child crying, and Hazel appeared at the entrance to the top-floor flat. She held Angus, still half asleep, over her shoulder and pressed the crying Esme against her legs. The folds of her thin nightdress accentuated the curve of her pregnant stomach.

'Will – what's going on?' Her husband shrugged. 'What's going on?' she demanded, turning on Brickall with a surprising viciousness. Her pale face coloured angrily.

'We've got a warrant to search the premises as part of our investigation into the deaths of Bruno Martinez and Emily van Meijer,' he told her calmly, refusing to make eye contact.

'But—'

Brickall held up a gloved hand. 'Please, you're best off just letting us get on with it. That way we'll be finished and out of your hair much quicker.'

The team worked their way from room to room, opening cupboards and drawers and flicking through paperwork. A laptop, an iPad and two phones were sealed in plastic bags.

'Can't I just download some of my work stuff?' Will grabbed desperately at his laptop as it was carried away.

'Sorry sir, no.'

'But when will we get these things back?'

'Impossible to say.' DC Tulloch said, without emotion. 'When we no longer need them.'

Rachel and Kirstie Blair were searching the MacBains' bedroom – Blair tackling the chest of drawers while Rachel worked through the wardrobe. The clothes were ordered and hung neatly, with shoes stored in their original boxes. In Will's case, they consisted of one pair of open sandals, one pair of black brogues and two brown pairs. Rachel removed a pair from their boxes and examined them. All perfectly smooth, and smelling of old-fashioned shoe polish. The smell triggered a memory, something important, but her brain couldn't quite drag it up from the depths.

As she turned over one of the shoes, a USB stick fell out. Rachel put it straight into an evidence bag, and handed it to Kirstie Blair. 'You carry on in here, there's something I need to check.'

She went into the sitting room and examined the contents of the drinks cupboard. There was no port, but there was a half-empty bottle of Southern Comfort. She bagged it and handed it over to the uniformed PC.

'Detective Sergeant,' she addressed Brickall. 'Come with me a second, please.'

He followed her down the stairs and out of the front door.

'Where the fuck are you going, Prince? We're supposed to be doing a full search.'

'I want to back up a hunch,' she told him. 'Can you open the garage door.'

It was locked. 'Better not pick it with your Swiss Army knife, not this time.' Brickall beckoned over one of the tactical officers, who forced the lock with one clean tap of his enforcer.

'What are we looking for?'

'Isn't it bloody obvious?' Rachel was standing on tiptoe, feeling her way along the wooden shelf on the exposed brick wall. She found oil, screen de-icer, WD40, tins of paint. And finally, there it was. She opened the bottle and sniffed it, then offered it to Brickall to do the same.

'Doesn't smell of anything.'

'Exactly. This is old-fashioned anti-freeze. Ethylene glycol.

Back in the incident room, Rachel debriefed the team and arranged for intelligence officers to analyse the portable devices and USB stick.

'Anyone have an update on Iveta Kovals?'

'I've got an Identification Bureau team searching for the murder weapon,' Sillars croaked. 'But chances are it's been chucked in the Water of Leith or the Union Canal. The search of the scene has thrown up some shoeprints – we reckon at least a size eleven, so male – which we're going to analyse, along with the material from under the fingernails. The victim was an itinerant worker who had no family or friends in the city, so we've no a lot to go on.'

'Can we do some door to door around the flat she shared with Balodis?' Brickall asked. 'And we'll need to either send an officer to re-interview Balodis, or get him brought over here in a prison van.'

'Aye, okay,' Sillars conceded, giving Brickall what passed as a smile.

'Thanks, Morag. You've been fantastic.'

Rachel thought Sillars would die of pleasure, watching the tiny woman positively glow at his words of praise. She waited until the group round the whiteboard had dispersed and then took Brickall to one side.

'Little job for you… we don't yet know for sure that Douglas Coulter and the man with the port wine stain who tried to molest Marie-Laure are the same person. She's back in France now, but can you organise for someone over there to show her a photo of Coulter and get a positive ID, then take a statement? There's an Interpol office in Lyon.' He rolled his eyes at being assigned a desk job, but she ignored him.

Rachel asked a passing constable to fetch coffee, then sat down at one of the desks, feeling faintly overwhelmed. Her mind was scrabbling like a hamster in a wheel, trying to hold on to all the threads in the case, trying not to forget or overlook anything. And having Joe to think about – delightful though that was – only added to the sense of pressure. While she had been speaking to the team a text had come in from him.

How's it all going? Any chance of a chat?

She replied, reluctantly: *Will probably be stuck in the incident room until quite late. Might be able to pop out for a coffee.*
Another text arrived immediately.

Was going to speak to you about Stuart. I think I'm ready to contact him now.

Rachel forwarded him Stuart's contact details, then typed.

Go for it. But bear in mind he and Claire have just lost a child, so don't expect too much to start with.

As soon as she had pressed 'Send', she wondered whether she had been a bit insensitive. She never used to worry about things like the note struck by a text message. This was motherhood, and it was turning her into an anxious wreck.

Another text arrived from Joe, of a sad face emoji, followed by a cow emoji, and a dagger. It took Rachel a few seconds to realise this meant the killing of a fatted calf. She laughed, relieved, and opened up her laptop. She found the copy of the file that Beth McAllister had showed her at Mail Boxes 4U. She watched the figure in the tartan Jimmy wig walk up to the post box, turn and walk back again. She paused the video and zoomed in.

And there it was – the detail that had seemed so incongruous when she first saw it. The smart shoes: shiny lace-up brogues. Exactly like Will MacBain's.

THIRTY-TWO

'So are you going to arrest someone?'

Rachel and Joe were heading to a Thai restaurant on Castle Street, near her hotel. It was late, and she had only just managed to escape the confines of the incident room after a twenty-hour day, but she tried not to let her son see just how exhausted she was. And, as he had correctly pointed out to her, her brain would work better if she ate a proper meal.

'Not just yet.' She was aware of the need to keep case details confidential, yet she enjoyed talking about her work to Joe, who in turn seemed genuinely fascinated. 'We're still in the process of putting the case together, piece by piece. You never want to risk the whole thing falling apart by making an arrest too early.' There was a distinct nip of autumn in the air, and Rachel hunched her shoulders so that her face and neck were covered by her scarf.

'But it is a murder case?' Joe persisted. 'As well as the child abuse stuff.'

'The problem we have is that the evidence pointing to murder is all circumstantial at the moment.'

'Bummer,' said Joe. To her great delight, he then hooked his arm through hers.

'Exactly. Which is why we have to be patient and just try and gather as many pieces of evidence as possible. So that if it does come to court, we can paint a convincing picture for a jury.'

'I spoke to my father today… not Dad, Stuart.'

'And how did that go?' Rachel asked carefully.

'Fine. Bit, like, weird.'

'I'm sure it must have been.'

'He was quite… formal.'

'I can imagine. But give him a chance. Stuart's a good guy, when all's said and done. Our marriage may have been a disaster, but that was mostly down to me.'

Joe grunted.

'I still have a great deal of respect for him though… Will you see him?'

'I think so. We talked about meeting for coffee or a beer first. Just the two of us. On, like, neutral territory.'

'Sounds like a plan,' Rachel leaned into Joe's arm.

'Rachel!'

When she looked up, a tall, dark figure was approaching them pulling a wheelie case, collar turned up against the cold.

'Giles… hello. You're back,' she added unnecessarily.

'Indeed, I had a call a little while ago about some… developments.' He looked warily in Joe's direction. 'And this must be your son?'

'Yes, this is Joe.'

He extended a hand. 'Giles Denton. Good to see you.'

'We're just heading out for a meal,' Rachel said, reluctant to prolong the encounter.

'And I'm just on my way to check into the hotel. Maybe see you later.'

To Rachel's discomfort he gave her one of his smouldering looks topped off with a faint wink, before walking away.

'Is that your boyfriend?' asked Joe.

'No, it is *not*.'

'Well I reckon he'd like to be.'

*

Rachel had just brushed the remains of the pad thai from her teeth and was planning on falling asleep in front of a Richard Curtis romcom when there was a tentative knock at her door.

She had half expected it to be him, and it was.

'Giles. I was just on my way to bed.' She indicated the hotel bathrobe, and her bare legs.

'Just what I like to hear,' he said roguishly, putting the Do Not Disturb sign on the door and closing it. He walked up to her, placed his hands on her shoulders and asked. 'How are you? Seriously?'

'Drained. Overwhelmed. Stressed.'

'That's what I thought…' Giles pulled her into an embrace and for a few delicious seconds she enjoyed the sensation of letting her weight sink into him, of being supported. He stroked her back, gently at first, then with more purpose, letting his thumbs stray up the sleeves of her robe to the inside edge of her bare arms.

'Giles…' she mumbled. 'Remember what I said… we can't get involved. Not now.' She pulled back from him. 'The case has moved up a few gears, and then there's Joe…'

'Ah yes, your lad. He's a long tall drink of water, isn't he?'

Rachel's expression told him that she had no intention of discussing her son.

'Anyway,' Giles persisted. 'This isn't "getting involved". We're just two colleagues catching up at the end of a long day.'

Giles went to the minibar and poured himself a whisky, sitting down on the edge of the bed, kicking off his shoes and swinging his legs up so that he was reclining against the pillows. He motioned to Rachel to sit down next to him, and too tired to resist, she sank down and allowed him to drape his arm over her shoulder.

'Can I get you a drink?'

'I think you'll find this is *my* room.'

He laughed. 'You know what I mean… you just need to rest while I wait on you.' He picked up the TV remote. 'Anything decent on?'

'I was going to watch a nice undemanding romcom. And then I was going to go to sleep.'

He reached over and kissed her; gently, platonically. Then he kissed her again, and this time there was nothing platonic about it.

'Sounds like a plan.'

Seven hours later there was another knock on the door, loud and abrupt, which signalled that it was Brickall. His room was on the same floor, and he was in the habit of calling for Rachel on his way down to breakfast.

She threw on her robe and tiptoed to the door, opening it only a few inches so that Giles' sleeping body wasn't visible.

'I'll be down in a couple of minutes,' she whispered. 'Just let me finish showering. And order me a coffee with hot milk.'

'You had someone in there with you, didn't you?' Brickall said accusingly as soon as she sat down opposite him in the restaurant. 'And I'm guessing it wasn't your son this time.'

Rachel shook her head.

'Don't tell me… Denton.'

Her lack of response gave her away.

'Fucking hell.' Brickall stood up and stomped over to the buffet, where he loaded up with the usual full Scottish. When he returned, he slammed his plate on the table and set about eating, ignoring Rachel.

'What is it you have against him?' Rachel asked. 'I don't get it. What's he ever done to you?'

'There's something about him that just doesn't sit right. Bit too good to be true; I don't trust him. So I'm hardly going to be thrilled about you dating him.'

'I'm not dating him.' Rachel poured milk into her coffee, feeling a little frisson as her mind raced back to the previous night's delicious non-date. She decided the best tactic was to change the subject. 'I wonder what delights will be waiting for us in Gayfield Square.'

Brickall ignored her, shoving a piece of black pudding into his mouth and settling into a grumpy silence.

'Ma'am, you need to see this. Straight away.'

DC Tulloch intercepted them in the front lobby as soon as they arrived, his body language bristling with adrenaline.

'The intel guys came back to us first thing this morning…' He continued talking as the three of them hurried up to the incident room. 'The mobile devices were all clean, but Will MacBain is certainly not. He'd deleted images from his laptop that we managed to recover. And then there's this…'

Rachel, Brickall and Tulloch crowded round a terminal, while Tulloch plugged the USB stick Rachel had found into the hard drive. Tentatively, Brickall took charge of the mouse and started to flick through the contents.

'Christ on a bike…'

They were pornographic images and video clips of children. There were both boys and girls, and some looked as young as six or seven. They were either alone and naked or being abused by a faceless adult. Hundreds of them.

THIRTY-THREE

Tulloch broke the silence.

'The restored stuff from the laptop was more of the same… shall we send someone round to pick him up, Ma'am?'

Rachel was trying to think but her mind was humming, rational thought temporarily crowded out by what she had just seen.

'We took prints from both the MacBains yesterday?' This was standard practice before a search, to be able to compare and identify any third-party fingerprints.

'Yes, Ma'am.'

'And were Will MacBain's prints on the USB stick?'

Tulloch shook his head.

'Okay, so he's been clever and either wiped it or used gloves – which means at interview he'll probably try and deny everything. There's still the laptop evidence, and I'd like to try and get him for organising the parties too… but we need to act fast: there are young children under his roof. And we need to alert Social Services and get the MacBain kids on the system, given what we now know about their father.'

Rachel stood up and paced to and fro, trying to prioritise the multiple new developments crowding in on them. 'The person who left the flyers for distribution in the Mail Boxes 4U shop looks very much like MacBain, but we need more… DS Brickall – can you get a photo of MacBain's face and get the Intelligence guys to run it through facial recognition, comparing it to our leaflet man? DC Tulloch – are we sure we didn't find a suspicious spare phone in the house, a burner?'

Tulloch shook his head.

'The man caught on CCTV left a mobile phone in the security box too,' Rachel was thinking out loud. 'Which would explain why there was nothing found on his regular phone.'

'Or: maybe he destroys the spare phone every time and gets another when he needs it. Maybe that's why they're called burners.' Brickall's voice was dripping with sarcasm. *He's still pissed off about Denton*, thought Rachel. It wasn't the first time he had sulked over one of her romantic liaisons, and no doubt it wouldn't be the last.

'If you could just organise the facial recognition test immediately, Sergeant,' she said, without making eye contact.

Brickall stamped off to one of the other desks, leaving Rachel with DC Tulloch.

'Do we know about the Southern Comfort bottle?' she asked him.

He retrieved a written lab report and flicked through it. 'Negative for ethylene glycol, Ma'am.'

'Fingerprints?'

'Just Hazel MacBain's and one other set we can't identify. Could be the cleaner?'

'Possibly… we need to rule her out. Radio control and get them to go to Valerie Muir's address and bring her in if she's there. Get a full set done, and hold on to her so I can talk to her again. We'll hold off on Will MacBain just a bit longer, as long as it takes for us to brief Child Protection, at least. He's not going anywhere.'

Rachel picked up her coat and bag.

'Got another assignation?' Brickall asked, curling his lip.

'If you can call paying a visit to Edinburgh Council's Fostering Services an assignation – then yes.'

*

Greta Wheedon lived in a characterless house on a modern estate in South Gyle. Rachel had been given her address after a very tedious hour and a half at the city council's offices, watching a willing but slow elderly clerk work his way through boxes of historic records.

'Can I come in for a quick word?' she asked, showing her warrant card. Greta, an attractive woman in her sixties who wore her grey hair neatly cropped and fuchsia nail polish on her fingers, took the card from Rachel and read it.

'Well,' she said, 'I can't think for a moment what a detective from the National Crime Agency would want to talk to me about, but do come in anyway.'

She smiled pleasantly and ushered Rachel into a bright open-plan reception room where a large fluffy cat basked in a patch of sunlight next to the French windows. 'Would you like coffee? I was just about to pop the kettle on.'

'That would be lovely, thank you.'

'And I've some scones?'

Rachel smiled gratefully. She'd consumed nothing but coffee since the Thai meal, and her stomach was growling.

While she was gone, Rachel looked around the room. There were a lot of framed photos; a couple of Greta with a distinguished-looking silver-haired man wearing a chain of office of some description – her husband presumably – and lots of photos of children of varying ages, some single, some groups.

Greta came back carrying a tray with a steaming cafetière and a plate heaped with the freshly baked scones, together with home-made raspberry jam. *Brickall would have been all over those*, Rachel thought, smiling ruefully.

As the coffee was poured, Rachel said, 'I understand from Social Services that you fostered a girl called Hazel Nevins. Hazel MacBain, as she now is.'

Greta narrowed her eyes slightly. 'Yes. Yes, I did.' Her tone was cautious. 'Why, has something happened to her?'

Rachel shook her head. 'No, she's fine. Nothing for you to worry about.'

'I hear she's expecting again.'

'That's right… are you still in touch with Hazel?' She took a sip of the coffee Greta had handed her.

'No, not exactly. I get a Christmas card from her every year, and I hear about her. Through her family on her mother's side, the Elricks. I've known the family for many years. In fact, that's how I came to foster Hazel when Barbara was… when she died. She was with us a fair few years. It was an informal arrangement at first, then I registered as a foster carer and took on more children. Quite a number over the years.'

'Do you have children of your own?' Rachel asked.

'Aye, two boys. But they were older than Hazel, almost grown-up when she came to us.'

She smiled at Rachel, and drank some of her own coffee. Setting down the cup, she said, 'I expect you'd like to know a bit about what Hazel was like as a little girl.'

Rachel nodded. 'I would, yes.'

'Has she… has she done something wrong?'

'I can't discuss details of our investigation with you at the moment. We're following up some enquiries into the company her husband works for.'

'That would be Will… och, I can't imagine *him* doing anything wrong.' There was a faint edge to Greta's voice as she said this.

'Why not?' Rachel was careful to keep her tone light.

'Well, you know, according to Hazel he's just so perfect. In every way.'

'Nobody's perfect.' Rachel smiled. *Ain't that the truth*, she thought, the images of naked pre-pubescent bodies swimming back to the forefront of her mind. She pushed them away, forcing herself to refocus. 'Tell me about Hazel.'

'She was a funny little thing when she came to us. It was 1993, and she was eight years old by then, but she was practically feral. Any good poor Barbara had done in trying to raise her had been completely undone by what that bastard Archie Nevins… sorry.'

'That's quite all right. He's a convicted wife-killer.'

'… by what he'd done to her mother.'

'Had Hazel been abused?'

'I think he hit her, aye. And treated her cruelly. But most of Nevins' rages were aimed at poor Barbara. So when Hazel came to us she was understandably silent and frightened, and developmentally delayed. She was quite a bright child, and she caught up, but she stayed a strange wee creature.'

'Can you describe how? It would be helpful.'

'She was quiet – almost timid – but when she set her mind on something, I've never known such doggedness. She wouldn't let anything else get in her way. You know when they say "quiet determination"… well, that could have been invented to describe Hazel.'

'How was she with the other children?'

'Well, of course, she was the first we took on. She got all the attention, and she thrived on it. But then we fostered another little girl called Annie, and she didn't like it at all. Played with her when anyone was looking, but when she thought no one could see her, I saw her pinch Annie on the arm, because Annie had a toy that she wanted. I've never seen a child act with such… such viciousness. She'd get bright red in the face with rage.'

'When did she leave you?'

Greta thought for a moment, pausing with a scone halfway to her mouth. 'She'd have been about fifteen. She went into a care home for teens – that was her own choice. I tried hard to keep in touch, but it was like she wanted to wipe out her entire childhood. Hazel always did well at school, but all she really wanted was marriage and babies. She desperately wanted the stable home she'd never had herself. Which is not surprising. So when she met Will through the Catholic church in the Cowgate, that was it. She set her sights on him, and nothing would deter her.'

'And was he as smitten with Hazel?'

She shook her head. 'No, I didn't really get that impression. He was very good to her, but I think he just wanted a wife, and any number of women might have fit the bill.' Greta poured herself more coffee. 'He's always taken care of her though, and from what I've heard, they've been happy. So, she escaped the curse of her parents' awful marriage. Which was what she wanted.'

Rachel's phone buzzed twice, and she took it out. The first message was from Giles, and simply read '*xxx*'. She deleted it, frowning. The second was from Brickall.

CCTV facial analysis back. It's MacBain.

As discreetly as she could, without Greta seeing, she typed back.

Bring him in. Now.

The initial interview with Will MacBain and his solicitor went very much as Rachel had predicted. The USB stick wasn't his: he knew nothing about it and someone must have planted it there. He even suggested that it could have been one of the White Crystal students. As for the laptop – whoever had searched for and downloaded the indecent images, it wasn't him. Again, according to him, the students could easily have used it. His demeanour was all wide eyes and shocked indignation.

'That's pretty low,' Brickall muttered to Rachel, during a break. 'The nonce pointing the finger at underage kids.'

'He's an upstanding member of the church. Hypocrisy rather goes with the territory,' Rachel observed drily.

'Are we going to try and nail him for the party stuff, too?'

'We'll give it a shot, but I'm expecting more of the same.' Rachel checked her watch. 'He was brought in at 13.10, so we've got him until tomorrow lunchtime. A few hours in a police cell might put some cracks into the holier-than-thou act.'

Rachel recommended the interview but, again, Will denied any involvement. The CCTV images captured at Mail Boxes 4U were of someone else. He knew nothing about the parties, and his whereabouts for the evening of the fifth of August could be verified. He didn't drink, and would never attend a social event without his wife. Rachel stuck with the plan, remanding MacBain in custody for the remainder of the statutory twenty-four hours.

'Are you thinking what I'm thinking?' Brickall asked as they went down to the canteen to grab a sandwich – or in Brickall's case, three sandwiches, a packet of crisps and a Twix.

'Probably.' They sat at one of the formica tables and opened their sandwich packets. 'Go on,' Rachel prompted.

'I'm thinking that MacBain has to be in the frame for finishing off those poor kids. He must have realised that if they talked about what had happened to them, his involvement in the parties was going to come to light, and with it, his particular… interest in the underage. So he drugs them and silences them permanently.'

Rachel nodded. 'I was thinking that, yes. But I've also been wondering how we're going to prove it, given he has an alibi for the night of Emily's death.' She thought for a moment. 'Did we ever get back the DNA results for the selfie stick? We need to chase that up, for starters.'

'And talking of chasing up leads, what's lover boy done about that list from the local sex register? I'm not sensing any urgency on that front.'

'I'll speak to him,' said Rachel, standing up with half of her sandwich still uneaten. 'But first I need another chat with our local friendly miracle worker, Mrs Muir.'

*

Valerie Muir was sitting on the edge of a chair in an interview room with her arms wrapped defensively around herself. She was crying.

Rachel offered her a tissue and sent a PC to fetch her a cup of tea.

'I've never been in trouble with the police before,' she sobbed. 'I've never had so much as a late fine at the library.'

'You're not in trouble,' Rachel said gently, giving her hand a quick pat.

'But they took my fingerprints.'

'That was just to rule you out. You're not suspected of anything. But, Valerie, I do need to ask you a couple of quick questions. Your fingerprints were on a bottle of Southern Comfort that was found in the drinks cupboard in 34 Campbell Road.'

'I expect I took it out when I polished inside the cabinet. I wouldn't have been drinking from it, not that stuff.' She pulled a face.

'Do you remember seeing it anywhere else in the house? You didn't find it in one of the student rooms when you cleaned, for example?'

Valerie shook her head firmly. 'Not that one, no. But I did find the other one.'

'The other one?'

'There were two bottles of that stuff, the Southern…'

'Southern Comfort.'

'Yes. The one in the drinks cabinet that was always there. And then the empty one that I found downstairs by the bin in the refectory.'

'Let me get this straight – there were two bottles of Southern Comfort? And the one in the student quarters was completely empty?'

'Yes, that's correct. Can I go now?' Her voice trembled and her face had an unhealthy pallor.

This was more than just routine nerves. Rachel held up a hand. 'Just a couple more things, do you remember what you did with it?'

'I put it out in the blue recycling bin. It would have been taken the next Friday.'

'And you really can't remember the name of the person who gave you the work in Grange? Please think very hard.'

'I've tried: I don't remember. Like I said, my memory's not what it was.'

Rachel's phone started vibrating insistently. She arranged a car to take Valerie home, then checked it. Four missed calls from Joe, and a follow-up text.

Something huge has happened. Call me!

THIRTY-FOUR

Joe and Charlie both talked at once when Rachel arrived at the flat.

'Slow down; one at a time.'

Charlie nodded at Joe. 'You tell her. She's *your* mum.'

Joe led her over to the sofa, clearing a pile of football kit off it so that they could both sit down. 'You remember Charlie was going to check that dark web forum we found, for updates? Well they're holding another of their special parties. And guess what… it's tonight.'

'At Grange Loan Terrace?'

Charlie shook his head. 'No, it's in Morningside.'

'Can you show me?'

Charlie pulled up a page on his laptop. Rachel made a mental note of the address: 141 Hellebore Drive. She would speak to Morag straight away; arrange for surveillance on the property.

'It's going to be dead exciting.' Joe beamed.

Rachel felt a shiver of alarm run down her spine. She put her hand on the sofa arm to steady herself. 'What do you mean? Are you saying someone's invited you?'

'No, they were advertising for "fresh-looking" waiters,' Joe made air quotes, 'aged eighteen to twenty-one. And we signed up. We thought we could go and, like, spy for you. Like an undercover operation.' He couldn't keep the excitement from his voice.

Rachel shook her head vigorously. 'No. Out of the question. Young people your age have been drugged and raped at these parties.'

'But we'd be together. We'd be fine.'

'Absolutely not. I'd be incredibly irresponsible as a parent if I let you go. What would Nick and Jane have to say about it? These people are predatory and they're dangerous. I'll definitely pass this information on to the team though: it could turn out to be extremely helpful.'

'But Rachel—'

'Joe – it's a no. That's my final word.'

At 9.50 p.m., Brickall and Rachel arrived in Morningside in an unmarked car. Brickall slid it into Hellebore Drive as unobtrusively as possible, taking up position within sight of the entrance to number 141. It was a double-fronted house with a gabled roof, set back from the road. The windows gave off a muted glow, through which the loud bass thump of music was just audible, and a row of flares lit the front path. At 10 p.m., guests started to arrive in ones and twos, hurrying up to the front door, some wearing carnival masks or with hoods pulled over their faces. Some even went so far as to drape their coats over the heads, like accused criminals arriving at court.

'Here we go,' Brickall said suddenly. 'I think we have a couple of… what do they call them?'

'Young Friends,' said Rachel, with a shiver of revulsion.

Two girls no older than their mid-teens approached the front of the house, giggling together. They wore short skirts and had made a lot of effort with their hair and make-up, stopping under the light of the front porch to check their reflections in their phone screens. Just as they would if they were going to a party with their peers. The door opened a fraction and they disappeared inside. 'Maybe we should go in now,' Rachel said.

Brickall shook his head. 'We don't have any grounds for arrest, and we don't have a warrant. People are entitled to hold a party in a private residence. And for all we know, those girls could just be there to wash glasses.'

'Come on – you saw the way they were dressed!'

'Leave it a bit longer, give things a chance to warm up.'

As he spoke, two familiar figures in black trousers and white shirts ambled up the path and were admitted through the front door.

'Christ, I don't believe it!' Rachel slapped on the dashboard. 'Joe and Charlie! After I told them not to.' She reached for the car door, but Brickall restrained her. 'Hold on a sec, who's this?'

A tall male figure emerged along the side path from the direction of the back door and walked briskly away from the property, seemingly in a hurry.

'Is that…?' Rachel tensed and leaned forward, but whoever it was continued onto the pavement and disappeared along the street, their identity obscured by deep shadows. She turned to Brickall. 'Okay, come on – I'm not leaving my son in that place.'

'Hold your horses. If you go rushing in there now, the whole party will fold, and it's only just started.'

'But—'

'They're eighteen, right?'

'Yes.'

'So they're technically adults. They're allowed to go to a party.'

'Not if they're at risk of harm.'

Brickall sighed. 'Okay, how about we give it thirty minutes? They're sensible lads, and they know you've flagged up that this party's happening. If anything worries them, I'm sure Joe will ring you.'

Rachel sighed. 'Thirty minutes. That's it.'

She refused the offer of Brickall's cheese and onion crisps, instead fidgeting and checking her watch continually for the next twenty minutes.

'Look!' said Brickall suddenly. 'Did you see that?'

In one of the front upstairs windows, a light was flashing on and off in a deliberate rhythm.

'That looks like some sort of distress signal,' Rachel said, scrabbling at the passenger door. 'We need to get in there!'

She leapt out of the car and started to run up the drive, but Brickall was too quick for her, intercepting her with a rugby tackle and dragging her forcibly back to the vehicle.

'No!' He spoke with uncharacteristic sternness. 'If we're going to do this, we're going to do it properly. Otherwise you're going to risk all sorts of trouble. And I – for one – do not want to end up being suspended again.' He reached for the car's radio handset and called the nearest mobile unit, stressing the importance of arriving on silent. 'Wait!' he told Rachel sharply as she tried to get out of the car again. 'Backup's on its way. Two minutes.'

A squad car with two uniformed officers arrived a few minutes later, minus sirens, and parked next to their vehicle. Brickall walked over to speak to them, then came back and stuck his head through the open passenger window.

'I'm going in, but you need to stay here.'

'But—'

'Forget it, Prince. You're too emotionally involved; you'd be more of a hindrance than a help.'

She nodded, and watched helplessly as Brickall and the two constables approached the front of the house. They banged on the door, and when there was no reply, one of them fetched an enforcer from the boot of the patrol car and hit it hard on the door's inside edge until it gave way.

There was an agonising wait. To Rachel it felt like an hour, but was probably only a few minutes. Eventually the front door opened. A few people attempted to leave, but were prevented from doing so by the uniformed police officers. Then the radio set crackled into life, and Rachel heard a disembodied voice request an ambulance and TAU. Within minutes, a tactical aid unit vehicle roared up, this time with blue lights and sirens, closely followed by an ambulance. Paramedics jumped out and walked quickly to the house, carrying their red kit bags, accompanied by half a dozen armed police officers.

Rachel could stand it no longer. She jumped out of the car and ran to the front door, just as two figures emerged through it, dressed in white shirts and black ties. Joe and Charlie.

'Joe!'

She only just managed to keep from hurling herself at him. 'Jesus, Joe… I thought I told you not to go!' She was half-shouting, her relief making her incoherent. 'Are you both okay?'

Joe gave her a weak smile. 'Yeah, we're fine.'

'Go and sit in the car, I'll be back in a minute.'

In the hallway, Brickall was watching as a stretcher was carried downstairs. One of the young girls was lying on it under a blanket, eyes closed, one arm flung out at a strange angle. A policeman helped the other girl as she stumbled down the stairs, wide-eyed with shock.

'We found one of them in the bedroom, out of it, and about to be sexually assaulted.' Brickall said quietly. 'Presumably for the benefit of a camera. We're getting a SOCO down here to check. IB unit, they call it here.'

Rachel groaned. 'We should have gone in sooner.'

Brickall shook his head firmly. 'We got there just in time: she's not come to any serious physical harm. And if we'd gone in any earlier, we'd probably never have caught them at it. That evidence is going to be vital.'

A few partygoers were attempting to sidle towards the open front door. Quick as a flash, Rachel stopped them, motioning to an armed officer to block their exit.

'Oh no you don't! All of you are under arrest, under the Protection of Children and Prevention of Sexual Offences Act. And –'

she ripped the mask off a distinguished-looking man with white hair – 'we need to see your faces.'

More guests were being led down the stairs, all of them middle-aged and well-dressed. 'I'll wait for the fun bus to arrive and take this lot away,' Brickall said to Rachel. 'You go and check on your lad.'

'Are you sure?'

'Yeah, go on. I've got this.'

Rachel gave him a grateful smile and slipped out to the car, where the boys were sitting in the back seat.

'I'm really hungry,' was the first thing Joe said.

'Me too.' Charlie nodded.

'We can go and get something to eat in a minute,' Rachel said. 'I just need to wait until the place has been cleared.'

'And we can't leave until we've got our phones back anyway,' Joe said. 'They took them off as us soon as we arrived. So we couldn't text you.'

'But you were okay? Nobody tried to… molest you?'

'This one guy did put his hand on Charlie's arse,' said Joe. 'But he told him to fuck off. The woman in charge of the staff—'

'Do you know what she was called?'

Joe shook his head. 'No, she never said, it was all very anony-mous. No names, no pack-drill. But I'd definitely recognise her.'

'Anyway, she told us off,' said Charlie. 'Apparently we weren't being "friendly" enough to the guests…'

'And then we spotted a girl being taken upstairs, looking completely stoned. We couldn't phone you or anything. That was when I got the idea to flash the lights on and off. In case the place was being watched.'

'It worked,' Rachel said, with a grudging smile. 'But you still shouldn't have gone.'

'We wanted to try and look through people's coat pockets to see if we could find their names, but they took the coats and locked them away,' Charlie said.

'But I did recognise someone,' said Joe. He was watching out of the window, fascinated, as the partygoers were led out in handcuffs and put in the back of a police bus that had just arrived. 'Whoah – Charlie look at that! Proper *Line of Duty* stuff.'

'I know. So cool.'

'Who did you recognise?' Rachel prompted.

'That friend of yours.'

She stared at him blankly.

'You know, the guy we met the other night on our way back from dinner. The Irish guy.'

THIRTY-FIVE

Rachel swivelled round in the front seat so she was looking straight at Joe.

'You mean Giles?'

'Yeah, that's the one. He was one of the guests.'

Rachel's felt her stomach drop, sharply. The faces of the boys blurred for a couple of seconds.

'Are you absolutely sure?'

'One hundred per cent. It was when we were handing out the welcome gifts. Only when he saw me looking at him, he must have left, because I didn't see him again.'

'You two, just wait here a second…'

She climbed out of the car and marched over to the police bus. There were around fifteen shocked-looking men inside, none of them Giles. There was no sign inside the house, where the TAU officers were carrying out a thorough search under the watchful eye of her Detective Sergeant.

'I thought you'd gone,' Brickall said accusingly.

'The boys' mobile phones are here somewhere; I said I'd ask for them… you haven't seen Giles Denton, have you?' she added, with forced nonchalance.

'Denton? No – why would he be here? You decided not to involve him.'

'Thought word might have got back to him… keep an eye out for those phones will you, and text me when you've found them.'

Rachel dropped the boys at Charlie's flat, stopping en route to pick up McDonald's burgers for them. Then, sitting in the car in Dundas Street, she phoned Giles's number. It rang out. She threw the car into gear and drove back to the hotel.

'I'm afraid we can't give out guests' information,' a bored receptionist told Rachel when she asked for Giles's room number, not even looking up from her screen. Rachel lowered her warrant card into the woman's line of vision.

'Room 315. But Mr Denton's just phoned down to say he's checking out,' she said, her eyes still on her screen. 'He's asked me to call him a taxi.' The receptionist finally looked up, turning to squint at the clock on the wall behind her. 'About… fifteen minutes ago. It should be here any minute.'

Rachel hurried to the lift and hit the button for the third floor, running down the maze of carpeted corridors until she found Room 315. She hammered on the door. It swung open. Giles turned away silently and sat down on the edge of the bed without meeting her eyes. He was dressed in a well-cut black suit, smart black loafers and a pale lilac shirt, open at the neck. His half-packed case was on the floor at his feet.

'Good party was it?' Rachel spat.

'Look, Rachel, sweetheart…'

He stood up and came towards her, but she backed away. He returned to his perch on the edge of the bed, placing shoes and a wash bag into the case and zipping it up.

'I could tell you I was there undercover, but that would be a lie,' he said quietly. 'And the last thing I want to do is lie to you.'

She folded her arms across her chest. 'So go on then Giles… what *were* you doing there?'

'I told you about my mate who lives here – the architect?'

'What's his name?' Giles did a double take as Rachel pulled out a notebook. 'Oh, didn't you know? We've arrested everyone there. So I can easily check your story, against my list.'

'Fairlie. Peter Fairlie. Look, Peter asked me if I wanted to go with him to a party. It was an unfamiliar address – you know, not Grange Loan Terrace – so I didn't think anything of it. It was only when I got there and I saw that it was all single men, some in masks, that the penny dropped. And then I saw your boy… Joe… coming through the front door with another lad, and I was… mortified. I left straight away, by the side entrance. I didn't even find Peter to tell him I was going.'

The vaguely familiar figure they saw leaving, Rachel thought. That had been Giles. 'I'm going to ask you something – something I won't be able to check up on – and I need you to answer it honestly. Did you know that this friend had an interest in sex with underage girls? Or boys.'

Giles sighed heavily and looked down at his feet. 'Yes. Well no, not the underage bit. But I mean, he was always a hard partier, and his private life was a bit… colourful. He always had an eye for a pretty young girl.'

'So as a Child Protection Officer, you still thought it was okay to go to a party with a friend you knew this about?' Rachel spat the words. 'You didn't see the massive conflict of interest looming? The compromise to your career?'

'Get down off your high horse, will you? Your own son was there, for God's sake!'

'And I had no idea about that until it was too late. Of course I didn't!' Rachel said hotly.

'It's okay, you don't need to convince me. But surely you can accept that my agreeing to go along was a mistake? A huge fecking mistake. And that all I feel now is utter shame. It's a mess. A horrible mess.'

Giles was right. She didn't know what was making her feel worse: the fact that her new love interest had attended a party for 'Young Friends', effectively torpedoing their relationship, or that her own son had been there, putting himself at risk. Her brain felt like a Newton's cradle, veering in one direction then the opposite. She sat down on the edge of the bed, rubbing her eyes so hard with the heel of her hand that it hurt.

Giles tried to reach for her hand, but she jerked it away. 'No. Don't.'

Eventually, when her breathing had slowed, Rachel looked up and asked, 'Where are you going? The sleeper train left an hour ago, and there are no flights until at least 6 a.m.'

'I'm getting a cab to Glasgow Airport, and then I'll crash out there until the first Dublin flight leaves.'

'You're going to Dublin?'

Giles nodded, then came towards her again and put his hands on her shoulders. This time she didn't resist.

'Rachel… you and I had such a good thing going. This doesn't need to be the end does it? It's not like I actually did anything… as soon as I knew what was going on I left, I swear to you.'

She shook her head slowly, and carefully removed his hands from her shoulders, placing them at his sides.

'You know it's the end, Giles. After this… I can't. Because there's another thing that's come out of tonight: I have to always put my own son's wellbeing first. Joe has to be my priority. There's just too much at stake.'

Rachel didn't mention Giles Denton's sudden departure to Brickall.

The following morning the two of them and Sillars stood together at the front desk in Gayfield Square to watch the custody sergeant charge Will MacBain with one count of causing or inciting provision by a child of sexual services and two of possessing indecent images of children, and to release him on police bail.

Will looked ghostly pale. His hair was greasy and he had two days' worth of stubble on his chin.

'Do you understand the charges?' the custody sergeant asked.

He shook his head. 'What's this "inciting sexual services" bit? I don't understand that.'

'We've evidence that you were involved in organising the parties at 21 Grange Loan Terrace and 141 Hellebore Drive,' Brickall said gruffly. 'At which several teenagers were assaulted, at least one of whom – Niamh Donovan – was underage.'

'I didn't do any of that. That's a lie.'

'Well, you'll have your chance to prove that in court,' Rachel told him. 'Meanwhile we will be carrying out further investigation.'

'So I'm allowed to go home now?'

Sillars shook her head. 'No you are not,' she rasped. 'Because of the nature of the charges, and because there are underage children in the house, you'll have tae make other arrangements. We need an address where you'll be staying before you can be bailed, and it has to be somewhere where you'll have no contact with anyone under the age of sixteen. Otherwise it's a bail hostel for you.' She turned to Rachel. 'I'll get Tulloch to chase up Child Protection's assessment on the MacBain kiddies. And we need to arrange an interview with the wife as soon as possible.'

'Hazel had nothing to do with this. Nothing whatsoever.' Will's voice trembled. 'And it's Angus's second birthday today. I need to be there for his birthday. I'm no risk to my own children, for goodness' sake!'

'The evidence would suggest otherwise,' Rachel said drily. 'And I'm afraid the law prevents it. You might, at some point in the future, be allowed court-ordered contact under a supervision order.'

Sillars addressed him again, pulling out her Mayfairs and lighter in readiness for her next cigarette break. 'But for now it'll be a condition that you stay away from your home address. Break that, and it's a stay at Her Majesty's Pleasure.'

'Good result,' said Brickall chirpily as they walked back to the incident room.

'No. It's not.' Rachel was only too aware that she sounded bitter. 'We've still got two dead teenagers and no one being charged over their deaths. And a Latvian girl with her head sliced off. Oh, and another teenager who was almost raped on camera last night while we sat outside eating crisps.'

'Wow – someone got out on the wrong side of the bed this morning.'

Rachel buried her face in her hands and took a long, jagged breath. 'Sorry. It was a late night and I'm just extremely tired.' But without even looking up she knew that Brickall had picked up that something was wrong.

'Tell you what,' he said, more gently this time, 'Why don't I get you a coffee, then chase down the cell tower records for MacBain's phone on the nights the two kids died?'

DI Sillars reappeared, breathing e-cigarette vapour all over them.

'Your other Latvian's just arrived in a paddy wagon. He's down in the cells, awaiting your earliest convenience.' She gave a cackle, exuding little gusts of vanilla flavouring.

Rachel beckoned to DC Tulloch to follow her, and they went to the cells on the ground floor. Maris Balodis was in the same male prisoner cell that MacBain had just vacated. He had lost so much weight that the prison sweats hung off him. Only the purple, bruise-like shadows under his eyes remained the same.

Tulloch led him, handcuffed, to an interview room and fetched him a cup of tea and a sandwich, removing the cuffs so that he could eat and drink.

'Maris,' said Rachel gently. 'You've heard that Iveta is dead?'

He nodded, closing his eyes briefly.

Tulloch pushed a still from the CCTV footage of Grange Loan Terrace towards him. It showed Iveta and the tall man, holding their heated discussion.

'Do you know who this man is?'

Balodis did not react. He picked up the ham sandwich and examined it suspiciously.

'Is it your friend Andrei?'

He shook his head.

'Iveta mentioned someone called Georgie? Is this him?'

Balodis nodded slowly. 'Gjerji.'

'Is that his first name? What's his surname? His family name?'

There was silence, apart from the sound of the sandwich being chewed and tea being slurped. It was like interrogating a piece of granite.

'Maris…' Once the last of the sandwich had been swallowed, Rachel motioned for Tulloch to put the cuffs back on. 'Iveta was brutally killed by someone, very possibly this man or one of his associates. You're in prison, and you'll be in there longer if we add a charge of obstructing a police enquiry. So please – if you know his name, we need you to tell us.'

'Dushku. Gjerji Dushku.'

'And how do you know him?'

Balodis shrugged. 'Everyone know him. Is Albanian. Albanians is like… mafia.' He mimed a throat being slit. 'Very bad men.'

'I've got some news,' Brickall told Rachel when they left the police station in search of somewhere other than the canteen for lunch. 'About Dolly.'

'I wish Dolly was here now,' Rachel sighed wistfully, 'She was a calming influence. Like a therapy animal.'

They had reached the café where they went on their first visit to Gayfield Square, during the festival. When Dolly had been with them. It was a few weeks ago, but felt a lot longer.

Brickall ordered a full Scottish, Rachel a toasted cheese sandwich and a pot of tea for them both to share. 'I heard back from my mate in Auckland – Dolly's real owner. I told him about leaving Dolly with your mum while I was working and he said he's happy for your mum to adopt her permanently. Do you think she'd like to?'

Rachel thought about this for a few seconds. 'Yes, probably, but don't you want her yourself?'

'Of course I want her. I bloody love that dog. But you know what it's like with our hours, and being called out on last-minute jobs… it's just not practical.'

'Fine,' Rachel poured them both tea. 'I'll have a word with Mum about it. If I ever get five minutes to speak to her.' She sighed heavily.

'Come on – tell me what's eating at you. I know there's something.'

Rachel took a long, deep inhalation of air. Then she told him that the mystery man they spotted leaving the party early was Giles Denton.

'Fucking hell. I told you there was something dodgy about him. Didn't I? I told you.' Brickall was triumphant.

'For what it's worth, I believed him when he said he didn't realise where he was going until he got there. I really do. Not that it makes the thing any less over.'

Brickall narrowed his eyes. 'Can you be sure though? Can you really?'

Rachel pressed her fingers into her brow bone. 'Christ, Mark, how can I be? How can any of us be sure about anyone, at the end of the day? I checked the list of people arrested at the party, and there is someone called Peter Fairlie among them, and I've googled him and he *is* an architect. So Giles's version of events stands up. But I also know that because of my job, and for Joe's sake, I simply can't take the risk. I can't have anything more to do with Giles.'

Brickall smiled slightly. 'You've only been a mother for a few weeks and look what it's done to you.'

Rachel gave him a weary smile over the rim of her tea cup.

'Seriously though: I'm glad I got to meet your Joe. He seems like a great lad.'

'He is.' Rachel desperately wanted to change the subject. 'I'm now wondering if this Albanian gangster had anything to do with Emily's death. Or Bruno's. But I just can't see it somehow.'

Brickall shook his head. 'Me either. It doesn't fit. Slitting the Latvian bird's throat – yes, absolutely. But I can't see him fiddling around with spiking drinks with ethylene glycol, which he then returns to a shelf in the MacBain's garage. In full view of the family and students. It makes no sense. And if a random Albanian turns up in your hall of residence are you really going to sit down and share a glass of Southern Comfort with them?'

'Agreed. It just doesn't stack up. And why would they want to silence Emily and Bruno anyway, when there's nothing overtly connecting them to those two students?'

Brickall stabbed a sausage with his fork. 'It's got inside job written all over it. It has to be Will MacBain. It just has to be. He's the link between the students and those dodgy parties, and everything was at stake for him if they blabbed.' He grabbed the brown sauce bottle and squirted it liberally over his plate. 'The only thing that doesn't quite add up, is that MacBain is into really young kids, but the parties are for much older victims. Some of them almost legal. So why is he bothering? Okay, the organisers could be paying him for providing 'Young Friends', but he doesn't look like he's into it for the money. His lifestyle's not exactly flashy: quite the opposite.'

'Ah, I think I know how that might work. It's all about access.' Rachel repeated Charlie's theory about bartering illegal content on the dark web.

'So let me get this straight…' Brickall drained the last of his tea. 'Our friend Will the Christian prefers pre-pubescents, so he trades his best-looking teenagers with other weirdos in exchange for material that's in his area of… specialisation.'

'As I understand it, that's how it works,' Rachel said, pouring them both more tea. 'Pretty Catholic virgins would represent a substantial bargaining chip. The choicest sort of 'fresh fruit'. And everyone gets their interests catered to without money changing hands. Less chance of being traced that way.'

'And MacBain can't exactly take his students to the parties himself, so he recruits someone to hand out invites to good-looking kids, and makes sure that the cream of that year's crop are in the right place at the right time, to receive them.'

'You'd never think it to look at him, would you?' Rachel said with a shudder. 'But then so many paedophiles are not what you would expect. I suppose viewing stuff through a screen allows them to disassociate the inner pervert from the straight-acting persona in their day-to-day life.' Rachel beckoned to the waitress to bring their bill. 'All of which begs a huge question: how much of this does Hazel know? Will says she's in the dark, but we can't take his word for it.'

'Christ no!' snorted Brickall.

'Tulloch's arranging to bring her in and ask her once the children have been risk-assessed, so we'll soon find out. '

'I for one can't wait to see what MacBain's phone location data tell us,' Brickall said. 'Then we'll nail the fucker.'

THIRTY-SIX

Gjerji Dushku had quite the rap sheet.

He had multiple convictions for robbery, assault and fraud in various European countries, and was wanted by Interpol for human trafficking. Rachel sat at her desk in the incident room that afternoon scrutinising his mugshot. Despite the ghetto clothing and the boyish appearance, he was actually forty-two years old.

'Excuse me – I'm looking for DI Prince?'

Rachel looked up into the face of a young woman with a shock of red hair in a fashionable undercut, multiple ear piercings and a diamond stud in one nostril.

'I'm Rachel Prince… and you are?'

'Celia. Celia Pownall. From JOC – sorry, the Joint Operations Cell. Our mutual colleague Giles Denton briefed me a few days ago, and told me you needed urgent help on a case?'

'Oh. Yes.' Rachel coloured slightly at the mention of Giles's name.

'I thought he'd be here to meet me, but I haven't been able to reach him on his mobile.'

'Well, your arrival is very timely,' Rachel said with a smile, avoiding the subject of Giles's whereabouts. 'Tea? Coffee?'

They took cups of coffee to an unused interview room, and Celia set up her computer. 'I've had some of the background from Giles, but maybe you could fill me in a bit more?'

Grateful for the opportunity to order her scattered thoughts, Rachel described the parties at Grange Loan Terrace and Hellebore Drive and the link with the shadowy figure of Gjerji Dushku.

'Is there any chance you can track him down online?' she asked, taking a much-needed mouthful of coffee.

Celia pursed her lips. 'I can certainly try, but if he's operating on the dark web he'll be using a code name, and his IP address will be obscured.'

'I see...' Rachel reconsidered for a moment. 'We found a hidden camera at one of the properties, and there's good reason to believe that videos of abuse are being shot at these parties and traded online. Is there any chance you could track those down?'

'It would be difficult,' Celia admitted, sipping her own coffee as she opened up a browser. 'There are various keyword chains we can use, but it takes time, simply due to the volume of stuff out there.'

'Apparently they advertise for staff on a forum called Edinburgh Extra... maybe you could start there?'

Celia started tapping buttons. 'Okay, I'll do a web scrape on the site and run some financial forensics... and it would help to know exactly who the victims are?'

'I'll get you all the details. Leave it with me.'

When she returned to the incident room, Brickall was tapping a biro on the edge of his desk, and scowling.

'What's up, my little ray of sunshine?'

'Something just doesn't make sense.'

'Go on.'

'Okay, firstly: MacBain's phone records. He wasn't at the house on either of the evenings in question. When Bruno and Emily were poisoned. On both occasions he was on the other side of the city.'

Rachel walked to the whiteboard and took down the photos of Emily, Bruno and Niamh to give to Celia Pownall. 'Everyone knows that cell-tower pings are unreliable as evidence,' she reminded him. 'So we can't be one hundred per cent certain of that.'

'Which is why I double-checked...'

Brickall showed her images on his computer terminal. 'Here... a picture on one of the White Crystal kids' Instagram account, posted at 21.58 on 7 August this year.' He showed Rachel a smiling group selfie, showing Will surrounded by students, at the Queen's Hall auditorium. 'And I checked through the archive posts on the White Crystal website and found this photo taken on a group outing the night Bruno went missing…' He showed her a photo taken on a dry ski slope at the Hillend Snowsports Centre. Will, resplendent in a country gent's wax jacket, was again at the centre of the shot.

Rachel sat looking at the images for a few seconds. Marie-Laure Fournier was there in the concert group, just as she'd said. 'And the second thing?'

'Kirstie Blair and one of our other Honeycomb uniforms tracked down an NPR capture of the MacBain's car heading away from 34 Campbell Road on the night of the seventh. No passengers, just the driver. At 21.08. MacBain can't be in both places at once.'

Rachel shrugged. 'The time stamp on a social media post is not indicative of when the photo was taken, only when it was uploaded. Maybe he was back from the concert by 10 p.m.'

'Surely the odds are that it would have been later than that? Most evening events don't end until at least ten.'

'Only one way to be sure – phone the auditorium and find out.'

Rachel's phone buzzed with a text. It was from Joe.

Got a minute?

She stood waiting for him on the steps of Gayfield Square half an hour later. He ambled into view, and the first thing she noticed was the rucksack on his back.

'You're leaving,' she observed.

He nodded. 'Charlie's got lectures starting on Monday, and I need to be getting on with finding some paid work. I'm just on my way to the station now.'

'Want me to give you a lift? I can borrow a pool car, or we could grab a taxi.'

'No, it's fine. I'll walk. Now that I know my way around this place so well…' He put his rucksack on the pavement at his feet. 'I just wanted to tell you a couple of things. First: I saw Stuart.'

'And how did that go?'

'Fine. Okay. Like, it's never going to be like it is with you…'

Rachel smiled. 'And how's that?'

'You know, just natural. Normal. But I'm glad I met him. We've made a start, at least.'

'Good. I'm glad. And the second thing?'

'I'm not going to tell Mum and Dad about going to the party.'

'Because you don't want them to think I didn't supervise you adequately, or…?'

'No, it's not that. Not exactly. It's just, I want it to be just between you and me. But Charlie and I both agreed it was the most badass thing we've ever done.'

Rachel smiled and looked up at him, this child of hers who towered over her. 'Well, I'll take that as a good thing.' She leaned into him and hugged him hard, inhaling the now-familiar smell. 'But promise me you'll never ignore an order again.'

'I promise.'

'And I'm so glad you came back. Really. It means everything.'

Joe sensed the emotion in her and stiffened, pulling away in order to shoulder his rucksack. 'Okay, cool, well I guess I'll see you in London?'

'Safe trip.' She kissed her fingers and waved them as he trudged away. 'See you in London.'

Celia Pownall was still working at 8 p.m., long after Kirstie Blair, Ben Tulloch and Morag Sillars had gone off-shift. Rachel hung around in the incident room, reading and re-reading the case file.

She was exhausted after the events of the previous twenty-four hours, but didn't feel she could go back to the hotel and leave Celia alone. She couldn't even rely on Brickall. His bag and jacket were still on a chair, but the man himself was nowhere to be seen.

Eventually Celia appeared and tapped gently on the open door. 'Rachel… I think you should come and see this.'

They went down to the interview room and sat together in front of the screen. Celia clicked on a thumbnail and a black and white video clip began to play. It showed a young girl on her back, motionless, possibly unconscious. Her mane of long blonde hair fanned out over the edges of the bed. Two men came into shot with their backs to the camera. One of them unceremoniously stripped off the girl's clothes, and the other started having sex with her unresponsive body. It was Emily van Meijer, being raped.

Rachel watched in silence, her knuckles thrust into her mouth.

'I think this is one of the girls?' Celia said quietly.

Rachel nodded, her hand still in her mouth.

'It was sold as a virginity-taking. Live.'

Fresh fruit, thought Rachel, with a shudder. 'When you say 'live' …?'

'By that I mean, at the time it was happening, people were paying to watch it on webcam. Like the pay-per-view set-up you'd get with a boxing match. It's not uncommon in child-porn networks.'

'Dear God. Can you find the people responsible?'

'Possibly. But it will take time: months probably. And there are almost certainly other organisations involved in supplying teenagers for the Edinburgh parties. The Albanians will be recruiting them from elsewhere too, as part of their network. Which will also take time to penetrate.'

Brickall came into the room, freezing when he saw what was on the screen. 'Jesus fucking Christ. Is that…?'

Rachel nodded.

Brickall rested his hands on the back of her chair. 'I need to talk to you, Boss.'

'Can't it wait?' she waved a hand, indicating the video.

'Not this time, no. I've been to the forensic lab to chase up the cross-checked results after the search of the MacBain place.'

Rachel swivelled in the chair to face him.

'The fingerprints on the selfie stick found with Emily van Meijer's body. They belong—'

Rachel finished the sentence for him. 'To Hazel MacBain.'

THIRTY-SEVEN

Brickall stared at her. 'How the hell did you know?'

He and Rachel were back in the deserted Operation Honeycomb room, after Celia Pownall had left.

'Couple of things. The first was something that came to me when I was re-reading Caitlyn Anderson's statement this afternoon.' There was an electronic clunk and hum as Rachel switched on one of the computer terminals and waited for it to finish booting up. 'She said that the woman she saw with Bruno was fat.'

'Yeah, I remember.'

'When we bailed Will MacBain he was whining about wanting to get to his son's second birthday party. If Angus was born in September 2015, it follows that when Bruno died, Hazel would have been eight months' pregnant. So at a distance, she would have appeared overweight.'

Brickall was shaking his head. 'But she was pulling Bruno from the car… and Hazel can't drive.'

'Can't she? She certainly told us she *didn't* drive, but that doesn't mean she doesn't know how. When I looked in her wallet the last time we were there, I think I spotted a driving licence.'

'That part's easy enough to corroborate, at least.' Brickall sat down and opened the PNC on the computer terminal. 'We just need to check the Drivers File… do we know her date of birth?'

Rachel shook her head, thinking back to her conversation with Greta Wheedon. 'Only that she was born in 1985. It could be in her maiden name – Nevins.'

'Here we are… yes, she holds a current UK licence. Valid since 2003.' He turned and looked back at Rachel expectantly.

'So – for one thing that solves the NPR mystery. Hazel could have been the driver of the family car when the number plate was picked up leaving Campbell Road.'

'But that's red. Caitlyn Anderson describes a brown car.'

'Rookie mistake, young grasshopper…' Rachel smiled. 'Anderson also said the car was under a street light. Sodium lights will make a red car appear brown. Ever tried to find a red car in a car park after dark? They don't look red. I can tell you that much.'

Brickall was frowning with concentration. 'So Hazel's heavily pregnant, which would make it difficult for her to manhandle someone more or less the same size as her – bigger in Emily's case: she was about 5'11" – unless she's given them a dose of ethylene glycol in a sweet-tasting drink.'

'Which would render them so incapable that all she has to do with Bruno is drag him to the water's edge and push him in, and in Emily's case, push her off the crags. Chucking the selfie stick after her to make it look as though she was attempting to take a picture of the city at night.'

'But why? If her old man's a paedophile, why would she want to protect him?'

Rachel swivelled in the chair to face him. 'Because she had too much to lose. She fought tooth and nail for her life of middle-class respectability and marital bliss. She must have found the porn on Will's laptop. Or maybe she'd known about his proclivities for even longer… so when first Bruno and then Emily threaten to get the authorities involved, she knows her perfect little life is under threat. She has to shut them up, so that she and the saintly Will can go on pretending to be Scotland's answer to Terry and June.

She must have emptied the bottle of port used to poison Bruno before leaving it in his room, and in Emily's case she bought a second bottle of Southern Comfort to allay suspicion. The one found in the drinks cupboard during the search was untainted, but their cleaning lady said she found a second, empty one in the rubbish. Hazel must have mixed the ethylene glycol into that one and put it somewhere Emily would be tempted to try it.'

'Didn't her friend say she wasn't that keen on alcohol?' Brickall reminded her. 'It seems unlikely she'd help herself to the Southern Comfort.'

Rachel shrugged. 'We may never know what happened. Maybe when Emily tried to talk to Hazel about the party, she invited her upstairs for a drink and brought out the second bottle, which was already laced with ethylene glycol. After all, she'd tried it with Bruno and got away with it, only on that occasion she didn't duplicate the bottle of port, she just washed out the poisoned one.'

'Perhaps she needed to duplicate the bottle because her husband was partial to a drop of Southern Comfort and she knew he'd miss it if it was gone from the drinks cabinet?' Brickall reached into his pocket and took out a packet of wine gums, dropping one into his mouth.

'So you don't think Will knew who killed the students? They could have been in it together.'

Brickall shook his head, still chewing. 'That's not his style. He's the man who hides behind a computer screen, remember? He's a coward.'

Rachel switched off the PC and reached for her bag.

'So what are we going to do now?' Brickall asked her.

'Well, it's nine o'clock in the evening, and everyone's pissed off home. But we ought to speak to Morag before we do anything else.'

She pulled out her phone and called DI Sillars number.

'*You've reached the voicemail of Morag Sillars. Don't bother leaving a message, because I willnae bother playing it.*'

They went down to the front lobby and asked the desk sergeant if he had any constables he could spare for an arrest. He shook his head.

'All my units are currently out on jobs… piss-ups and punch-ups. The usual.'

'Any idea where DI Sillars would be?' Brickall asked him.

'Aye, I do. She'll be down the Stag's Head.'

They walked round the corner to the Stag's Head pub. It was a traditional Victorian establishment at the bottom of Broughton Street, all dark-wood panelling, black and white checked floor and old-fashioned pub chairs. A TV screen in one corner was showing a football match. They fought their way through to the bar and found a lairy Sillars, straggly ponytail down, lipstick smudged, dwarfed by a loud after-work crowd.

'We need to talk to you,' Rachel mouthed. The music from the jukebox in the corner was so loud it was impossible to hold a conversation. She jerked her head in the direction of the door, and the three of them struggled out through the crush.

'What d'yous two want?' Sillars immediately lit a cigarette and puffed away on it silently while Rachel went through the evidence pointing to Hazel MacBain's culpability.

'Well,' she said finally. 'That's quite a theory yous have got there.'

'We need to bring Hazel in for questioning, but there's no spare manpower back at the station.'

'Aye, well, that's because Thursday's the new Friday. Piss-ups—'

'—and punch-ups. Yes, we know.'

Sillars narrowed her eyes at Rachel.

'Morag,' Brickall wheedled. 'Surely you can call in a couple of off-duty bodies? We need to get over there now.'

She tossed her cigarette butt, and it fell to the ground in a shower of orange sparks. 'I dare say I can. Leave it with me, and I'll make a couple of calls.' She pulled out her phone. 'Yous two go back and wait in the incident room and I'll be with you as soon as I can.'

'Have you still got the keys for that unmarked pool car, or did you give them back?' Brickall asked Rachel as they walked back to Gayfield Square.

'Still got them…' She stopped in her tracks. 'You're not suggesting we go over to Campbell Road now?'

'Why not? Will MacBain's not there, remember, so it's just her and two tiny kids. Two of us and one of her: it'll be fine.'

Rachel stared at him a beat. 'Okay. But we're going prepared.'

THIRTY-EIGHT

Campbell Road was the archetypal sleepy suburban street, silent apart from the flicker and murmur of television sets from behind curtained windows and the occasional clatter of a fox rooting through bins.

Rachel and Brickall parked outside number 34 and sat in silence for a few seconds.

'Ready?' asked Brickall. Rachel nodded.

They climbed out of the car and opened the boot, taking out stab vests and fitting airwave sets at the shoulder and attaching handcuffs to their belts. Rachel's phone vibrated and Morag Sillars' number flashed up on the screen. She hesitated, staring at it.

'She'll probably be looking for us.'

Brickall snatched the phone and cut the call. 'Come on; we've only got to get one small-ish pregnant woman into a police car. Let's just get on with it before she offers a poisoned liqueur to anyone else.'

He walked up the steps and rang the bell for 'Enquiries'. There was no response. Brickall took a step back and tilted his head to look at the windows on the top floor.

'Lights are on. Try again.'

Rachel pressed the bell hard for several seconds, and banged on the front door. It opened, and Will MacBain stood there. The colour drained from his face when he saw who was standing on the front step.

With impressive speed, Brickall pulled out his handcuffs and slotted them onto Will's wrists.

'Look, there's no need for this. I just dropped by to make sure the children were okay. I'm staying round the corner.'

'Will MacBain, I'm arresting you for violating the conditions of your bail. You do not have to say anything, but it may harm your defence if you do not mention when questioned something you later rely on in court. Anything you do say may be given in evidence. It's a trip back to the nick for you, old son.'

He led Will down the steps and out to the empty car, opening the rear door and guiding him onto the seat.

'Might as well take the two of them in together,' Brickall said when he re-joined Rachel. 'A Mr and Mrs special. That would be fitting.'

Hazel MacBain was standing in the doorway of the top-floor living room. As Rachel and Brickall came up the stairs, she called out 'Will? What's going on down there?'

Then she saw Rachel and Brickall and her eyes widened, a surge of colour flushing her face crimson.

'What are you doing here?' she demanded. There was an aggressive edge to her voice that had never been there before, and she backed away from them warily.

'Hazel, we're here to talk to you,' Rachel said calmly. 'We need to speak to you about the deaths of Bruno Martinez and Emily van Meijer.'

The red colour intensified. 'You've got no business being here! I want you to leave.' There was a whimper from one of the children's rooms, and she darted in there, coming out again with a sleep-tousled Angus in her arms. He was wearing a blue velour Babygro and had a security blanket clutched tightly between his chubby fingers. He whimpered at the sight of the strangers, and bored into his mother's neck.

'I said I want you to leave!' Hazel spat.

Rachel reached for her handcuffs, nodding to Brickall to indicate that he should take the child from his mother's arms.

'Hazel MacBain, I am arresting you on suspicion of murder. You do not have to say anything but it may harm your defence if you do not mention when questioned something you later rely on in court. Anything you do say may be given in evidence.'

'No!' Hazel screeched at Brickall as he reached for Angus. 'Get away from me.'

She backed into the kitchen, using the toddler as a shield, and pulled a large kitchen knife from a magnetic holder on the wall.

'Hazel, there's no need for this. Let's just keep things calm here, eh?' Brickall tried again to take the child, but she lunged at him with the knife blade, catching him on the wrist. As he swore and doubled up with pain, Hazel pushed past him and hurtled down the stairs, still holding Angus, who emitted ear-piercing shrieks of terror.

She reached the ground floor, ran to the back of the passageway that led to the kitchen and yanked open the side door that gave access to the garage. Rachel and Brickall ran after her, leaving a trail of blood spatter from the cut on his wrist.

'Fucking hell, it wasn't supposed to go like this!' Brickall muttered. There was just enough light coming into the garage from the main house for them to see Hazel pressed against the wall in the far corner. She gripped a squirming, distressed Angus with her left arm and held out the knife with her right.

Rachel tugged the airwave from her shoulder and switched it on.

'This is Control…' a disembodied electronic voice crackled.

'No!' Hazel hissed. 'Don't call anybody. If you do…' She brought the blade back and laid it against her son's throat.

Rachel and Brickall exchanged a shocked glance.

'Hazel,' Rachel said quietly. 'You don't want to harm your child. You're a good mother.'

'I'm not though, am I?' The glitter of tears was just visible in the half light. 'I'm an evil person. I'm messed up, just like my dad. There's something wrong with me, in here…' She thumped her chest with the hand that held the knife, the blade coming within millimetres of Angus' neck. 'That's what they used to say to me when I was in care. That I was a weirdo, not normal.'

'Hazel,' Rachel took a step nearer. 'Give Angus to me.'

The blade flashed as it went back to the child's throat.

'How do you think this can possibly end?' Brickall asked her. 'Come on Hazel, you're not thinking straight. *Think* about what you're doing.'

'It's already ended,' Hazel's voice was thick with tears. 'When he… when Will… started looking at that stuff… he spoiled it all. But I thought if nobody found out then we could go on as we were, and we could still have our lovely life together.'

Rachel tried coming forward again, but instantly the knife was back at little Angus's throat.

'I want you to leave. Leave now, and it'll all be okay. If you're not gone in five seconds, then I'm going to do it. I *will* do it.'

Rachel nodded to Brickall and the two of them started to back away slowly, still keeping their eyes on Hazel. As they were reaching the garage door, it cracked open and Will crashed through it, hands still cuffed in front of him. Without saying a word, he lunged at Hazel and tried to knock the knife from her right hand. She stumbled back then lost her footing and lurched forward, sinking the knife into Will's chest as she fell.

He collapsed onto the ground just as Rachel leapt forward and pulled Angus to safety, a dark lake of blood pooling around his body. Then the child's high-pitched cries were joined by the scream of sirens.

THIRTY-NINE

'Just what the fuck did you think you were doing?'

Morag Sillars had pulled herself up to her full four feet ten inches and was bellowing at Rachel and Brickall. Paramedics were carrying Will MacBain's body out of the house, covered in a blanket. Hazel had already been taken away in a van after being tackled by two officers in body armour, and a distressed Angus was being checked over by a third paramedic. A uniformed PC held a confused, sleepy Esme. The swoop of circling blue lights lit up the cordoned-off street, and there was a constant background crackle of police radios. Suited forensic officers shuffled between their van and the house.

'I told yous two to wait for me to come back!' she screeched, emitting little puffs of smoke from the ever-present cigarette. 'But oh no, you two little London heroes have to go off and round up the double murderer all by yourselves.'

Brickall opened his mouth to speak, but she cut him off. 'After a commendation were you? Because you'll no be getting one now. Not now a man's been stabbed to death.'

'We didn't know Will MacBain would be there,' Rachel said. 'We wrongly assumed it would be straightforward.'

'You never assume it will be straightforward. That's why we use backup units! Even if MacBain hadn't been breaking his bail, she could still have gone for a knife.'

Rachel and Brickall exchanged glances. Sillars drew in a long hit of nicotine then blew it out, her anger deflating. 'Aye well, we all know things don't go to plan in police work. At least you had the nous to leave your airwave set open, so Control would know there was a problem.'

Rachel gave her a brief nod. She was not in the mood for an argument. Not after seeing Will MacBain bleed out at her feet, and being unable to do anything to help. And in truth, she did not have much of a leg to stand on. Sillars was right.

'And yous did a brilliant job working out that it was MacBain's wife in the first place.' Sillars' tone was conciliatory now. 'DC Tulloch's still lined up to deal with her, even though you got ahead of yourselves.'

Rachel nodded again, still unable to speak.

'You'll be in need of a brandy,' observed Sillars. 'Anyone want to come back to the Stag's Head with me?'

Rachel shook her head. There was blood all over her shoes and the hems of her trousers. All she wanted was a long hot bath and her bed.

'Sounds like a great idea, Morag,' said Brickall. He placed his hand on the small of her back to propel her to her car, giving Rachel a discreet eye roll as he did so.

Sillars was unable to hide her gratification. 'Good lad.'

Hazel MacBain's demeanour in the interview room was catatonic. As she sat there the next morning she was completely still, her fair complexion so waxy that she might have been a statue.

'I'm doing this interview,' Sillars had growled at Rachel when they arrived at the station earlier. 'And Ben Tulloch will take the second chair. We don't want any more fuck-ups.'

Rachel and Brickall watched in silence from behind the one-way glass in the viewing room. Unlike her husband, who had lied and obfuscated, Hazel answered every question in a flat but open manner. *But then*, thought Rachel, *she had lost everything she prized most, and so had nothing to gain by denying the truth.*

Bruno Martinez had come to see her on the night before he left, and told her he thought he might have been assaulted. Having recently discovered the child pornography on her husband's laptop, Hazel had been terrified that Will might have been involved or, at the very least, that his laptop would be examined. When this happened, Will had been out with the minibus and about half of the students, and the children were asleep. The boy had become very worked up, so she had told Bruno that she would get him a drink to calm him down. She ran up to the flat for the bottle of port that had been a gift from a Portuguese student, stopping first to knock out Esme with a double dose of Medised.

It was when she reached the ground floor again that she had had the idea to spike the drink. She went through the connecting door into the garage and tipped a bit of antifreeze into the port bottle. She wasn't sure how much, but at least 100 millilitres. Then she had taken the port to Bruno's room and made him drink a glass of it, using the fact that she was pregnant to avoid drinking it herself. Once Bruno had become disorientated and incoherent, she had put the boy's arm around her shoulder and dragged him into the garage. She planned to say that Bruno was unwell and that she was taking him to the doctor's if anyone saw them, but nobody did. Her toddler daughter was out cold, and the students who had not gone on the dry ski slope expedition were all playing pool and watching TV, with the volume turned up loud.

She had heaved Bruno onto the back seat of the car and driven to Leith, parking the car as near as she could to the entrance to Lighthouse Park. She had dragged Bruno – barely conscious at this point – into the park and pushed him off the edge of the wall into the water, hurrying away without looking back. Once back at the residence, she tipped the remains of the tainted port down the sink, washed the glass and replaced it, along with the empty bottle, in Bruno's room.

The students had still been playing pool in the TV room, Esme was still fast asleep: it was as if nothing at all had happened.

'And did you tell your husband about it?' Sillars demanded. 'Did he know?'

Hazel shook her head with a robotic movement. 'No. He doesn't know any of what I've done.' She spoke as if Will was unharmed, and not lying on a steel post-mortem table in the pathology lab.

'And your conscience didn't prick you to come forward when his body was found? Or later, when you'd thought about what you'd done?'

Hazel stared at Sillars as though she was speaking a foreign language. 'I hadn't planned to do it; the thing with the anti-freeze just came to me at the last minute. It was ruled an accident,' she said dispassionately, as though this meant the death was no longer anything to do with her. 'Life carried on. Things went on just as normal.'

'Except you knew your old man was still looking at pictures of naked kiddies,' Sillars snarled at her. She pulled out her e-cigarette and took a couple of forceful puffs. 'That was hardly normal.'

'Can we move on to the death of Emily van Meijer?' DC Tulloch cut in.

'That wasn't so easy,' Hazel said, her voice still flat. 'For a start, she was very calm and rational about everything. She wasn't keen on having a drink. And she was a strapping girl. Statuesque.'

'So this time you did plan it?' DC Tulloch asked.

Hazel nodded. Her body was inert, her eyes barely open. 'She'd said she had something very serious that she wanted to talk to me and Will about. So I went out and bought a second bottle of the Southern Comfort because I knew someone might notice if the one upstairs went missing. And I baked some Dutch-style cinnamon cookies. I thought that would make it easier to get her to drink. I poured myself a glass of Southern Comfort from the original bottle, poured a second glass from the bottle with the anti-freeze in it and put both glasses on a tray with the cookies. I handed Emily her glass, so there was no chance she'd pick up the wrong one. I only had a sip from mine, because, you know…' She indicated her pregnancy bump. 'She said she wasn't keen on spirits, but I convinced her it went well with the cookies, and she drank half a glass. Just to be polite, really. Before she became incoherent, she said something about having been drugged and assaulted, and making a complaint to her lawyer. So you see, I was right. I had to do it. Otherwise everything would have been over.'

'What about the selfie stick?' Tulloch asked.

'That was left behind by one of a previous group of students. It was in a box in the garage, and I saw it when I was filling the bottle with anti-freeze, and thought it might make a hillside walk look more believable.'

'And you got her in and out of the car all by yourself?' Sillars demanded. 'A young woman nearly six feet tall and weighing over seventy kilos?'

'It was really hard. In fact, at one point I thought I was never going to get her to the edge of the Crags. I had to drag her some of the way, and she got cuts on her arms. But at least I wasn't heavily pregnant this time.'

'And when you got her there?'

'I pushed her over the edge and threw her phone and the selfie stick with her.' Hazel described the event as though it were a trip to the shops.

'So you took this bright, beautiful young woman – with her whole life ahead of her – and you chucked her to her death as though she were just a heavy bag of rubbish? Is that what you did?' Sillars snarled.

'I had to,' Hazel's voice was monotone. 'I had to—'

'Yes, yes, yes! You had to protect your precious life as a surrendered Christian wife!' Sillars held up the flat of her hand. 'I don't want tae hear it. Not any more. Interview concluded at 9.56 a.m.'

*

'Are we going to pack up and head back to London now?'

There was a hopeful note in Brickall's voice when he came outside and found Rachel sitting on the steps of the Gayfield Square station. He sat down beside her and offered her a plastic cup of machine tea.

'That would be nice,' Rachel said. 'But not just yet. We've got a whole house full of party guests to round up and interview.' She sighed heavily.

'You all right, boss?'

'I just need a bit of fresh air. That testimony was hard to hear. Especially the stuff about poor Emily. Such a waste... all that potential. Dries van Meijer messaged me yesterday asking for an update, and I told him I'd be providing one very soon. God knows how I'm going to tell him about all of this. Especially about the on-camera rape.' Rachel rubbed her hand over her forehead, burying her fingers in her hair. 'It's strange, but I don't think I've ever felt so gutted about the death of a victim.'

'That makes perfect sense to me.'

She looked at Brickall. 'It does?'

'You've got a teenager of your own... must make it so much more real.'

Rachel managed a smile. 'What are you now – a shrink?' She stood up, stretching her limbs. 'I'm going to go back to the hotel and head out for a run. Then I'll meet you back here, and we can make a start on following up with Edinburgh's child-abusing elite from the other night's party.'

'Was it really only a few days ago?' Brickall stood up and mirrored her stretching movements. 'Feels like half a lifetime.'

Rachel sighed wearily. 'Doesn't it just.'

FORTY

It took four whole days to take statements from the two girls at the Hellebore Drive party, and then interview the entire cohort of guests.

For every minute of those days, Rachel fantasised about being back in London, back in the familiar and orderly space of her flat. They had arrived in Scotland in high summer, but now autumn had taken a firm hold. The weather was damp and drizzly, turning Edinburgh's blackened sandstone buildings dour and unfriendly. She was homesick for red double-deckers, white stucco and sparkling shop windows.

Both girls claimed to be sixteen, but when their information was double-checked, one of them turned out to be three weeks shy of her sixteenth birthday. She was not the girl who had been drugged and molested, but she described being pawed and fondled against her will by at least two of the men there. Her age opened up the possibility of charges of causing or inciting provision by a child of sexual services. It also meant that Douglas Coulter's freemason friend, Eric Gourlay, who was one of the attendees, faced a charge of failing to comply with the requirements of the Sex Offenders' Register.

'Good,' said Brickall, who had interviewed him and declared him 'odious'. 'With luck he'll be banged up.'

Rachel shook her head. 'I doubt it. The maximum's six months, but since he wasn't one of the men who molested either girl, he'll probably only end up with a community order.'

All of the guests were male, middle-aged and professional, and they included a judge, an orchestral conductor and a barrister. The man who had assaulted the drugged sixteen-year-old – a leading plastic surgeon – was charged with sexual assault. The remaining party guests were encouraged to opt for a caution in exchange for total candour, and by piecing together all of their statements, the complete picture emerged.

Douglas Coulter was in charge of the guest list, and had been the point of contact for most of them. Young girls were procured by a fixer – almost certainly Gjerji Dushku – who had contacts within several educational establishments in the city who also supplied selected 'Young Friends'. The most renowned – and sought-after – parties were the ones that took place in August during the festival. An international crowd was in town during those weeks, among them various high-powered individuals who wanted their preferences catered for. The young Catholics supplied by White Crystal were the most prized on this dubious circuit; selected for their looks and their purity. They were promoted on the dark web as virgins, and as such attracted a premium. Kenneth Candlish liaised with Douglas Coulter about these highly specialised soirées.

This was also where Will MacBain came into play. It appeared that he had been hand-picking individual students and arranging for them to be invited to the parties by the likes of Maris and Iveta, so that they would never suspect that White Crystal Tours had any connection with the events. But with Will MacBain dead, the full story of his involvement would probably never be known.

As Sillars dispatched officers to arrest both Douglas Coulter and Kenneth Candlish, there was one last party guest to interview. The architect, Peter Fairlie.

'This one's mine,' Rachel said firmly.

She and DC Tulloch went into the interview room, where Fairlie was waiting alone, having opted not to have a lawyer present. He was a heavyset man dressed in chinos and gingham shirt, his hair spiked with gel in an attempt to make him appear younger than he was.

He smiled at Rachel. She did not smile back, but kept her tone scrupulously neutral. 'Mr Fairlie, I'd like you to start by telling me how you came to be at the party at 141 Hellebore Drive.'

'A contact at my golf club mentioned it to me… someone he'd met through the freemasons had told him about it. You know, word of mouth stuff. But look,' he leaned forward on the table, his manner authoritarian, 'I didn't… you know… do anything.'

Rachel played dumb. 'I'm sorry, I don't know. What does that mean?'

'I didn't touch either of those girls. Or the wait staff.'

'So why were you there?'

He shrugged.

'Are you married, Mr Fairlie?' DC Tulloch asked.

'Yes, yes I am. But—'

'So why did this contact think you would be interested in going to this event on your own? Why didn't you take your wife?' Rachel remained cool on the outside, but inwardly she was burning. This man took Giles Denton with him to the wretched party, and in doing so messed up what could have been something great.

'Please bear in mind that if you cooperate fully, you will in all probability only receive a caution,' DC Tulloch interjected.

Fairlie sighed, and spread his hands on the table. 'I suppose it was because they knew I have a weakness for… younger women.'

'How young?'

'Very young. But not illegal. Nothing like that. Just what you might call age-inappropriate.'

Rachel fixed him with a steady gaze. 'Did you go to the party alone?'

He shook his head. 'I took a friend of mine. Giles Denton.'

DC Tulloch looked startled. Rachel shot him a warning look and went on, forcing her voice to remain level. 'And was that because he shared your interest in *age-inappropriate* girls, as you call them?'

The head-shaking was more vigorous this time. 'Good God no. Not Giles. It's just because he was in town for a while and he's good craic, and I thought he might enjoy getting out of his hotel for a bit.'

'And is this the same Giles Denton who's a Child Protection Officer?' Rachel's voice was cold with fury.

Fairlie nodded.

'And you didn't think it was poor judgement to take him along to that kind of gathering, given his job description?'

Rachel spat the words with such venom that Tulloch looked at her in alarm.

Fairlie pulled at his shirt collar, sweating now. 'With hindsight, yes. Obviously. But bear in mind I'd never been to one of these… things… before. I had no idea what to expect. I certainly didn't think I was getting into anything illegal. I have something of a profile in this town, a successful business.'

'Indeed. As did many of the other people there. Didn't stop some of them from crossing the line though.'

'I don't know what happened to Giles: I've been trying to contact him, he's avoiding my calls. But I do know he didn't stay very long.'

'Wait here please, Mr Fairlie…' Rachel picked up her notebook and beckoned Tulloch out of the room. 'Issue him with a caution please, Ben. And what he said about Superintendent Denton stays strictly on the record. As in no gossip about it around the station, okay?'

'Absolutely, Ma'am. I won't say a word.'

FORTY-ONE

On Rachel's last morning in Edinburgh, she set off alone towards Inverleith and went into a coffee shop near the Botanic Gardens. She ordered a double espresso and sat down to wait.

The door eventually opened and he came in, seating himself opposite her at the table. He smiled.

'So?' said Rachel.

'So,' said Stuart. 'I met our son.'

She nodded. 'He told me.'

'We made a fantastic child together. As I always knew we would.'

'I don't think we can take all the credit for that,' Rachel told him, with a slight smile. 'But it would be nice to think we had a little bit to do with it.'

Stuart became serious. 'Rae, you know this isn't how I would have chosen things to be—'

'We've been over that…'

He held up a hand. 'I know. I know. I was just going to say that I'm glad to have had the chance to get to know him a bit. And I hope to do so more in future.'

She nodded, sipping her coffee. Stuart summoned the waitress and ordered.

'I really just asked you here to say goodbye,' Rachel told him. 'I'm flying back to London this evening. Finally.'

'Case all tied up now, is it?'

She rocked her hand to and fro. 'More or less.'

'Well, I'm very glad you contacted me before you left. Because I have some news of my own.'

His excitement was infectious, and Rachel found herself grinning. 'Go on...'

'Claire continued feeling unwell after her miscarriage... she went to her gynaecologist to be checked and she was told she was still pregnant. Still pregnant...' His voice broke slightly. 'She'd been carrying twins. She lost one of them, but the other...'

Rachel's eyes widened. 'Go on...'

'The second baby's doing fine. We're going to be parents in the new year after all.'

The Operation Honeycomb incident room was being dismantled. Brickall and Rachel stood and watched as the whiteboard was wiped, the computers unplugged and the files taken away to be archived.

A noise behind them grew louder as its source got closer. A familiar phlegmy cough and the whiff of a vape.

'Yous two still here?' she croaked. She bent double as her diminutive body was wracked with another bout of coughing.

'Those fags really are doing you the world of good, Morag,' Brickall said. 'By the sound of it you're on track to live to a hundred.'

'Shut it!' she rasped. 'I just came to say goodbye and good riddance. I cannae say I'm going to miss having poncey London detectives stealing all my officers and making the place look untidy.'

'The feeling's mutual,' Rachel said, but she was smiling.

'I also wanted to tell you that I've spoken with the Procurator Fiscal's office, and now that Hazel MacBain has been charged with the manslaughter of her husband, there'll be no further enquiry into the circumstances surrounding her arrest. Which means this: the two of you piss-artists may have been out of order going out to the house without adequate manpower, but as far as Police Scotland's concerned, it stops here. I managed to bury it.'

'Thank you Morag.' Brickall gave her his most boyish smile.

She poked a finger at him. 'But you're no forgiven for that fag joke, sunshine! Who wants tae live to a hundred anyway?'

'Fair point.'

'I fully intend to smoke myself to death, and ah'll do so quite happily, thank you.'

'I gather Candlish and Coulter have both pleaded not guilty,' said Rachel. 'So we may be back before you know it to give evidence at their trials.'

Sillars rolled her eyes.

'And the Joint Operations Cell are going to continue pursuing the Edinburgh paedophile network on the dark web. So I'll be keeping you updated about that from time to time.'

'Aye, well.' Sillars looked almost emotional, faking another coughing fit to hide it. 'Forensics have just told me the skin cells under Iveta's fingernails are definitely a match with Dushku's DNA. Interpol have issued a red notice for him, so as soon as they catch up with him, he's off to the big house for a life term.'

Rachel gave her a brief nod.

'And ah just wanted to say that was a great piece of investigation. Your work on the deaths of those two kids.' Sillars exhaled vapour like a diminutive dragon, almost smiling. 'Good job.'

FORTY-TWO

Rachel looked up at the handsome red-brick facade of the Dutch Embassy with a sense of disbelief. Back to the exact place where this all started, she thought. Only two months had passed, but it felt like two years.

'Are you ready?' asked Nigel Patten. He took in her smart navy skirt suit, her hair swept into a French pleat, and her heels.

'I think so. It feels pretty strange.'

Patten gave her shoulder a paternal squeeze. 'I'm proud of you.'

They were led into one of the Embassy's formal function rooms, all gilt furniture, framed royal portraits and velvet drapes. And there – watched by Patten, Dries and Annemarie van Meijer, Luuk Rynsberger, his parents and a handful of diplomatic staff – Rachel walked up a short length of carpet towards His Excellency Carolus Visser.

'I have great pleasure in awarding you the Orde van Oranje-Nassau – the Order of Orange-Nassau – in recognition of the way you have carried out your duties on behalf of our citizens.' He pinned a blue-and-white enamelled chivalric cross onto Rachel's lapel, bending to kiss her on both cheeks. The tension of the moment was broken by one of his attachés sending a champagne cork ricocheting into one of the floor-to-ceiling windows with a resounding crack.

Annemarie van Meijer embraced Rachel warmly. 'Thank you so much, DI Prince. For all you have done for our precious girl.'

Rachel thought of Emily, and then thought of her own son, and felt tears prickle in the corners of her eyes. 'I'm so sorry that her story ended the way it did. What we found out... it wasn't an outcome that could give you any comfort.'

'Oh but it did,' Annemarie assured her. 'Because now at least we don't need to wonder why, and we can begin to come to terms with losing her. We don't have to think that she wanted to leave us.'

Dries van Meijer shook Rachel's hand. 'Anything we can ever do for you, just say. We're forever in your debt.'

Patten paused to admire the Order before he and Rachel got into the car that was going to take them both back to Tinworth Street. 'Apparently, it's a bit like a Dutch OBE,' he said, making the cross sparkle as he turned it to and fro in the October sunshine. 'A very fine thing to have. Well done.'

'Thank you, sir.'

'I don't know whether you've heard, but Giles Denton has resigned from his post at the NCA.'

Rachel stared out of the car window so that he couldn't see the expression on her face. 'I hadn't, sir, no.'

'It was very sudden, apparently. You wouldn't happen to know why?'

'No. I'm afraid I don't.' Rachel crossed her fingers behind her back, and hoped that Patten would never get round to checking Fairlie's statement.

'Yes, well... on a more positive note, you may be hearing from the Inspectors Branch of the Police Federation,' he said, as the car slid out into the traffic on Kensington Gore. 'There may be promotions to Chief Inspector available before too long. Not that it's easy to get through that recruitment board though. In fact, it's very challenging.'

She smiled at him. 'I'm sure. But then so is anything worthwhile.'

EPILOGUE

DECEMBER 2017

'Everybody – this is Joe.'

Rachel led her son into the living room at her mother's house in Purley. Her mother, wearing her best apron, looked as though she might faint from pleasure. She darted forward and gave her grandson a hug, then disappeared into the kitchen, flapping about finishing the icing on a specially baked cake.

'Welcome, Joe.' Rachel's brother-in-law Gordon stepped forward and gave Joe a brief handshake, and for once Rachel was grateful for his customary reticence. Her nephew, Tom, raised his hand in a barely visible wave of greeting and her niece Laura mouthed a shy 'Hi'.

'It's lovely to finally meet you, Joe,' said Lindsay, bustling forward to kiss him on both cheeks. 'It's—'

Rachel shot her a look and she backed away without completing her sentence, which was undoubtedly going to be something along the lines of '*It's a shame we had to wait eighteen years.*'

Joe shuffled his feet awkwardly, unsure what to do. When Rachel sat on the sofa he took his cue from her and perched next to her. Dolly trotted into the room, squirming with delight when she saw Rachel, followed by Eileen Prince pushing a hostess trolley. Joe, who had clearly never seen one before, widened his eyes at the sight of this mobile cornucopia of baked goods, then caught sight of Rachel watching his expression. The two of them suppressed laughter as if in on a private joke, which led to pursing of the lips by Lindsay.

'I've done coffee cake, Joe,' Eileen said anxiously. 'But I know not everyone likes it, in which case there's Battenberg, or shortbread…'

'I love cake,' Joe reassured her. 'All cake.'

Lindsay poured them all tea and half an hour of polite small talk ensued, lightened by Dolly's benign presence. Joe gamely endured a grilling from Lindsay about his academic achievements, and ignored the veiled comparisons with Tom.

Finally, Gordon and Lindsay drove their children away to take part in some wholesome activity, and Rachel was left to help Eileen clear up the tea things while Joe walked Dolly round the block.

Eileen grasped her daughter's arm. 'Oh Rachel, he's wonderful!'

'Yes, I think so too. Although I'm a bit biased.'

'And he's so like you.'

'Do you think so?' Rachel was genuinely surprised. When she looked at Joe she mostly saw Stuart.

'Oh yes, very much so. And he's got your spirit, I can tell.'

Once the washing-up was done, Eileen gathered up Dolly's bowls, lead and accessories and put them in a bag. 'You're sure you'll be all right with her? Make sure she wears her coat when it's cold.'

'She'll be fine Mum, don't worry.'

'I'll miss her dreadfully.'

'Mum! It's only five days.'

With Dolly on the back seat of the car, she drove Joe to East Croydon station, to catch his train back to Sussex.

'Well, that was…'

'… awkward as hell.'

Joe finished the sentence for her, and she laughed. 'But I guess it was always going to be. And now it's out of the way, things should be easier from here on in.'

As they headed onto the platform, she took a small box from her pocket, wrapped in red paper and tied with a green ribbon. Inside were silver cufflinks, monogrammed with 'JBT'.

'I know it's a bit early, but since I won't see you at Christmas, I thought I'd give you this now.'

He looked down at the parcel with an anxious expression. 'But I haven't got anything to give you.'

She smiled at him, the broadest of smiles. 'Oh, you've given me more than enough already. More than I could ever have hoped for.'

Rachel drove round the South Circular to Forest Hill. She parked outside Brickall's flat and rang his doorbell.

'Somebody here to see you.'

'Dolly!' He knelt down next to her and she plonked her paws on his shoulders, her tail quivering with delight. 'Hello, baby girl!' He kissed her repeatedly on the top of her silky head. 'And look how smart you are!' He pointed to her blue and green tartan coat.

'My mum's going down to Torquay for a few days with her gardening club, so I said I'd take her. Thought you might fancy a walk.'

'I'll grab my coat.'

Brickall ran back down the stairs a few minutes later in his waxed jacket and a trapper hat, and the three of them set out along Dartmouth Road to Crystal Palace Park, past windows lit by sparkling Christmas lights. It was almost dark, but there were a few remaining families heading back from their Saturday afternoon outings, dressed in colourful scarves, bobble hats and gloves.

They walked in silence round the upper lake, with Dolly trotting happily at their heels. 'Bit like being back in Scotland,' Brickall said at last. 'Bloody cold enough anyway.'

'Do you miss it?' Rachel asked.

'What, working with Morag? Nah,' he scoffed. 'Well, maybe just a tiny bit. It had its moments.'

'It certainly did.'

'And you ended up with the Dutch Order of the Garter, or whatever the hell it is. Who'd have thought it.'

'It's only an honorary title, seeing as I'm not a Dutch citizen.'

'Whatever next, Prince – Chief Constable?'

'Don't be a plank, Brickall.' She paused a beat. 'Although, Patten did make noises about promotion to Chief Inspector being on the cards.'

'Fucking hell.' He gave her a sidelong glance. 'You'll be even more unbearable than you are already.'

The light had almost completely left the sky, leaving it streaked with crimson and purple. They turned and headed back towards the flat. Without looking at Rachel, Brickall said: 'I heard Denton left CEOP.'

'Yes, that's right.'

'Heard he went back to Ireland.'

Rachel nodded slowly. 'He did.'

'Bit of a shame, isn't it? Given you and he were—' He caught sight of Rachel's expression and swallowed what he was about to say, simply asking, 'Did he say how long he was going for?'

Rachel hesitated. 'No,' she said. 'He didn't.'

Brickall gave her a sharp look. 'But you really liked him.'

She nodded slowly. 'I did. I liked him a lot.'

'So maybe you should head over to Dublin?'

Rachel shook her head. 'I've got more important things to do. I've got a kid now, remember?'

She didn't mention that once her initial anger had died down, she had tried phoning Denton but his number – the NCA-issued mobile, which was all she had – was now out of service.

'And you've got a promotion to chase,' Brickall reminded her.

'And your useless arse to keep in line!' As she swatted him playfully on the arm, her phone rang. It was work.

'Who was that?' Brickall asked, after she'd ended the call.

'Interpol in Belgium have picked up Gjerji Dushku. They want someone from our end to head out there to question him.'

Brickall grinned. 'That'll be us then. Or maybe a girls' trip – you and Morag Sillars.'

'I guess we should ask her if she wants to come along. Only fair.'

'Either way, we'd better get our backsides over to the office immediately.'

They both quickened their pace as they walked up the road, Dolly trotting happily between them.

A LETTER FROM ALISON

I want to say a huge thank you for choosing to read *Now She's Gone*. If you enjoyed reading it and would like to keep up to date with all my latest releases, just sign up using the link below. Your email address will never be shared, and you can unsubscribe at any time.

www.bookouture.co.uk/alison-james

It's been incredibly rewarding taking Rachel Prince on this second investigation, and developing her journey in an unexpected direction. There are more exacting cases and further personal challenges ahead for her.

If you loved *Now She's Gone*, I would be very grateful if you could write a review. I love hearing what readers like most about the characters and story, and it really helps new readers discover my books for the first time.

I also love hearing from readers – so do get in touch via my Facebook page, Twitter, Goodreads or my website.

: @AlisonJbooks

: Alison-James-books

Lightning Source UK Ltd.
Milton Keynes UK
UKHW02f2314241018
331145UK00014B/476/P

9 781786 814142